D1147424

Mark Rusher

The Body on Scafell Pike is the first DI Jess Chambers and Margot Voyce murder mystery, a series set in the spectacular Lake District national park in northwest England. S J Brooke lives in Kent and used to be a newspaper crime reporter.

The Body on Scafell Pike

S J BROOKE

WILDFIRE

First published in 2023 by
WILDFIRE
an imprint of HEADLINE PUBLISHING GROUP

First published in paperback in 2023 by
WILDFIRE
an imprint of HEADLINE PUBLISHING GROUP

2

Cataloguing in Publication Data is available from the British Library

ISBN 978 1 0354 0018 8

Typeset in Dante MT Std 11.25/15.25 pt by Jouve (UK), Milton Keynes

Printed and bound in Great Britain by Clays Ltd, Elcograf S.p.A.

MIX
Paper | Supporting
responsible forestry
FSC
www.fsc.org FSC® C104740

Headline's policy is to use papers that are natural, renewable and recyclable
products and made from wood grown in well-managed forests and other
controlled sources. The logging and manufacturing processes are expected to
conform to the environmental regulations of the country of origin.

HEADLINE PUBLISHING GROUP
an Hachette UK Company
Carmelite House
50 Victoria Embankment
London
EC4Y 0DZ

www.headline.co.uk
www.hachette.co.uk

Something was wrong. Very, very wrong.

James couldn't understand it. He'd completed the run many times before, studied the map before setting off, in fact done all the things he should have.

But now he was heading down the steep rock-strewn scree, his knees bent and his steps short, Scafell Pike seemed to be playing with him. And it wasn't a fair game.

The reasonable weather he'd set out in had been, James discovered as he reached the top, too brief an interval between the storms of recent days. The patchy fog and wind had abruptly shifted on him, the rain slashing sideways. The summit was said to be routinely ten degrees colder than at the base, and James shivered through his clammy waterproofs, convinced the temperature was actually dropping as he continued down.

He'd had to go slowly so far on his descent – well, slow for him, at little faster than a jog – as after his hugely successful Instagram posting of the night before, and the follow-up social media he'd done at first light, the last thing he needed right now was an injury.

He came back to a walk, realising after a while that he was

quite alone – a rarity on Scafell Pike these days as usually it was besieged with walkers on all the routes. But gone were the usual hordes of those desperate for photos at the top of England's highest peak, driven away by the foul weather.

He stared up at the sky. It was only early afternoon, but it could have been much later. The day was slipping away from him.

He must have strayed from the path or missed its swing to the left, James realised a little later. *Shit.*

He halted and turned slowly in the murk, meaning to retrace his steps to the right route. But all this did was disorientate him further, as suddenly he couldn't tell from the scrubby grass and rocks all around – hazy in the mist – which way was up or down, nor the direction he had come from. In normal conditions there'd be no problem, but James was astounded at how confusing it all seemed in the blink of an eye.

A noise behind – or perhaps above – but it was just a scatter of small stones he must have dislodged a moment earlier, a few skittering past his feet.

James reached for his phone, but he only had one bar of signal and that faded out immediately.

He tried his compass app, Google Maps and What Three Words but there just wasn't enough reception. He'd been foolish to do this without an actual map, he realised. He patted his pockets for the old-fashioned compass he carried and then remembered it was in his other running jacket, the one currently nestled in the boot of his car.

James felt a shift in the air and shuffled a few steps forward. His foot slipped, and then a lurch.

He was suddenly teetering very close to the precipice, almost at its edge, and the deep gunmetal of the vertical rock face descending into the mist was dizzying. As a swirl of cloud cleared he could see a corresponding sheer wall on the other side of the deep gully, the trickle of a river far below between the rock faces.

He'd come so close to falling, he thought, shivering and stepping backwards sharply.

But then – without warning – he felt something slam into him, and he was falling.

Patience really was a virtue, thought the stranger, glimpsing the surprise on James's face.

The plan couldn't have gone better.

James was too easy to read, too wrapped up in his social media boasts, too obliging in setting out the precise route for his run before setting off. And the poor weather was the cherry on the cake.

No one else around.

James disorientated in the mist, thinking of other things, his guard down.

Conveniently standing right beside the drop.

Honestly, it was almost too easy.

He couldn't save himself.

As he whipped his head around, over his shoulder James caught the merest glimpse of a stranger dressed in waterproofs of green and dull khaki, and the last thing he saw as his body hurtled past the lip of the rock face and bounced downwards was a pair of well-worn mountain boots.

*

3

The sound that left James as he hurtled downwards was deeply primal. It reverberated against the sheer walls of the gully, stretching out for almost too long.

There was the oddly soft sound of a bump from far below, and the other crouched down to peer gingerly over the lip of the drop.

The stranger felt a surging heartbeat, goosebumps rising from the thrill.

A peek over the edge showed the body of the famous fell runner lying twisted and still, one leg at a sharp angle.

The peek lasted more than a minute, each second settling the adrenaline in the stranger's veins. Then finally, the body still motionless, peace.

The chances of James coming to – if indeed he was still alive – and getting out of this predicament were absolutely minuscule.

It was a shame. They'd had some good times, but it had been unavoidable.

Life was like that, sometimes, wasn't it?

James couldn't tell what time it was when he came to.

It was properly dark now, the rain falling heavily still, with a dank haze closing in from every direction.

Groggy, he was in agony, lying partly submerged in the freezing stream at the base of the gully, but as he looked at the steep vertical pitch of the rock face in front of him, he forced himself to try to sit up.

He couldn't do it.

James knew he was in trouble, but he got his bearings, nonetheless. He had to be lying at the bottom of Piers Gill, the deep-cut canyon descent notorious for serious accidents. *Do not follow the bed of the stream in Piers Gill.* That was the advice given to all climbers and runners on Scafell Pike, no matter their level of experience.

And yet this was precisely where he was.

Many have died in this gill, James knew. If he wasn't to be another statistic, he needed to get out, and fast.

He took an inventory of his injuries. Right off he could tell he'd torn the rotator cuff on his right shoulder, as he'd done this before and recognised the same wincing pain. He felt a numb tingling of his right hand – even through his black gloves he could see he'd dislocated his fingers, and very probably he'd also sustained a greenstick fracture to the radius bone in his left arm. As if that wasn't enough, he felt unnaturally woozy, and so he was concussed.

These injuries were certainly painful and distressing, but they were unlikely to be life-threatening, thankfully. But then he found the real problem.

His thigh. Indeed his leg was at such a strange angle that James knew the femur had snapped. More dangerous than this, though, was the blood saturating his running tights.

James knew he had to raise the alarm, otherwise he would almost certainly die of exposure if he remained on the mountain overnight. More importantly, though, he needed to staunch the flow of blood if he was to make it that long.

Gingerly he touched his thigh, and although there was a lot of blood, presumably from a nick in the femoral artery, there might be something in the way he was lying that was slowing down the flow. If it had been severed completely, he would've been long dead by now.

Death didn't feel imminent, James decided after his initial examination, and so the priority needed to be to get to his phone first, in case he passed out while dealing with the leg injury.

His jacket was rucked around, making it almost impossible to unzip his left-side pocket, especially with his useless fingers, but when he finally managed to pull it out, the phone was entirely shattered and bent out of shape. He shook it and jabbed at the screen, but there wasn't even the sniff of an erratic signal. He shouldn't have been surprised. Piers Gill had atrocious signal reception, especially in bad weather.

What do I have to do to get a break? James thought, but he was determined. He hadn't got this far in life by giving up, even when the odds were stacked against him.

New priorities. He had to deal with his leg, which could kill him in minutes, and then the very real threat of hypothermia, which could kill him in hours. But he had food with him and a spare coat in his rucksack, and he was out of the wind, and if he could just hang on overnight, there would be walkers near Piers Gill he could shout to.

Suddenly shock coursed violently through his body . He struggled against it, and when he eventually got his system back under control, he managed to pull off his GoPro harness to use as a makeshift tourniquet on his leg. The camera itself was long gone. But though he managed to wrap the harness around his thigh and was about to pull firmly enough to quell the blood flow leaching from him, James experienced a wave of weakness and then a rushing in his ears. Even though he was lying flat, he felt dizzy and as if he were falling once more.

6

Determined not to lose consciousness until he'd stemmed the bleeding, James closed his eyes and forced himself to curl forward as much as he could to muster one last burst of effort.

But at that moment he realised that there was another reason for the rushing sound.

In terror he watched as a wall of brown water cascaded towards him, pushing a mass of rocks and plant debris with it.

The flash flood hoisted James up, the abrupt immersion in the fresh iciness sharpening all of his senses as he found himself swallowing mouthful after mouthful of muddy water. His body was helplessly batted from one side of the gully to the other as it swept him along. One moment his knees were above his head, before being upended once more.

Then, just as James lost consciousness, the neck of his nylon jacket snagged on an outcrop on the vertical rock face, brutally plunging his head downwards. In the maelstrom one of his running shoes was ripped off, slamming against his open mouth as the current dragged him face under and pinned him there.

James's very last thought was *Fuck, so that's who did this to me.*

But with that his head was dunked under the water once more, and this time it stayed there.

And when the water level dropped as abruptly as it had risen, James was very dead indeed.

DAY ONE

Margot Voyce was still familiarising herself with her old stamping ground. It looked and smelled pretty much exactly as she remembered, and it felt the same underfoot, yet it all seemed different somehow, disconcertingly so.

She'd been back for well over six months but she was yet to find the sense of belonging she'd anticipated would come sooner. She was getting bored with waiting for this to happen.

She'd grown up nearby, and as a child had loved the majestic sweep of the awe-inspiring mountains – much quieter then in terms of visitors, and with parking definitely easier to find – and the way the glassy surfaces of the lakes would reflect the peaks rising high above the national park. Never one for school, she had always itched to be outside, walking or climbing or swimming or horse riding.

And then she'd become desperate to leave these mountains and lakes, as the life she'd grown up with had come to feel not enough. She wanted – no, needed – bigger challenges and more exciting people.

It had taken some turbulent times since to convince Margot that there really wasn't anywhere in the world like home.

Suddenly she found herself craving what she knew. And, generally, coming back had worked out well. She'd got a job as a walking guide on the peaks as it seemed to offer both freedom and a general lack of stress. But it did mean brushing up on routes that previously she'd known like the back of her hand, and hence this outing, early enough that she wouldn't be distracted by the walkers so that she could concentrate on memorising the titbits of information she planned to tell her clients.

Margot tried to imagine them, but this unnerved her. She had decided to be a mountaineer back in the day as she hadn't wanted to talk to people. Of course the community she'd joined back then turned out to be one that functioned with people at every turn, and she'd never been able to get a moment to herself. Older now, she craved solitude once more. But she needed a livelihood, and escorted guiding was the best she could come up with, though she couldn't say the idea filled her with enthusiasm.

But Margot was diligent, and so she had been clambering all over Scafell Pike and nearby fells each morning for weeks now, checking routes for novice, intermediate and experienced walkers, although she couldn't seem to get back the fitness she'd once found so easy. Her long and lithe body might look the same, but that was as far as it went.

As she climbed, Margot savoured the chill but clear autumn weather.

Following the downpour of yesterday, this morning had broken calm and sunny, making the world before her look washed clean, and she loved the tones of earthy scent lifting from the ground still in the deep shadows where the sun was yet to hit.

The air felt sharp and almost spicy, very different to the tang of other mountains she had known. And as Margot stood on Scafell Pike and breathed in deeply, out of the blue she felt a sense of immense well-being. Perhaps guiding wouldn't be so bad after all.

Still, she couldn't deny that even though she had been in the gym a lot recently, with the rest of her time devoted to riding her horse Trojan, which she'd recently moved up from a livery stable in Hertfordshire, the extent to which she wheezed negotiating a not particularly steep incline was embarrassing.

A little later and unable to ignore any longer the burn in her legs, she tapped the stopwatch on her phone to halt it, and crouched down to catch her breath.

Not very good at doing nothing, after a short recovery Margot stood to shoot a 360-degree video around her. The sunshine was causing the odd shimmy of mist to rise from the warming damp ground, while the ice-blue cloudless sky contrasted dramatically with the deep hues of the peak rising above her.

She made a note on her phone of how long it had taken to get to where she was. And then she looked carefully at her video to see if a closer analysis suggested anything she'd not previously thought about that she could mention to clients.

She couldn't see anything obvious but then, on the edge of a patch of shadow, Margot noticed something that looked peculiar, an unexpected clump of something darker. Her interest piqued, she shuffled closer to the edge of Piers Gill for a better view at what it was that her video had picked up.

She took some photos of the opposite rock face, and when she stretched them on her phone, she took a sharp breath. What had alerted her looked now for all the world like a body suspended high up on the rock face, the legs and one arm akimbo towards the sky, but with the head and the other arm hanging low. The deep blackberry colour of the face and livid fingers poking through a ripped glove told Margot, who had seen several gruesome outdoor accidents, that this was blood pooling through gravity over at least fifteen hours. And this level of lividity meant the person was definitely dead, and beyond her help.

She moved away, staring at her phone. It was a while until she had phone reception and she was able to dial Mountain Rescue.

'My name is Margot Voyce, and I've just discovered what looks like a body hanging quite high up off an outcrop at Piers Gill.' She then looked at her phone and added her map co-ordinates.

'Stay where you are,' came the reply. 'We're already on the mountain searching for a reported missing person. I'll send them up and over to you. Near the Corridor Route?'

She retraced her steps. Standing well away from the lip at the top, Margot peered into Piers Gill and took a long look at the body. Then she turned her back to the distressing sight and walked a fair way away before perching on a large rock to await the rescue party.

Not too long afterwards they arrived, trailed a short while later by a pink-cheeked, breathless woman a little older than Margot who was woefully underdressed for a Cumbrian fell in November, especially one as brutal as Scafell Pike. The woman was accompanied by a face Margot remembered well from yesteryear, that of Councillor Robert Newman.

Dressed in old-fashioned gumboots and a calf-length waxed

14

coat that looked like they'd done sterling work for decades, Bob Newman was a local bigwig who even when Margot was a child seemed to have a finger in many pies.

After a few words to the first team, who paused for a few seconds before they went over to Piers Gill, Margot stayed where she was as she knew Mountain Rescue would be otherwise engaged for a while as they came up with a way to retrieve the body. Unhelpfully this was snagged in such a manner on the igneous rock that there wasn't an obvious way either to hoist it up or guide it down. Logistically this retrieval was going to be a challenge, she knew. They would talk to her properly when they were ready.

The woman and Councillor Newman looked across at the rock face where the man was – Margot was increasingly convinced the body was male, although she wasn't quite sure why – and then the woman turned towards Margot and tilted her head on one side as she looked at her.

Margot was slightly surprised that the woman, who tried to make a call and then angrily jabbed the Reject button, although obviously irked over the lack of mobile reception, didn't seem to be ruffled otherwise by what she'd seen. Normally unflappable, Margot was herself rattled, and so she couldn't help but wonder at her seeming so calm.

The woman strode towards Margot, her steps verging on a cross stomp, a peevish look on her face. The councillor seemed stricken by what he was still looking at and remained where he was.

Margot sighed, her legs stiff now, and with a small groan she stood up.

'I am Detective Inspector Jess Chambers,' the woman announced in a gruff voice that wasn't local. 'You call this in?'

'I did. I'm Margot Voyce. I came across the person about twenty minutes ago,' said Margot as she studied the flimsiness of the inspector's trousers and the inadequate footwear. If ever somebody had planned for a day that wasn't going to be spent tramping around the peaks as the weather turned wintry, it had to be Jess Chambers.

Margot felt a twinge of sympathy as the detective had to be cold, and then she added, 'But I wasn't expecting Mountain Rescue to arrive quite so soon nor for the police to be here at all.'

DI Jess Chambers stared at Margot for another long second, and for no reason she could fathom, Margot felt self-conscious.

'It's coincidence I'm here, as what was a courtesy visit to the volunteers led to watching the team in action and a real-life rescue. Or what now seems a retrieval,' the police officer said at last, after wondering about the experience of the woman before her, who seemed to know her way around a mountain rescue in a way that most people wouldn't, a way Jess Chambers envied right now.

'A-ha,' said Margot, who decided the lilt to the DI's voice was probably Northern Irish. And then she explained what she was doing on the mountain, how she had come to discover the body, and how she had had to move away to find reception on her phone before she could report it, indicating where she had stood with a toss of her head.

After Jess had watched Margot's video and inspected the photographs, Margot asked if they knew who it might be.

16

'We're expecting it to be James Garfield, Councillor Newman's nephew.' Jess didn't see any point in withholding this information, seeing how upset Newman was and that he would definitely give his nephew's name if Margot were to ask him.

'Oh!' said Margot, clearly taken aback, and then she couldn't stop herself twitching slightly under another scrutinising look from the detective inspector, who had immediately looked at Margot with renewed interest at her exclamation.

'You know him?'

'Well, yes. Sort of. Once. A bit. A long time ago, but yes. If it is James. I didn't recognise him though. In fact I wasn't totally certain the person over there was even male, although I suspected so. I didn't know James was related to the councillor.' Margot knew she was rambling, but she couldn't seem to stop herself.

'Thoughts on what you've seen?' interrupted Jess. 'How would you interpret the body hanging there?'

But Margot Voyce didn't seem to notice as she stared into the distance, before saying, 'It doesn't make *any* sense if it is James Garfield, as if ever somebody knew what they're about on a peak or on a mountain, then it's him. This terrain normally wouldn't cause him any problems at all. I can't believe it is him, but if so, something extreme and catastrophic must have occurred. A really horrible . . . um . . . accident.'

'Go on.' There was silence as Jess Chambers waited for Margot to elaborate, but she couldn't think of anything else to say.

'I'll need to talk to you further, Ms Voyce,' the detective told her with an emphasis on the 'Ms'; Jess had noticed Margot's blink rate rise and her eyes moisten. 'Don't go anywhere.'

And if Margot found the woman's previous stare uncomfortable, it was nothing to the piercing look she was now subjected to, before abruptly the detective strode back to stand beside the Mountain Rescue team, who were still debating with one another the best way of handling things. Jess didn't even glance at the councillor as she passed.

Margot sat back down on her rock, and then took off a glove to nibble a nail as she looked about her, the instruction to not go anywhere rankling slightly.

She watched the volunteers, who now appeared to have come to a decision about dealing with the retrieval. Margot recognised their experience as they went about their preparations, noticing the deft way they were going through their rucksacks, how confidently they withdrew what they needed, and the way each member of the team seemed to understand instinctively what everyone else was doing. She was pleased James would be handled by people who obviously knew what they were about.

And then Margot realised how they had acquired that sort of experience, and once she'd allowed that thought to settle, she felt even worse.

Her breathing, unbidden, began to quicken, and as she looked the other way, down the corridor, Margot realised the colours of the fell that not long before had seemed romantic and ethereal had now morphed to brash Technicolor, and suddenly she felt lightheaded and an almost overwhelming desire to lie on the ground. She'd experienced altitude sickness on several occasions, and the feeling was similar.

Damn it, thought Margot. *This is a terrible thing to happen to*

James. But what feels as bad is that I hate myself for thinking that it's tarnishing my upcoming guiding. I just couldn't have had a worse springboard to a new way of life.

As the horizon in front of her began to tilt, Margot realised she was in the early stages of a panic attack, and that finding the body and then the discovery she knew the victim was sending her into shock. She had no doubt now the body belonged to James, and although things between them had soured, she wouldn't have wished this upon him.

Margot had seen bodies being brought off mountains but she'd never known any of the dead personally, and by the time she'd seen them they'd been wrapped up and prone in a mountain stretcher, and so it had seemed something clean and sanitised. The way James has been suspended shouted the agony of his death, and Margot was deeply perturbed by what she'd seen. And she'd also let thoughts of her own position creep in – what did that say about her as a person? Not much that was good, she felt.

Margot dropped her head and studied her knees as she forced herself to breathe more slowly and deeply.

Slowly she began to feel, while not better as such, more in control of herself.

How on earth had James ended up like this?

He was incredibly experienced, and accustomed to much bigger and more dangerous mountains than Scafell Pike, Margot knew, and his mountaineering and fell-running know-how should have prevented such an outcome. She'd climbed with him, and so she knew precisely how thorough and safety conscious he was. What she'd seen seemed incredibly out of character. And very wrong.

Indeed, the more she thought about it, the less sense it made.

As Jess turned to frown at her again, Margot had the sensation that James's spirit was calling to her.

Walking to where Margot had indicated she would likely get a signal, Jess Chambers made some calls to her police station, then returned to stand by Councillor Newman for a minute before edging closer once more to the lip above the gully to take in all she could. This wasn't how her morning should have gone and she felt thoroughly out of sorts.

Hungry and cold, without a hat or gloves, with her suit trousers offering next to no protection against gusts of biting wind, and her wool Crombie overcoat not doing much better, the final straw was her boots blistering her heels. It all combined to pretty much sum up her increasingly dismal time in Cumbria so far. At first she'd enjoyed the Instagram-ready vistas of high peaks and tranquil lakes, bordered by quaint old houses and pretty gardens, as well as the endless tones of grey in the stone walls and the wry Cumbrian humour in the shops and eateries. And the array of lively characters who ended up at the police station had made her smile on several occasions.

But Jess had struggled to make much headway into the community. People seemed suspicious of her, and she felt forced to spectate rather than participate.

While nobody had been unpleasant to her face, she couldn't say she'd had a warm welcome at the station in the month she had been there. No one else seemed knocked out by her arrival either, other than Bob Newman of course, and she thought that was driven more by calculation than him being genuinely pleased to meet her.

Controversial staffing rota adjustments and internal policy changes were already afoot when she was seconded in to take the place of a popular detective inspector signed off long-term sick, and although none of this was anything to do with her, Jess had detected a distinct whiff of rancour from her colleagues that suggested they'd expected an internal promotion to fill the spot she had taken.

Jess felt like telling them she was just as unsettled about the situation as they were. A stint in the Lake District hadn't been at the top of her agenda, and she'd agreed to it on a whim. In part to allow her colleagues to get used to the idea of having a new boss, at least until everyone felt a bit more settled about the situation, so far Jess had spent quite a lot of time away from her desk. This was also because she needed to orientate herself to a different sort of policing than she was used to.

Right from her first few days, the difficulties of covering a rural area largely in the midst of a national park revealed themselves as polar opposites to the urban policing Jess had experienced previously.

While there wasn't the thrum of potential havoc she'd experienced when she'd been based in Belfast, instead she'd discovered the trials of narrow roads and inadequate parking, and low-wage communities plagued by extortionate housing costs caused by second homes belonging to affluent townies and the plethora of Airbnbs, which resulted in many people being forced to live far from where they worked, with no option of public transport. While these issues were less obviously incendiary than

21

Jess was used to, it didn't take long for her to realise they could be just as fraught.

Organised thefts from farms and animal rustling were rife, as were drugs coming in via the coast, burglary rings plundering second homes and badly behaved visitors. Regular drownings in the lakes and deaths out on the peaks were, sadly, merely another facet of the job, she'd been told.

The area was breath-takingly beautiful of course. But wonderful vistas didn't put food on the table or keep people out of hospital. The contrast was disconcerting, to say the least.

Early on Bob Newman had taken her under his wing.

Jess found him – from the moment she clocked his self-satisfied expression, round belly and the drinker's nose that shouted he was quite the bon viveur from two generations before hers – irritatingly patronising, but she had made a conscious choice not to challenge his attitudes. An old dog wasn't going to change his tricks, and Jess could just tell that Bob had decided long ago how the world functioned, especially when it came to women. But although it grated on Jess's nerves when Bob said 'my lady wife' when talking about his spouse, and he liked to drop into the conversation a bit too often that his local golf club had a prize he sponsored, Jess made sure to keep the same bland expression.

She had a more important reason for not challenging Bob Newman. Jess had always found it a useful tactic to allow people to underestimate her. And Bob wasn't without his uses. He was happy to share his deep knowledge of local affairs, having been prominent on the local council for years. And everyone seemed to know him. As they drove around, Jess felt she was getting a crash course in living in the Lake District, and who its movers and shakers were.

Still, a little of Bob went quite a long way, and already Jess had decided their time together was enough. The visit to Mountain Rescue was going to be the last day she'd be spending in his company, although Jess hadn't said as much yet.

And then in an instant it had all changed earlier that morning, as within moments of arriving at the rescue centre, its volunteers and a search dog were preparing to set out on a mission in the early light, to hunt for someone reported missing.

It was immediately apparent that Councillor Newman's nephew was the person they hoped to find.

The older man went ashen and suddenly seemed so diminished in stature when James Garfield's name was first mentioned that for a moment Jess thought the councillor was about to have a cardiac arrest. She made sure he sat down and had a drink of water.

He was made of stern stuff though, and it wasn't long before Bob rallied and insisted he accompany the search. There would be an innocent explanation for why James's car had remained overnight in a remote parking area, and even though James had missed his regular evening social media update, Jess should go with them too as she might never get another 'perfect opportunity' to see a real-life operation unfurl, Bob had insisted.

A mountain rescue wasn't something Jess felt she needed to see as she could imagine all too clearly how it would function. But Bob and the team's eager expressions seemed to say for her not to go along too would be a black mark against her that could well take her more trouble to recover from than it was worth. So Jess agreed she would head up the mountain

23

alongside Bob in the wake of the rescue team. The fact that she'd not had any breakfast or the discovery in the first couple of minutes trudging up the fell that her boots were in no way waterproof had not improved her mood.

An hour or so after they had left the centre, the discovery of a body had been reported, the last thing Jess wanted to hear.

After they'd scrambled around to Piers Gill, it was clear the manner in which the person was strung up on the rocks made immediate positive identification impossible, although almost immediately Bob Newman appeared convinced it belonged to his nephew James.

Jess phoned for a doctor for death to be pronounced and discovered this would happen at the mortuary. She sighed, unused to the way it worked out here, and then saw Bob's face had turned grey once more.

'Let Councillor Newman have that rock you're on,' Jess called to Margot and then strode over to the minuscule spot of reception to telephone for an ambulance.

'The ambulance will be at the bottom,' Jess announced a few minutes later. 'You'll accompany us, Ms Voyce.'

Margot nodded she understood.

Jess stood there uncharacteristically indecisive. She felt she was leaving an unusual incident scene much too early, and in a perfect world she'd be delegating this escort duty to a more junior officer while she got on with what she was good at, which was looking for anything that seemed to stand out. As quickly as she could she shot a video and a string of photographs, just to make sure she had some sort of record aside from what the volunteers were filming.

Was what she had now in digital form a suspicious death, some sort of bizarre accident or a suicide? How on earth had the body come to be snagged on a vertical rock face, with his limbs so ridiculously splayed?

The more Jess considered what she'd seen, the more flummoxed she was, an unexplained mountain death so far out of her professional experience.

She peered again at the tangle of clothes and flesh, and then above and below; there was no sign how it had got up or down there, which seemed ridiculous. Still, although she had no idea what made her feel this, something seemed wrong.

Jess was all too aware that perhaps this was more the result of her time with the Police Service of Northern Ireland. During her time in Belfast, Jess had found that pretty much everything suspicious *was* suspicious. And still easing herself in after a sabbatical following an investigation gone wrong that had made Jess wonder if she needed a different career, she couldn't decide what to make of the woman who had called the body in. Was it even normal for a lone woman to be out on the fells this early or indeed at any other time?

Jess glanced across at Margot. She seemed distracted and thoughtful as she stared at the body with every bit as much concentration as Jess. Margot Voyce was composed, and capable and strong too in the physical sense, and certainly she was more comfortable outdoors than Jess. Maybe she shouldn't assume too quickly this woman's non-involvement.

Jess sighed. It was so difficult to make any sort of judgement call in such unfamiliar surroundings. Should she get a forensics team up here, just in case? And could the local force afford to send one, even if she did make the call? It looked an expensive proposition, one that probably needed higher authority.

With an exasperated hunch of her shoulders, Jess reached for her phone to discuss the situation with her superior. It was shaping up as a long and unrewarding day of precisely the sort she hated.

Thirty minutes later Jess was walking in thoughtful silence. Bob Newman had rallied once more, and seemed physically able to get to where the ambulance would be without too much of her help, even though there remained a bluish tinge to his lips. Jess noticed Margot was adept at helping him over any rough pieces of ground or when it got slippery.

Once the going got a little easier, Margot began talking to the older man. The wind was picking up, and she told him to zip his jacket up so as not to lose any more core temperature. She handed him her water bottle and insisted he sip slowly, adding that she remembered him from when she was small and would watch him on the local television news at teatime, and she was very sorry if the person she'd found did turn out to be James, as she had known him too.

'Aye,' said the councillor in a way that didn't really say anything, as Jess tried to look as if she wasn't listening as intently as she was.

Margot explained to Bob Newman that she had come across the deceased earlier that day because she was preparing herself to become a walking guide, but that 'back in the day', she and James had made several ascents together on mountains in other parts of the world. They had lost touch with one another in recent years, although she'd heard on the grapevine James had taken his mountaineering skills and combined these with ultra-fitness and speed running targets over rough terrain, making him an online star.

Jess willed Margot to go on in this vein.

'Someone told me that James did a lone run of the equivalent of a double marathon over incredibly steep inclines in the Mojave Desert in 120 degrees,' Margot added.

'Aye, he did – the daft bugger,' said Councillor Newman with a small chuckle at the memory, as the blue sky was over-whelmed suddenly by dark clouds. Jess felt a new breezy chill. 'And maybe a month later he did the same again in some forest in Alaska. Tongass National Forest, was it? I can't remember for certain. He told me just a couple of days ago that next summer he was going to Namibia to run over seventy miles, and if that went well he wanted to join a hundred-mile annual desert and mountain run in Tennessee where hardly anybody finishes. He said part of the route is called Little Hell, and that stuck in my mind. I think he wanted to post about me sponsoring him, but I said I'd need a business plan before I'd let him shout about his connection with me. I believe family comes first, but that doesn't mean I don't want it done properly, I told him.'

Jess smiled to herself about the deft way Bob Newman kept inserting himself into James Garfield's story. If the body did turn out to be that of his nephew, Jess didn't doubt that the councillor would be mightily upset, but that that wouldn't over-ride Bob Newman's desire to make his family connection clear as crystal to whoever he was speaking with.

Bob added, 'I might have done it too and given James the

sponsorship he wanted; he's many fans, you know, and some of them will be local voters, and never let it be said that I'd turn a voter away if I could help it. But James was restless and had a lonely life, I'd warrant – people felt they knew him, and I'm not sure they did.'

Margot nodded. 'Keen on having admirers, but keener on being alone?'

'He were always the same,' said Bob Newman. 'I'd hoped he'd have settled down by now, but there were never any sign.'

Margot gave a small snort, but when Jess glanced in her direction, Margot's expression was inscrutable, and the snort could have been anything.

During her sabbatical Jess had flown over the Tongass National Forest, and she'd been struck by the dark, mysterious sight of the endless tall firs crowding over the many steep rises. She'd felt at the time it looked intriguing on first glance, although not so much the more one stared. Sinister was how she'd thought of it later.

Although Jess had been meaning to listen rather than join the conversation in the hope that Margot Voyce and Bob Newman would forget about her and then say something they each might not have if she'd asked them directly, Jess couldn't help butting in. 'Why would he put himself through these ridiculous challenges? His body must have hurt constantly. I don't get it.'

Margot replied, 'When I knew James the outdoors was where he said he felt at home, and I understand that as it's how I feel. His physique was perfect for endurance, and so extreme challenges would have been easier for him than most of us, and I guess somewhere along the line he just gave up on being a career mountaineer. It's very expensive and competitive, and the recognised climbs feel more like tourist traps these days, with too many inexperienced people paying large sums for organised climbs, and then queuing to summit in a short window of weather or daylight.

'James and I didn't part on the best of terms, but I guess he decided to monetise his ability for physical challenges. Running up Scafell Pike is relatable enough to ordinary folk, so that's where the numbers of social media followers are – it's the numbers that the sponsors pay attention to. He presented himself as being ordinary, but better, faster, more determined. He's the sort to check the view stats each day and strategise for his next post if there was any drop-off. At least that's what I assume.'

Jess stuck out a hand for Bob Newman to grab as they were stepping down a steep bit of scree just as she wondered if there had been a slightly acerbic note to Margot's words.

A heavy squall cut out further conversation, and as Jess tried to imagine what James Garfield would have been like should she have met him, she was doused with icy water that made its way straight through her outer garments and on to her skin.

Fortunately they then crested a small rise and saw the ambulance, and it wasn't long before the councillor was wrapped in foil with blankets on top, and on the way to hospital for a thorough check-up.

As the ambulance door was about to shut Jess noticed his fingers were now the same grey-blue as his lips. 'I'll ring you later with an update, Bob, and to see how you are.'

Shakily, the councillor raised a hand in acknowledgement, and the door closed as the ambulance bumped away.

A minute or so later Jess exclaimed, 'Hell, I didn't ask Bob Newman for his car keys.'

The two women watched the ambulance bounce around a corner and out of sight. There was a short silence.

'Where is your car?' said Margot.

'Mountain Rescue.'

'I'll take you.'

Jess thought the subsequent twenty-minute trek to Margot's car was the most unpleasant physical experience of the whole of her life. She was sopping wet and chilled to the bone, with the tops of both ears painful through repeated stings from the slashing raindrops.

Margot didn't seem bothered by the weather, and Jess tried not to look at her.

Margot's ancient car seemed barely roadworthy, with dented and scratched bodywork and faded paint.

Margot saw Jess's disapproval and said, 'Runs like a dream.'

'A nightmare?' Jess replied.

They got in, and Jess noticed the milometer was well in excess of one hundred thousand miles.

It took Margot a couple of goes to encourage the engine into life, and Jess said, 'I suppose I shouldn't mention an MOT?'

'Probably not before we're out of the car park.'

Oddly, Jess's ears stung more once she was in the car, and she lifted her hands to press them. Wordlessly, Margot reached over to the back seat, handed Jess a microfibre towel and a Thermos of coffee. Jess blotted as much water as she could from various bits of her and tried to warm her sodden hands on a cup of coffee.

'You're better negotiating these roads than me,' Jess admitted after Margot expertly guided the car to within a centimetre of a stone wall on Jess's side in order that someone coming in the opposite direction could pass.

'Well, I learned to drive here,' said Margot.

'Hmmn,' said an unconvinced Jess. 'I think it's more than that. Not even afraid of stone walls.'

'Well, if you hate stone in Cumbria, you're in for a bad time,' laughed Margot.

At the Mountain Rescue centre Jess thanked Margot, passed her a business card and then asked for Margot's details, adding she'd probably need to talk to her again, but if Margot thought of anything in the meantime, even a very small thing, then she must let her know.

Jess made as if to get out of the car, but then sat back in her seat as she said, 'So how well did you know James Garfield?'

Margot frowned. 'It's hard to say. We went back years to school, and we hooked up for a while a few years back. But our paths didn't really cross much, and so it was very casual, although there was certainly a period when I very much liked seeing him. He could be fun and witty, and always I loved his energy. The problem was that everybody else felt the same, and this made James really keen to build on his reputation as the cool fun guy but not always nicely. But he was sexy, although he made it clear I wasn't the only one. So for someone like the me back then, I thought he was glamorous and I enjoyed the way I felt when everybody wanted to talk to him but it was *me* who was beside him. But . . .'

Margot stared down at the steering wheel.

Jess waited and when Margot didn't continue, she prompted, 'But?'

'Oh, it's not really to do with me and James as such. But I realised after a while that *everybody* thought him *the Man*, not just me, and actually him most of all, and being alongside someone like that is really depressing. I had no special privileges, no matter how many times we shared a bed, and it became tiresome to see how quickly he'd spring out of bed after we'd had sex, or how when we went out, hordes of other people were waiting for their chance with him. And then, completely through my own fault, I had a bad fall in the Atlas mountains in Morocco, and I broke my back. He was on that expedition, but he didn't give a shit what had happened to me.'

Margot was surprised that without warning there was a crushing ache in her throat that made her voice quiver. She never talked about this dark time normally and now she knew why.

As the engine gave the ticking sound of cooling down, Jess found she was holding her breath. There was something about Margot Voyce she liked, but Jess reminded herself that she must keep in mind Margot's discovery of the body, and her being a potential suspect if anything suspicious did turn out to have happened.

Jess felt a corresponding stab of recognition at the tone of Margot's voice when she mentioned her injury. Jess's stint in Northern Island, the end of it anyway, made her feel shaky too, deep down inside.

Margot added quietly, 'I was in hospital for a long time and had to learn to walk again. It was very difficult as the doctors told me my mountaineering days were over, and I struggled with this. James turned away in all senses when I was lifted off the mountain – he never knew I *saw* him do this at the time – and in the weeks that followed he hardly got in touch and never visited.

'We FaceTimed one day, and all I could see on his face was that I was now the person he never wanted to be, the poster girl for how badly it could all go. And it made me end the conversation abruptly. And he never called back, and the upshot was that he and I never spoke again. It hurt a lot at the time, but I think probably he never gave it – or me, come to that – a second thought. He was like that, I think now. It was all about him. He was not that nice a person after all, no matter how great everybody always said he was. Not that I think about it much.'

'You've recovered well,' said Jess. 'I couldn't see that you'd been injured, and I'm good at noticing that sort of thing.'

'Oh, I work hard at it. I know my limits, and I try not to get close to them. And the limits are pretty much governed by constant gym sessions for strength and yoga for stretching, and hiking relatively gentle inclines,' Margot said with a dismissive exhale.

Jess didn't feel there was anything gentle about the incline she'd scrambled up earlier, but she didn't say anything.

'And I do a lot of quiet horse riding as it's relaxing. The rest of my time I try to eat right and get enough sleep. And I take painkillers. A lot of painkillers, but over-the-counter stuff, not prescription. It all means I can move around on the peaks, but only to a level.'

Jess thought Margot's life sounded limited.

Margot smiled at Jess in a way that suggested she'd guessed

what Jess had thought and had to agree. 'Me as a walking guide is my compromise – it's the best I can manage and, depressingly, it's the best I can achieve. I know guiding would be a dream come true for a lot of people, and no disrespect to anyone for that, but it seems second best to me in comparison to how I started out. The irony and, what I find most galling, is that I slipped over on some loose stones at a base camp, scree that wasn't difficult, yet somehow totally wrecked my back. I wasn't even out on the mountain proper, and that hurts as much as the fall did, only in a different way, of course.'

'If that is James up in Piers Gill, what's your best guess about what happened?'

'Hard to say,' said Margot. 'It could be a freak accident or weather. Odd things happen out in the open, and nature doesn't treat us as we expect it to. So there could be an innocent explanation. But it's completely out of character with the man I knew. It must have happened yesterday, as the blood had pooled in his face and sunrise is late at the moment. James wouldn't have set out running in the dark as that's a fast track to taking your cruciate ligament out, and he wouldn't have risked that as his sponsorship deals would demand him active, and in any case I was up on the fell early and he'd been on that rock for literally hours already when I found him. He was definitely running when he was on Scafell Pike; his shoes tell me that.'

Jess agreed with the timing Margot estimated, but she hadn't noticed the footwear.

'Did Mr Garfield ever express any suicidal thoughts to you?'

'Never, no. He was a person who embraced life like nobody I've ever met, and he was an ambitious man on a mission.'

'Mission?'

'World domination, more or less, in the extreme challenges arena.'

'So not one for laughing on the outside and crying inside?'

'Absolutely not,' said Margot. 'Okay, his extreme record attempts could be taken as having something of a death wish, but I think only as death by proxy. Actually, more likely death by glory, dying in attempting a magnificent achievement where it wasn't even part of his equation. But a lonely tumble into Piers Gill where conceivably he might not have been found for months, and without his followers already prepped, and nobody filming? Please! He'd never want such an ignominious end.'

Jess knew Garfield's digital footprint would help narrow down timing as well as what might have happened. She must find out what had been his intention when he had gone out on Scafell Pike.

'And do you follow James now on his media outlets?' said Jess. She'd detected a deliberate distance in the way Margot spoke about him, but she was curious as to just how familiar the woman beside her would be with his movements.

'There's vague gossip from the outdoor community here, and through that I know he does sometimes post locally. But the gossip says he's here, there and everywhere, so the way he presents his activities is more what'd he'd describe as pan-global. I suspect some of it will be flimflam designed to keep his follower numbers growing and please his sponsors,' said Margot. 'But since I came out of hospital five years back, I've made it a point of principle to give James Garfield exactly what he gave me: zero attention, and so I don't look at his posts.'

They looked at each other, and Jess couldn't detect anything about Margot's demeanour or voice that suggested she wasn't telling the truth.

'Do you remember the last time you saw him? Or had contact?'

'Absolutely nothing since the time just after I broke my back. Seriously.'

The rain splattered viciously against Margot's windscreen once more as Jess's phone rang, causing both women to start slightly.

She answered and after an 'Uh-huh' jabbed the Off button and then stared at her damp knees. 'Sod it, I've got to go up there again,' she said.

'Hang on a minute then,' said Margot. She got out of the car and went round to the boot, returning with an armful of clothes which she thrust towards Jess.

'There's a silk vest and long-sleeve under-top, a couple of climbing fleeces, tights, waterproof gloves and a pair of trousers to go on top of the tights, socks, a snood and a proper jacket. You get yourself sorted, and I'll get you a refilled Thermos and a bottle of water and some snack bars. And I've got some sandwiches I made this morning – you'd better eat them now in the dry before you do anything else.' Margot retrieved the sandwiches from the glove compartment and put them on top of the clothes.

Jess gazed at Margot blankly. Who on earth kept such a vast array of stuff in their boot?

'Snood?'

'Better than a scarf as it doesn't come undone,' said Margot as she lifted it so Jess could see.

'Thank you. Bob Newman said when I first met him there would be times I'd need to go out on the fell and I'd need to tog up, advice I ignored. Big mistake.'

'I shouldn't for a moment think that's the first time someone has not listened to Bob's advice. You'll get the hang of everything. What size boots are you, as those must be crippling? There's always a pile of old boots in the centre, so I'll see if I can dig you some out.'

'I don't suppose they have blister plasters too?' said Jess, and then asked how there came to be such a selection of boots at the centre.

'Donations of serviceable but no longer needed boots when people have traded up,' said Margot, 'for precisely this situation.'

Twenty minutes later Jess was ready to go. Although she'd eaten the sandwiches and polished off the coffee in what felt like seconds, it had taken a while to get all the clothes on. Margot had shown her a way of tying her laces so the boots didn't move, and with an extra pair of thick mountaineering socks on they would do, although they were still a touch too large. Margot had even found a waterproof walking rucksack for the water and snack bars, and popped in a laminated map, a compass, whistle, goggles and a head torch 'just to be on the safe side as phones can die, and there's never decent reception at Piers Gill. Best to have backup so you can work out where you are and make your way down in the dark if need be.'

Jess caught a glimpse of her reflection in her car window. She wasn't knocked out by the garish jacket but wasn't going to complain.

'Last thing before I leave,' Jess said, who was feeling very hot now wearing the outdoor gear in the shelter of the car park. 'Have you any idea, assuming this is James Garfield and if it does turn out to be a suspicious death, of anybody who might have had it in for him?'

'I've been wondering about that. But nobody springs to mind,' said Margot. 'Take care of that jacket please – it's a proto- type from when I once almost got sponsorship, so it's got sentimental value.'

Jess went to take it off with an 'Oh, I couldn't possibly—'

Margot put up her hand to stop her. 'It's what you'll need, so keep it on. I've just thought of something though. Who reported James missing?'

Jess could have hit herself. She hadn't already established that, and it was such a basic error. 'That's a very good question,' she said.

'Well, somebody must have known he'd gone up Scafell Pike and hadn't come back down,' said Margot.

Both women looked up to where the surrounding peaks would be visible if they weren't shrouded in cloud. After a few seconds of silence Jess got into her car, plonking her wet clothes in the boot, where they lay in a crumpled heap beside a tatty and forlorn bag-for-life. The last thing she saw in her rear-view mirror was Margot standing by the door to the rescue centre watching her make a rather tentative turn out of the parking area on to the narrow country road.

Late afternoon and a very weary Jess made her way into the incident room at the police station, where the first thing she did was to connect her phone to her computer to download the images and the videos she'd taken.

She'd felt so much better earlier once she'd had the sandwiches and the hot drink – Margot had been right about that – and she resolved not to skip breakfast from now on.

Jess hadn't enjoyed making her way back to where the body was, her thigh muscles complaining ferociously all the way as she climbed. But decent clothing made a huge difference. She knew she'd sleep deeply that night, as she wasn't used to being out in the fresh air for such a long time, let alone such punishing exercise.

As she looked around what passed for the incident room at the police station, Jess could feel her cheeks throbbing bright red after their blasting from the rain and wind.

This was the first time she would work with her immediate team on a possibly suspicious event. Although they had the support of some backroom staff, essentially she could call on a staff of two: Detective Sergeant Tony Peters and Detective Constable Bill Harper. They were older than she was and had worked at the station for years, and so her briefing would bear little resemblance to the much larger and frequently fraught internal briefings she had conducted in Northern Ireland.

She wasn't detecting a sense of urgency in the room, but she tried not to read anything into that one way or another.

'Right, listen up,' said Jess in as energetic a manner as she could, and then gave a small inward quiver of embarrassment for the "listen up" that sounded uncomfortably TV detective. 'As you'll know by now, a youngish and fit man died in Piers Gill after presumably climbing Scafell Pike – that is the normal route, I'm told. It's too early to say exactly what happened, or quite when the death occurred, although it seems likely that it was just over twenty-four hours ago in the bad weather when the mountain was quiet. But –' one of her colleagues gave an audible intake of breath as with a tap on her keyboard she brought up on the whiteboard a photograph of the suspended body '– it looks at the least an unusual death. I left the scene this afternoon after the body had been retrieved and it is now at the mortuary. He will be formally identified in the morning, but all indications are it's Councillor Bob Newman's nephew, James Garfield. He's a local man and an internet celebrity in the world of mountaineering, extreme fitness and fell running. The PM will take place tomorrow after the identification.'

'Ah, I follow him on TikTok – he's good,' said DS Peters, suddenly perking up and looking engaged.

'Yes,' said Jess. 'And is – was – James Garfield as special as they say?'

Peters rubbed his chin, and Jess could hear the scratch of his beard. 'I'd say so. I enjoy his live feeds, and he's good at explaining technicalities. He's very personable, and funny at times.'

'I didn't have you down as an avid TikToker, Tony.' DC Harper gave a small snigger at Jess's comment, but she ignored this as she continued, 'Meanwhile the woman who found Mr Garfield used to know him – she told me everyone thought of him as the proverbial good guy. She's a walking guide called Margot Voyce, recently moved back to this area. Either of you know her?'

Peters and Harper shook their heads.

Jess wrote Margot's name on the board. 'Tony, as you're already familiar with Mr Garfield's world, you can dig into everything online about him, and see if anyone made any threats – that sort of thing. Get everything in a single file, going back three months. And while you're about it, find out what there is to know about this woman, Margot Voyce; she's got mountain experience and seems to know a lot about what James Garfield did – the physical challenges and so on. And she and Mr Garfield had a thing a while back. She seems all right, but really dig into her past and see if you can find any animosity in the last five years between her and Mr Garfield. I've got his phone, but we'll need to send that off for specialist analysis as it's waterlogged. It's dead anyway.'

Peters nodded.

Harper said, 'I might be able to dry out the phone, rather than having to wait for the tech people. A phone in a bag of uncooked rice on a radiator can work wonders.'

Jess passed the phone across. 'Knock yourself out, Bill. The only fingerprints on the phone belong to Mr Garfield – I've had those checked. You can look into his background aside from online. Whether anyone had a vendetta or long-standing gripes against him, money woes or a disgruntled lover, or he'd upset people over parking or planning permission, or been involved in any domestics – the usual drill. I believe he was single and lived alone, but check into that too.'

Jess had a thought and added, 'It might go without saying, but don't either of you take it for granted all Mr Garfield's sexual partners were female. I've been told he was popular, but let's make no assumptions. Also, make a list of other deaths on the local peaks of experienced runners, climbers or anybody else that seem odd.'

'Is it suspicious then?' said Harper more dubiously than Jess Chambers felt the unexplained death of a fit and healthy man merited.

Jess didn't say anything, and after a pause Harper added, 'I mean, I know it *looks* odd. But very strange accidents happen on the Cumbrian fells all the time, and they're pretty much always down to human error or heart attacks or strokes, or occasionally allergic reactions to bee stings. And James Garfield died at an accident black spot. We don't usually go all out on getting involved if we don't have to, as we don't have the manpower . . .'

Jess snapped, 'I've no idea yet whether it is a suspicious death, and I've no idea what my superiors will think, and so you could both get reassigned first thing tomorrow. But I'm not really that interested in how you *used* to do things around here. It could even be that Garfield was a jumper and it was suicide.

'But look at it this way for now: should the body turn out to be James Garfield – and all the signs are that it will – then Bob Newman is going to be over us like a rash, even if ultimately his nephew's death proves to be the result of an accident. Everyone – Bob especially – keeps telling me he has the ear of the press and he's never off the local news programmes on the telly, so we need to act from the get-go as if we know what we're doing. We don't need any negative headlines if we can possibly avoid them. I understand we have time and money constraints, but let's be cautious and cover ourselves right from the start.'

Peters and Harper glanced at each other.

Then Jess added less stridently, 'Look, we'll know more tomorrow. But from what I saw, a body suspended high up on what I heard called a vertical pitch doesn't look like a normal death in that terrain. And while you're about it, Bill, ring the hospital to find out how Bob Newman is – he wasn't looking too good when I last saw him. Meanwhile I'm assuming that Garfield had an accountant or somebody who helped him on the business side, and so we'll have to track whoever that is down. And aside from Bob, does he have any next of kin? Bob said on the way down from Piers Gill that Mr Garfield's parents had both died and he was an only child, and that he'd never married or entered a civil partnership, but let's check that's the case.'

An office phone rang, and Harper answered it, then turned to Jess. 'Ma'am, that was the pathologist who's at the mortuary putting the body into the cold room. Apparently the deceased may well have been wearing a camera to film his run, something like a GoPro.'

' "Skip" or "boss", please. The latest ones are even more tiny now, I guess?' said Jess.

'The webbing harness looks to have been used as a makeshift tourniquet,' added Harper, just as Peters said, 'And GoPros are nearly always black.'

'Convenient,' Jess murmured, thinking of the myriad nooks and crannies out on the peak.

'One of you needs to establish if the feed from the GoPro is sitting on a digital cloud, and if you can, get too what's on his phone – there must be a laptop, so cross-reference. Overnight I'll be senior investigating officer and will open the policy book now, but it could be we'll need to join forces with a neighbouring team, and/or a higher ranking officer will take over from me. Either way, can one of you look also into who alerted Mountain Rescue?'

Jess wouldn't give up the role of SIO without a fight, but at this moment she was really too exhausted to care, with what felt like every muscle in her body still complaining over climbing the fell not once but twice. The day had been a shit-show, and so far tomorrow was shaping up to be more of the same.

'I might be in late in the morning,' Jess said, declining to elaborate further, and as she picked up her laptop and left the room she ignored mutterings about needles and haystacks presumably to do with the missing camera.

Then she turned to stick her head back into the incident room. 'A couple of last things. See what you can find out about Margot Voyce's car. Has it an MOT, tax up to date and valid insurance? I'm not interested in chasing her up on these, but want to know if she's a rule-follower. And maybe ring round solicitors to see if anybody has a will made by James Garfield lodged with them. And don't forget the information on the person who reported the disappearance, please.'

'So we're not waiting on a formal identification before we make enquiries about a will?' said Peters.

Jess looked at him, making sure he was the first to turn away.

While Jess had been gloomily contemplating her life choices as she'd plodded back up to join the rescue team at Piers Gill and accompany the body off the mountain, Margot had headed to the stables where she kept her horse.

She parked the car, and as she got out, looked back across to where she had come from. It looked to be bleak and overcast still there, although the weather was lifting where she was. It was typical Cumbrian weather – in a single hour in any season, it was possible at just about any time of the year to experience wind, rain, fog and sunshine.

In spite of a weak sun suddenly breaking through the clouds, Margot didn't feel like riding, and so she turned out the rugged-up Trojan in the small stone-walled field behind the big modern barn that housed the stables American style, unable to prevent a smile as he trotted away to find the muddiest part of the field for a good roll. And then she went to speak to yard owner Tom Drake.

Actually Tom was much more than a yard owner as the stables were only part of a large and presumably profitable enterprise that Margot joked was his version of 'destination tourism'.

Aside from the 1,000-plus Herdwick sheep out on the fells that underpinned Tom's business, there were some pig and sheep rare breeds housed conveniently close to the parking area for visitors to spend time with, and a large farm shop selling produce and home wares from other local farmers and small businesses. The farm shop had a space for tables so customers could enjoy coffee and some food, while Tom also ran pony trekking in the summer and, round at the back, had facilities available all the year round for more serious horse owners who kept mounts in livery. Tom employed quite a team of workers, but Margot was always surprised how little she saw of them, though apparently it was very different during lambing in the spring.

As expected, Tom was in the farm shop as he usually was at this time of day, doing his accounts by the look of it, his favourite

45

collie breeding bitch curled up nose to tail nearby on some folded horse-blankets that were no longer fit for purpose. The shop was empty of customers and he looked pleased she'd come in as he was always happy to be distracted from paperwork.

'I thought you were up on Scafell all day,' he said.

Margot frowned. 'You've not heard, then?'

'Heard?'

Tom's amiable expression slipped to one that indicated a sharp mind as he ran a hand through his unruly hair and then tugged at his ancient seaman's gansey beneath several worn-out quilted gilets.

'I came across a body this morning.'

'Nasty,' said Tom. 'Happens though.'

Margot felt unsteady for a moment or two, and she reached for the countertop.

Out of all the people she knew in Cumbria, Tom Drake was probably the one whose opinion she valued most. He was sensible and quiet, and not unattractive if one liked that sort of thing, with the bonus of a wicked sense of humour, although he could be choosy about when to laugh.

Although they were both single, they had never even come close to getting together, possibly because she'd knocked out one of his baby teeth at primary school in a playground tussle during a game of kiss-chase, and since then there'd always been an implicit agreement not to get too close.

Margot didn't see that changing. Tom was far too valuable a friend to risk upsetting with anything more complicated than what they already had. In her experience good friends were much harder to find than lovers.

Immediately Tom could see something was more amiss with Margot than simply discovering a dead person up on Scafell Pike. He thought her one of the least panicky people he knew, the epitome of a person able to deal calmly with life's ups and downs.

'Pour us a coffee and I'll close for a bit,' Tom said as he flipped his laptop shut and stood up.

This was what Margot liked about Tom: his ability to cut to the chase without unnecessary drama.

He came to sit with her at a table a minute later, and then he peered at her for a moment before springing up. 'You look like you need to eat.'

'Ah, yes. I had to donate my sandwiches and coffee to a police inspector who happened to be out on the peak too,' said Margot. 'She'd no idea what she was about and hadn't got any food with her.'

Speaking with her mouth full, Margot described what she had seen and how she'd reported it to Mountain Rescue.

Tom didn't interrupt and let her tell the story in her own way.

Then Margot pushed her plate away, feeling overwhelmed by what she was about to say.

'It was horrible, just so bizarre, but the really foul part came later. They think it's James Garfield, Bob Newman's nephew.' Tom let out a low whistle that Margot ignored. She added, 'You, me and him were all at secondary school together. I think you know things developed between me and James a few years later, although I've not seen him since I hurt my back, and I didn't recognise him as he was upside down with a purple face. When I first spotted the body, there wasn't any obvious indication of who it was, and I was just too far away to see the face clearly. The body hadn't been officially identified when I left, but Rescue was already out on the mountain searching for James – he'd been missing since yesterday – and Bob Newman, who was there too, seemed in no doubt once he saw him.'

Tom's brow wrinkled as he got up to refill his cup. 'If you're right about it being James, that doesn't make sense. He knows that peak like the back of his hand, as well as what to do in an accident. In fact I was looking at his posts only last night and thought he seemed the most fit and determined I've seen him. He's got an astronomical following these days, you know.'

Margot nodded and gave a damp sniff. 'So I hear. I don't know why I feel so upset now – I wasn't like this earlier. It's not as though I know him any more, or that we ever meant any-thing much to each other.' Tom lifted one eyebrow at this point, but Margot didn't notice as she was looking at her half-eaten food. 'I guess it's because we had some good times and every-body thought he was so great. And it's always sad to see someone cut down in their prime.'

Tom grunted softly and stared out of the window. The way his face was angled meant Margot couldn't see the doubt in his eyes. Then he glanced towards her. How she'd spoken of James Garfield made it impossible to believe that they'd never been more than good friends.

Tom wasn't certain how that made him feel.

Complicated, he decided.

Later that evening, Margot received a WhatsApp: 'Thank you for the loan of the waterproofs – it made such a difference. Do you want me to drop them off at yours, or will you collect from the station? DI Jess Chambers.'

'No hurry – I'll pick them up from the police station when I'm next that way,' Margot tapped back immediately. She thought for a minute or two, before sending Jess a second message: 'BTW, JG had a fan who shot a lot of drone footage of him, most of his runs locally it looks like. I've just seen online as I just had to check what JG had posted in recent years, and this led me to his fanbase. Might this person have been out with the drone yesterday? Only a thought – I don't want to step on anybody's toes . . .'

Jess saw Margot's messages on her dashboard screen as she drove home. She was exhausted but nodded to herself. It was good to deal with someone efficient, a quality she felt many people lacked.

And then Jess reminded herself that her new colleagues might well be amazingly brilliant and efficient for all she knew. She hadn't really given them the chance to show what they could do. Jess wasn't proud of this. It wasn't like the person she wanted to be.

She really had to make a new start here, and stop hankering after what she'd known before, she told herself. If she didn't make more effort, she would only hurt herself, and she'd done enough of that already. She'd been at a loose end when the Cumbria secondment came up, and it was a good option for her. At the very least she needed to be the most professional officer she could be.

Promising to concentrate on savouring the good things about the Lake District and stop dwelling on the negatives, Jess drove along the narrow road, gingerly making the difficult turn into the parking space next to her grey stone cottage and then parking so that she could wriggle out of her half-open car door, her right foot already on the step up to the back door. The cottage was adorably pretty from the outside, but she could almost touch the walls on either side when she stretched out her arms if she stood in the middle of her living room.

Standing in the kitchen, she realised it was probably colder than outside, and Jess remembered this was because she was out of gas and that very possibly she had not ordered a new gas canister to be delivered.

Hell! This meant she'd have to tackle the cast-iron log burner, an unfamiliar appliance which she had so far proved spectacularly unsuccessful with.

She tried to get a draw on some kindling in the stove, but the wind seemed to be in the wrong direction and the flames were hard to coax into life.

All Jess wanted was to have a hot bath and get something out of the freezer to eat.

Double hell! She'd forgotten to replenish both fridge and freezer, which had been her plan that day, until hijacked by the death on the fell.

The cottage had looked so quaint when the estate agent sent over the details that Jess had fallen for the romantic idea of living in the middle of nowhere and had signed the rental agreement without visiting. But the reality was a different story. The wind whistled constantly in the roof, and even with the central heating at full blast it always felt cold to her, while the picturesque but minute windows meant it was always dim inside, even on the sunniest days. And it was only a matter of time before she scraped one of her front wings in the incredibly tight parking place.

Jess had tried to back out of the agreement, but the landlord wasn't having it, and so she was stuck in this gloom-box for the next ten months until her release clause at a year, miles from anything like a pub or even a small store, let alone neighbours.

Not bothering to take off Margot's multicoloured waterproof jacket, Jess poured herself a glass of red wine and then plonked herself down on a rather hard armchair. It was going to be a challenge in the short term to remain upbeat about her new job and home. But the wine definitely helped.

She picked up her phone. 'Mike, I've a favour to ask,' she said and spoke for a few moments.

Jess hung up, only for the station to ring before she'd had a chance to put her mobile on to charge, asking if they could patch a call through.

She almost said no as she felt completely done in, but when she heard it was James Garfield's agent and business manager, she agreed to take the call.

'Detective Inspector Jess Chambers.'

'Kate Summers. I'm James Garfield's business manager.' It was the posh voice of somebody used to getting her way. 'I am getting unconfirmed reports of an incident involving James, an event or accident that may have led to his death?'

'All I can say at this moment is James Garfield was reported missing first thing this morning, and a body of a man around Mr Garfield's age has been found at Piers Gill on Scafell Pike.

We are yet to get a formal identification or conduct a post-mortem, and so I won't say any more.'

'I see,' said Kate Summers. 'And what makes you think the body is that of James Garfield? He's at the top of his field, you know.'

'I am not going to talk about identification further at the moment,' answered Jess, who didn't care for the snap in the other woman's voice and so decided to be less helpful than she might have been. She could have said she'd had James's uncle with her and there was currently little doubt as to who the body belonged to. 'However, Ms Summers, assuming that you are not currently in direct touch with James Garfield, and find yourself unable to reach him overnight, if you could make yourself available for a face-to-face interview at my police station tomorrow afternoon, then that would be sensible. By then I might have information to suggest whether the death is suspicious.'

'Tomorrow? In Cumbria? That's very inconvenient. I'm based in London, and I am a very busy person.'

'Not as inconvenient for you, I'd imagine,' said Jess, 'as for the person I watched being retrieved from the mountain today.'

Jess exhaled carefully and leaned back in her chair as Kate Summers rang off without saying goodbye.

DAY TWO

The next morning Jess woke early and lay in bed for half an hour scrolling through social media for the latest updates. The suspected death of James Garfield was trending, which it hadn't been the previous evening.

Then she got up and went for a short run after she had warmed up – well, managed a couple of stretches – on the nearest off-road path. The going was steeper and trickier than it looked, and a large number of sheep had recently been moved along the path to judge by the amount of droppings, so it wasn't long before Jess's enthusiasm evaporated, and she stopped for a moment to gaze at the valley below.

For the first time since she had been in Cumbria Jess decided the way it smelled and looked had some merit, and as she breathed in deeply, the fresh air made her feel clear-headed, strong and vital. This was in spite of the droppings, and even though her trainers, while perfectly adequate for speed work in a gym or city park, offered nowhere near enough support for such rough going.

Aside from a single car in the distance twisting its way along a road, Jess couldn't see anybody else at all, and she realised that this was perhaps the first time she had ever experienced such a thing. She'd pretty much always been in the company of others. But as she contemplated the vista, which stretched for miles, she began to notice signs of the non-human life pulsing around her.

There were the calls of some birds high in the sky, possibly gulls, she thought, and closer to her was the soft, almost musical sound of a trickle of water, although she couldn't see where this was coming from. And, if she concentrated, far away she could hear a faint mechanical noise that she thought could be a quad bike. Jess remembered Bob Newman telling her that farmers often used quads to check on their sheep or deliver food to live-stock once the forage died back, although she had no idea if this was year-round or just in winter. And she could see many shades of green but hadn't a clue whether any of them indicated plants that sheep could eat.

Jess made her way home, deep in thought. It was quiet where her cottage was located, not on the tourist fell-walking routes, and so it wasn't surprising she hadn't seen anyone. But where James Garfield had been found – after checking his posts like Margot had done, Jess was convinced the body she'd seen com-ing off the mountain was his – it was a different story, as the whole of Scafell Pike was popular with all sorts of people in nearly all weathers, which meant he was unlucky not to have been discovered sooner, bad conditions or no. And if it turned out to be a case of foul play, then whoever had been up there with him had been taking a terrible risk, which in turn said something about that person's personality.

Following Margot's text, Jess had found online the poster with the drone and the habit of filming James – somebody who had chosen the tag @FanBigRunClimb001 – and Margot had been right: they seemed to have been unnaturally keen on James Garfield over the last eighteen months or so, putting up a story most days, even if only a short clip accompanied by music or a segment of James talking about what he was up to. Annoyingly, whoever this was used an anime image of a bird as a profile image in their personal details.

She'd direct-messaged whoever it was, asking them to get in touch, but with no joy as yet.

James also had an official fan club, but as far as Jess could tell, @FanBigRunClimb001 wasn't anything to do with it. She'd emailed Tony Peters asking him to track this person down as a matter of urgency.

Freak accidents did happen, but although somebody like James was all about testing his limits, this very fact meant he'd be incredibly aware – much more so than most – of what his limits actually were. It didn't pay people like him, whose financial and professional success depended on his exploits, to risk injuring themselves. They might deliberately *seem* reckless, but that was an act designed to grow their profile, and actually they'd be very risk-averse. It was all about the spin people like James Garfield put upon themselves, Jess was convinced, and Margot Voyce's comments backed this up.

After they'd eaten the takeaway her old mentor Mike Bowers had brought over the previous evening, he and Jess had spent several hours going over James's online footprint, and sure enough his followers had started to post about rumours of something bad having happened. Suddenly there were reams of people eulogising James to a ridiculous extent.

Jess tried to ignore all the speculation – Tony Peters could look into that to see if anything or anyone seemed pertinent to what had happened – and the seeming dead end for the moment with @FanBigRunClimb001, and instead insisted that she and Mike concentrate on how James had presented himself on social media.

A bit to her surprise, Jess found herself impressed with how organised and methodical James appeared in terms of his training and the clever way he went about posting on his various accounts. He had the knack of making multiple posts about essentially the same information – him – seem familiar but endlessly fresh, and he absolutely didn't come across as any sort of fool.

And Jess could definitely see James Garfield's metrosexual appeal. He came across as manly but in a contemporary, intelligent, non-threatening way that was likely to appeal to people of nearly all sexual persuasions. But when Jess asked herself whether she would have been tempted to climb into his bed, she found herself less keen and wasn't quite sure why. After deliberating further, she decided her reluctance was to do with something closed occasionally flitting across his face and a certain guarded quality about his movements as he spoke directly to camera that made her doubt he'd be a satisfactory lover.

Mike Bowers was a retired chief superintendent who had been Jess's fatherly mentor in her early years in Belfast. He had encouraged her to take the job in the Lake District as he now resided there in a rather grand house about five miles away from Jess's cottage. Jess still didn't know why Mike had ended up in the Lake District; like her, he didn't have ties to the area.

He'd laughed when she'd asked him about it when he suggested she move there too and said, 'Good times, Jess, and good people.'

Jess had thought retirement must be suiting Mike, as he'd verged on the perennially grumpy back in Belfast, a quality she rather liked as she could see that in herself too. And she'd wanted a bit of whatever it was that was making him so relaxed, so thought that maybe Cumbria would work for her too.

The previous night Mike had initially laughed when Jess said she had doubts about James as a lover, although then he said she'd hit the nail on the head. James Garfield seemed to have something of a chameleon about him; underneath it all he didn't seem authentic. That wasn't to say, Mike added, that Garfield's general posts didn't signify a man who knew what he was about.

'I'm more interested in him than I expected, Jess. The more I see, the more I want to see. He's big business,' Mike said, 'to judge by the calibre of his hashtag sponsors and the number of followers, and he seems very keen on orchestrating it all. In theory, your James Garfield isn't the sort of person I'd expect to rate, but looking at what's here, he's got something, although I can't see anything obvious going on that would lead to foul play. Perhaps his death was a simple accident after all, and you shouldn't spend too much time trying to make it something it's not.

'But if there is more to it than bad luck, maybe somebody felt he was stepping on their toes and skimming off too much for himself. Or is it a case of the old saying that handsome is as handsome does, and he's acted out of line in his personal life? If that's the case, what's going to be most important is what others think of him. Or it could be a mixture of the two.'

Jess sighed. Suspicions like this were always the very devil to prove.

Mike rubbed his brow thoughtfully and then added, 'Either way, I can't help thinking that whatever happened to him is likely to end up a bugger to prove for whoever's appointed SIO. I mean, there's serious money driving what James Garfield was about, so it's easy to see how somebody could have wanted a piece of it. And in my experience focused determination almost inevitably means he's trodden hard on a lot of people on his way up.'

'Goodness knows if I'll stay as SIO, but I can't square what has happened. I don't know what it is, but something doesn't feel right. Everybody online is saying James Garfield was a "very nice" person, heart and soul, but without much being there to back it up.'

'Well,' Mike said, 'it could be he had a dark side and the "nice" was a deliberate ploy to mask this. Or he was a total pain in the backside, and people claimed he was great to close him down. Or people are following the crowd, and they haven't a clue. Either way, it wouldn't be a bad thing to distance yourself from this one, as it has the stamp of a shit-show about it.'

'You cynic, Mike!' Then Jess smiled and added, 'I'm inclined to agree. His former occasional partner Margot Voyce described somebody superficial but craving attention. She said James Garfield never gave her what she wanted or needed, not even after she broke her back on the same expedition as him. When he's photographed with others, it's all about him looking at the camera and owning the shot in a way that ignores the others. He's got the knack of annoying people, even if only about diet or methods of fitness training, but maybe that's intentional. He doesn't acknowledge anybody else in his posts, and only name-checks people or organisations if he has official dealings with them. There's no mention of the Joe Bloggs of the world, which is a bit odd seeing as that's where his fanbase is. And without his fans, those sponsors would be dust.'

'My mother had a phrase that might sum him up: "all fur coat and no knickers",' said Mike.

Jess laughed. 'I'm liking your mother! I agree. It's as if each post seems impressive on its own, but somehow all together not so much so.'

Back at the cottage after her run, Jess gave the kitchen a quick tidy, had a shower and organised for gas canisters and food to be delivered the next day, Mike having volunteered over their takeaway to let himself in to wait in for both. Jess realised that despite playing golf and doing all the things that single retired men did, time was probably hanging more heavily on Mike Bowers' hands in the Lake District than he'd anticipated, and she had given him one of her spare keys.

Jess rather wished she had that problem; her own timetable for the day looked distinctly frantic.

Annoyingly, all of the clothes she'd borrowed from Margot Voyce were still damp, either from yesterday's wet weather or the quick wash Jess had put them through the previous evening, when they had shared the machine with her own clothes from yesterday.

Jess had called the hospital while Mike dished up their curry, and had learned that Bob would be kept in for observation over-night, but provided nothing untoward was found, he would be released at doctor's early rounds.

Bob had other ideas. He'd texted her before 7 a.m. to say he was much better and would be out of hospital within the hour. Jess was pretty certain this was earlier than the doctor would advise, but she could imagine Bob kicking up a fuss, and it was likely he would get his way as he had that authoritative bluster that the older generation liked to employ on occasion. How-ever, she had persuaded him to stay put until she got there.

Jess rang Margot.

'Inspector,' Margot answered on what felt like the first trill of her ringtone.

'I wanted to thank you again for the loan of your gear yester-day, Ms Voyce, and to apologise. I didn't have proper heating last night, so I've not been able to dry it properly.'

'Margot, please. And no problem,' said Margot. 'That doesn't sound good – the heating.'

'I've had warmer evenings, that's for certain,' Jess replied.

There was a silence as both women sought something to say.

Then they spoke together. 'Anyway, I just wanted to say I am very grateful,' said Jess. 'It won't take long for you to work out what you need in terms of outdoor gear,' said Margot.

They each heard the smile in the other's voice as Jess added, 'Got to run,' and Margot said, 'Let me know if there's anything I can do.'

Five minutes later, in the car, Jess rang Margot again. 'I'm sorry to interrupt your day, especially as this isn't a work-related request. But actually there is something you could help me with. I was wondering if you could come with me to an outdoor-gear shop and point me in the direction of what I need.'

'Yes, I can do that,' said Margot. 'You'd better have deep pockets though as the good stuff is eye-wateringly expensive, and you might as well get everything in one go. Yesterday might have felt cold and wet, but if you have to go up on a snowy February day then what you experienced yesterday will feel positively balmy. Get the best you can afford; it'll last much longer if you look after it. And your life might depend on it one day. It took me a while to learn that scrimping ends up costing more in the end.'

'Like so much in life,' said Jess.

They arranged for Margot to come to the police station mid-afternoon, when she could give her statement formally about the discovery of the body, and from there they'd go in Jess's car to Carlisle to get her some outdoor gear.

After she'd ended the call, Jess turned the car around and drove back to the cottage to collect a second credit card – one with a higher spending limit. After a moment or two peering out of the small window up towards the top of the nearest fell, she reached for a third.

'Yes, I confirm that is my nephew James Garfield,' said Bob Newman without prompting, as he and Jess looked down at the body, which was mostly covered by institutional mortuary sheeting.

He reached out as if to lay a hand on James's shoulder, but Jess put a hand gently on his arm to stop him.

Jess thought the councillor sounded like he was acting in a police procedural TV drama, but then she peered a bit more closely at the older man and saw that his lips were trembling and had a blue tinge, and she realised it was more that he was trying to contain his upset.

'My condolences, Bob. I'm sorry for your loss,' said Jess, her voice genuine as she caught the hovering mortuary attendant's eye to signal she wouldn't be long but that the post-mortem wasn't to go ahead until she was present. 'Come on – let's go and find Maureen.'

The councillor and his wife Maureen – or Reeny as Bob called her when he forgot to say 'my lady wife' – had been sitting in the room where patients waited to be collected to go home when Jess arrived, Bob Newman obviously pensive as he twisted the brim of his tweed trilby in his hands. The mortuary was in the basement on the other side of the hospital.

Ordinarily Jess would have got a relative to come back later in order that the identification could take place after the PM, so that as much forensic evidence as possible could be preserved in initial findings, some of which could subsequently be compared to medical or dental records, CCTV and the like. But one glance at the councillor's face and general demeanour told Jess that that the exertions of the day before had exacted a heavy price and Bob needed to rest. It was hard to think of the Bob Newman she had seen in the waiting room as the bumptious man she had encountered yesterday, and so she'd said, 'Give us a few minutes to get ready, and then you can come in.'

Now Jess drove them all to a café in the town and over tea said, 'I expect you understand this already, but James's body can't be released yet, and it might take a while. We need to work out what happened, and should it go as far as an arrest being made for some sort of crime, it's possible we'll hold the body long enough for a second, independent autopsy.'

'It makes no sense.' Bob had the light from the window on his face as he spoke, and he looked exhausted.

Jess said, 'Tell me about him.'

'He was a fine chap,' Bob said.

'James was always headstrong, just like his father. He wasn't easy, you know that, Bob,' said his wife sharply as she stirred some sugar into her cup. 'He was always wanting something from you.'

'Nobody deserves what happened to James,' Bob replied.

Maureen said, 'That's not what I mean, and you know it, Bob.' And she shook her head in an irritated way.

Jess thought of the outpourings of emotion about James on the trending posts, and although she knew social media worked like that, it occurred to her that Reeny Newman was one of the few people who didn't immediately have something positive to say.

She wanted to probe further, but decided it would be best to get Maureen alone.

Jess was just forming her next question for Bob when the alarm on her phone gave a beep to show the PM would begin in fifteen minutes, and with the question instantly forgotten, Jess said, 'I need to go. Do you want me to arrange for you to be taken home? I'll have your car collected too if you give me your keys.'

Before either Bob or Maureen could answer, a dishevelled

man with lank hair and a bald spot who'd been sitting at a table nearby lumbered over with the sort of 'oof' that people with arthritic knees tend to say, and butted in: 'I'll take them.' Jess thought the man young for obvious arthritis or joint issues, but he had a large frame and so possibly that made a difference.

Anyway, Bob and Maureen seemed to know him and were happy to accept his offer, and as Jess headed to her car she phoned DC Harper to arrange for someone to collect Bob's car keys from her at the mortuary and then pick up his car and drive it to his house.

The man in the café was a timely reminder that in rural areas everybody seemed to know everybody. She needed to be careful what she said.

The forensic pathologist was scrolling through her laptop while waiting for Jess, looking at what she could find online about James Garfield.

'Well, it's going to be a surprise to no one who's died, as social media is alive with rumour and speculation. The surprise is that he died at all.' Although she and Jess had met at the edge of Piers Gill as James Garfield's body was brought round to where Jess and those waiting to take it off the fell were gathered, and the pathologist had quickly taken several samples, she reintroduced herself as Rose Thorne.

'We'll release a press statement later,' said Jess.

She admired the undercut of Rose Thorne's hair and the tattoos on her fingers, as these suggested somebody with a strong sense of self.

Mike Bowers had told Jess that it would be great if they could get Thorne allocated to the case as apparently she was the best. She was much in demand though, and worked a wide area.

'Rose Thorne?'

'Rose is a nickname from when I was a toddler, but I'm so used to it now that it's what I call myself and so does everyone else. Seeing as I'm so dainty and all.'

Jess raised an eyebrow as she took in Rose's strong, corded forearms, her muscular legs and height. She looked like she could bench-press over a hundred pounds.

Garfield's clothes were labelled and in bags ready for forensic testing, and there was a folder of dental and medical records, as well as emailed reports from Mountain Rescue and the doctor who'd pronounced life extinct, and even detailed printouts of the weather on various bits of Scafell Pike. X-rays of the body had already been taken.

Jess examined the webbing GoPro harness that had been wrapped around his leg, which was now curled in an evidence bag.

Naked, James's lithe body was covered in bruises from the tips of his toes to the top of his head, while the gash on his thigh had clearly been life-threatening. He didn't have an ounce of superfluous fat anywhere on his body; he was long and lean, his musculature perfect for endurance feats.

Jess realised she was probably heavier than James, and was pleased to discover she had moved on from when such a thought would be depressing, and instead just accepted it.

Rose Thorne checked the scans they'd already taken against James Garfield's dental and medical records, confirmed that the man in front of them was the subject of those records and then pointed out past healed injuries that featured in the reports and X-rays, and in her own scans. 'I've swabbed for DNA. He wasn't a stranger to injury, that's for certain. And I can see he put many hours into training.'

'Any old injuries that look suspicious?' asked Jess.

'I'd say not. I haven't seen anything I wouldn't expect to see on someone with James Garfield's mountaineering experience,' said Rose Thorne. 'I've taken samples too for toxicology. I'd assume that's unlikely, unless he was given drugs surreptitiously by a third party, but we'll test for alcohol, drugs – illegal and prescription – and poisons. We'll do our own tests, but as sports enhancement drugs change all the time, I'll send samples to a specialist.'

'I see,' said Jess. 'Yes, I suppose he might have been taking illegal performance stimulants.'

'I'd be surprised,' said Rose. 'While he may have been up for that sort of thing when he was building his reputation, it's hard to imagine he'd still be doing it. If he'd been caught, the negative publicity would have led to his sponsors dropping him. The risks would be too great.'

This was Jess's thinking too.

Rose pointed out foam in his airways. 'Indications of drowning, but blood loss from that leg injury or exposure overnight would have led to the same outcome unless he'd received immediate medical help. His clothing was activity gear, designed to keep out the wind and wick sweat away but not keep a stationary body warm, at least in Piers Gill on a rainy November night.'

'Any indications of how he came to be suspended so high up on the rock face?'

'It is odd,' agreed Rose Thorn. 'There's debris in his mouth that entered with such force that his teeth are chipped, and so my guess is he was injured first, probably during the fall into Piers Gill, and then he got swept away in a flash flood, his teeth damaged by stones in the water. His femur was cleanly broken, which suggests a fall from a great height rather than a stumble, so that probably happened before the water. And he couldn't have moved to lessen the impact of the water once he was at the bottom of the gill – he has several intracranial haematomas too, and so he might not even have been conscious. I can't say definitively whether the haematomas occurred before his immersion in water and subsequent drowning, or after that. But the fact the harness was wrapped about his thigh although not pulled tight suggests he was trying to staunch the flow of blood from the gash when he was drowned.'

'He couldn't have been trying to tighten the harness while he was in the water, assuming he was caught in a flash flood?' said Jess as she flicked through the weather reports. There hadn't definitely been a flash flood, although there was a comment that the gulley was known to flood and there were signs of a recent body of water moving down it.

'I doubt it,' Rose answered. 'For his body to be suspended that high suggests he was caught in a quick-moving rush of water, and trying to do anything in that would have needed a lot of strength. He was right-handed, I think, to judge by his muscles, but those fingers are dislocated. And if that happened prior to the immersion, then he would have been severely incapacitated, especially with the head injuries and his broken leg. He had also injured his shoulder. And look at this.'

Jess stared at the area of James Garfield's neck that Rose Thorne was pointing to. The skin was puckered, and as Jess bent to look more closely, she thought it looked as if some of the top layer had sheared off.

'The video of his removal from the pitch showed that at some point the neckline of Mr Garfield's outer garment caught on a jagged piece of rock, and when I X-rayed him earlier, his hyoid bone in his neck had a tiny fracture. There's water in his airways, so his death wasn't strangulation as such, but the catching of the clothing around his neck may have contributed to him drowning as he might have lost consciousness. Although there are contributing factors, drowning is the cause of death.'

'He really wasn't going to get out of that gully alive, was he? The irony is there was so little water when I looked into the bottom of Piers Gill yesterday,' Jess said.

'Flash floods disappear as quickly as they come, and the rock formation at Piers Gill lends itself to them. It's rare but it could happen. I did some work in Australia in a rocky area where a lone kayaker on a river had disappeared and wasn't found despite numerous searches. Months later he and his kayak were found wedged at the top of a tree. He'd not been found because the search parties had been looking at the riverbed, as this was where they expected to find the body. When winter came and the leaves dropped, the body and kayak were exposed. The water in the river had risen very high and dissipated extremely quickly.'

'But if James fell into Piers Gill on his descent, how on earth did that happen?'

'Ah well, that is the question, isn't it?' said Rose Thorne. 'And very likely one more for you than for me. But if it were me directing a new inspection along the lip above Piers Gill, I'd be suggesting a search about two hundred or so metres up, a bit more towards the peak of Scafell Pike, from where he was found, but on the same side of the vertical rock face as where you were when you initially stood across from him. That's the biggest drop. There may be evidence there if Garfield made the mistake of running off the lip in thick fog. That area would also be relatively speedy for somebody with an ulterior motive to exit the scene as the going is soon much easier. Use a drone inside the gully though as there's more bad weather forecast.'

Rose Thorne put some photographs up onscreen for Jess to look at. 'There's a faint contusion on the centre of Mr Garfield's back which doesn't match the others. Could it be a handprint? His outer garments need checking, although I'm not hopeful about them yielding much. But this contusion doesn't have the broken skin that the others have, presumably because the other marks were made by the skin being scraped hard against the synthetic fibres of his clothing in the flood. The cause of this injury just looks different to me.'

Jess couldn't make out anything from the mark just below his shoulder blades. 'Before I go, any sign he'd had sex with anyone?'

'Again, it's not definitive because of the immersion in water, but I've done a sweep and the swabs are negative.'

'Thanks,' said Jess. 'Hard to tell if that's helpful either way, but good to know.'

Rose Thorne lifted a hand in farewell as she added, 'I'll send you a preliminary report as soon as I can. Hopefully we won't be waiting too long for the results from the other labs.'

At the station Jess was pleased to discover her colleagues had been more thorough in their investigations than she had anticipated, and that James's car had been removed from where he had parked it and was now sitting in the police pound, something Jess realised she had forgotten to request.

She'd always been good at seeing all the angles but felt rusty at the moment, if she were honest. It wasn't a good feeling, so Jess told herself to acknowledge it but then move on quickly, as she needed to concentrate and keep her focus. She had managed to wing it so far, as neither of her colleagues gave the slightest hint they suspected she might be floundering.

Normally by now she would have a working hypothesis she'd use to direct the investigation. But the fact it wasn't clear whether it was an accident or not seemed to have smothered any plan other than to keep casting the net wide. But with little manpower and few financial resources, they couldn't keep doing that, Jess knew, which made her uneasy. And then her confidence was given a fillip by an email that she would remain SIO at least until after the inquest had been opened and adjourned, which would probably happen the next day or, if not, the day after that. Her status could change at that point, she was told, but in the meantime she would be allowed to send a forensic technician up to investigate where Rose Thorne had suggested was the most likely place an incident, if it had occurred, would have taken place.

'Ma'am . . .' said Bill Harper.

Jess gave a deliberately heavy sigh, and the detective constable mouthed a silent 'Sorry' back. She hated 'ma'am' for reasons she couldn't quite articulate, although they were something to do with perpetuating old-fashioned attitudes in the police force.

'There's a Trevor Walton waiting to see you. I asked him to come in – he's the person who reported James Garfield missing,' said Harper.

'Put him in the interview room while I talk to the press office as we need to get a statement out,' said Jess. 'And has anything come of the enquiries I asked about? Margot Voyce will be here to give her statement, so she's a priority.'

'Nothing suspicious has come up on her. She's had a few boyfriends, although none flagged on our system. Her credit rating's not so hot, but her car documents are up to date.'

Jess smiled. She was impressed Margot had teased her over the MOT with such a straight face.

'She told me she'd broken her back and had a long recovery when she wouldn't have earned, and she didn't strike me as the sort who'd have insurance or health cover,' said Jess, 'so I'm not surprised she isn't flush. Dig a bit deeper, just in case.'

Jess emailed the PR department requesting a bare-bones press release. She gave them James's full name and date of birth, that he had grown up locally and supported himself as a social media influencer, that he had been reported missing the previous morning and his body retrieved from Piers Gill a few hours later, that his body had been identified that morning by his uncle Councillor Robert Newman and a post-mortem had already been conducted, and an inquest would be opened and adjourned to allow enquiries to continue. And that the police would be making no further statement at this point in time, nor revealing the details of the post-mortem.

Jess pressed Send and headed to the interview room to conduct her first interview since arriving in Cumbria.

'Mr Walton,' she began, and then stopped as she immediately recognised the person sitting at the table as the lank-haired man from the café who'd offered to drive the Newmans home. 'I trust you took the Newmans where they wanted to go.'

She stared at Trevor Walton without blinking, and after initially puffing out his chest, he visibly wilted.

'Was Mr Garfield a relative of yours? A close friend? An acquaintance?'

Trevor Walton shook his head to each of Jess's questions. He didn't seem a naturally chatty man.

'With that in mind, why don't you tell me how it was you came to report Mr Garfield missing?' Jess asked.

Trevor Walton described himself as James Garfield's number-one fan, and the more he said, the sadder Jess thought he was. She doubted that in return for his devotion James Garfield had noticed much about Trevor Walton, beyond seeing him in various car parks with depressing regularity.

'How come you have so much free time?' she asked. 'Don't you work?'

'I had some luck a while back with the lottery, so I gave up my job.'

Jess was surprised; he didn't look like a man with a surplus of cash. She changed tack slightly. 'Would you call yourself a friend of Mr Garfield?'

'He'd nod at me, and sometimes we'd pass the time of day.'

'What was it about yesterday morning that made you think that Mr Garfield was missing?'

'He never came back to his car from the previous day. He did that once before, but it turned out then that he was with some girl. But when the car was still there at first light yesterday, I knew it was wrong. I've followed James Garfield for such a long time that I know all of his routines, and he wouldn't have done that with his record attempt so near. And in any case he wasn't an all-night sort of person. And I could see by the way all the things in his car were the same as the day before that he'd not been back when I wasn't there.'

Jess gazed at Trevor Walton. He was very devoted. And verging on the creepy. Still, he'd confirmed the impression she'd got from Margot Voyce that James, while happy to have sex, didn't go a bundle on staying the night afterwards.

'Tell me about the café earlier today, Mr Walton.' Jess changed the subject again.

'Well, I'd been to the place they always use when they bring bodies down, the place where they're kept first. And it was quiet there first thing this morning, so I went over to the hospital. I watched Bob Newman leave the main part of the hospital and then head to where I was waiting. I hung around some more, and then I went to the café after you took them both there.'

Jess hadn't noticed Trevor Walton when she was at the café with the Newmans, she remembered. She looked at him with fresh eyes and understood why. There wasn't anything unusual about him in any way; he was the sort of person who simply merged into the background and nobody ever paid any attention to.

'Anything else I should know?'

'No,' he said cautiously as if Jess was setting a trap.

She hadn't been, but she wondered why he might think so.

'Don't leave the area, Mr Walton,' she said. He looked as if he were about to object, and Jess added quickly, 'Poor James Garfield. Who better to help us find out what happened to him other than his most prominent superfan? In time, it could be that we'll mention your help publicly and tell everyone how you have been a key component in our investigation.'

Trevor Walton gave a little shiver at Jess's words. He was flattered, which was precisely what she'd intended. There was a quality to him that suggested he craved admiration, or was it just acknowledgment?

Jess returned to the incident room and was immediately collared by Bill Harper. 'Skip, there's a Miss Kate Summers here for you. And she says she hasn't got long as she has a lot that she needs to do and your speedy attention is required.'

'Remind me in a while to speak to her,' Jess answered.

'Ten minutes?'

Jess stared at the detective constable, realising she was being chippy for no reason other than she hadn't much cared for Ms Summers' tone with her on the phone the previous evening, but somehow she couldn't quite bring herself to be more conciliatory.

'Twenty?'

She thawed. 'Now you're talking my language, Bill.' Jess

noted how the DC's ears pinkened as the ghost of a smile dimpled his cheeks just for a moment. It was the first time she'd addressed him by his Christian name or given him a compliment.

Perhaps this team isn't going to be so bad after all, Jess thought.

She immediately made Bill Harper exhibits officer, and told him to assemble in one place everything that had been found out so far about James Garfield.

'He wasn't scared of an online spat from all accounts,' he told her a little later. 'The comments on his posts showed he rubbed some people up the wrong way, although lots of people always sprang to his defence.'

'I thought that when I had a look online, so dig further,' said Jess. 'Meanwhile, any sign of a will, Tony?'

'Not yet.'

Twenty minutes had allowed Jess a deep dive with her computer into what she could find out online about Kate Summers.

It was clear she was a pushy operator who liked to gloat over her successes. While this might be good for her clients, some of whom were very high profile, as she was obviously good at striking business and sponsorship deals, and improving her clients' presence across all sorts of media, Jess guessed that Kate Summers was probably rather obnoxious in the normal run of things, and especially so if she felt in the mood.

And she probably didn't care much for women, as the vast majority of her clients were men, although Jess told herself to remain open-minded on this, as that could be something to do with the people Kate Summers needed to do business with on her clients' behalf, quite likely old-fashioned men mainly interested in supporting other men.

All the same, Kate Summers' Twitter account had many more male faces on it than female, in spite of James's 'eco' sponsors priding themselves on their low global impact and their equal treatment of everybody, and in spite of women making up a sizeable proportion of the spokespeople and CEOs of those companies who had backed the exploits of James Garfield.

Jess's impression from their phone conversation of Kate Summers being an irritating woman who tried to bully people into submission was not altered by meeting her in person. Even before she entered the interview room, she could hear a tapping noise from within. This turned out to be the sound of Kate Summers drumming the emerald-green acrylic talons of one hand on the table, while with the other she angrily thumbed her phone.

Jess noted her expensive cream trouser suit and Hermès Birkin handbag. It wouldn't be an accident that the handbag, which from a previous case Jess knew retailed at over seven thousand pounds, had been left in clear view on the table. Jess knew the handbag could be rented, but when she noted the agent's Christian Louboutin boots peeping out from the bottom of the trouser hem, she thought probably not. Kate Summers was clearly keen to point out, without actually saying so, that her earning power was far in excess of what ordinary mortals possessed.

Jess had seen the boots in a Sunday paper fashion spread a couple of months previously, when she wondered who wore that sort of thing. Now she knew. Another thing she knew was that the extravagantly pointed stiletto nails were a signpost of

78

heterosexuality – something else Jess had discovered in a previous case – but when Jess studied the woman sitting opposite her, she concluded quickly that James's agent was a woman who got her kicks by other means than sex, very probably by manipulating the rich and famous.

'At last,' Kate Summers barked after Jess had introduced herself. 'It's my first time in this part of the world, and the long drive and the wait for you has really eaten into my day.'

It took a while for Jess to sit down and make herself comfortable. And then she made sure her face was set in a pleasant expression and her voice soft before she said, 'Thank you for making the time, Ms Summers. I'm sure James Garfield would have been most appreciative too. We did earlier today formally identify the body taken down from Scafell Pike yesterday as his.'

Jess had read the word 'harrumph' in novels, but had never, until now, experienced anyone actually saying it. But as she didn't want to further alienate her interviewee, she avoided any sort of power contest. 'I'd be very interested to hear you describe what James Garfield was like, Ms Summers.'

'He was everything an agent wants from a client,' Kate Summers retorted. 'Ambitious, organised, dedicated, smart, determined to hit the big time.'

'All qualities replicated in a good personal agent, I should imagine?' said Jess.

Kate Summers looked at her in a way that for the first time suggested interest and then said more agreeably, 'It's fair to say that James and I shared the same objectives, and we had a mutually beneficial professional relationship. We understood each other.'

'May I ask what your percentage was of his earnings?' Jess asked, expecting the agent to sidestep the question.

'Well, it varied. This is market sensitive and so I assume you will keep it confidential, but generally I'd say twenty to thirty per cent depending on what was being sold, but for some things it was more, and for others – things James may have set up himself, for instance – it was less, although I would still get a cut as my legal department always oversaw contracts and invoicing. His turnover in his last taxable year was lowish six figures, plus VAT of course, but we expected to at least quadruple that in the next set of accounts submitted.

'I had a terrestrial television deal in the offing on how to train for the type of challenges he excelled in, as well as a four-part series he would present on famous mountaineers for a television subscription service, then there were guest appearances lined up on several Christmas TV shows of the "light entertainment" variety, while towards the middle or end of next year two high-profile reality TV appearances were currently under negotiation, one of the romantic variety and one of the so-many-celebs-begin-and-each-week-one-gets-knocked-out type. That last one was extremely high profile and in the run-up to Christmas on a Saturday night, after which his earning potential would have gone stratospheric.

'I also arranged bespoke luxury goods lines with a luggage company that would be personal to him, and there were deals with a footwear company and a watch manufacturer. I'd just begun to look at sunglasses, top-end bed linen, interior furnishings and deals with a camper-van manufacturer and a water-sports clothing supplier. And in the new year I was hoping to strike a deal with a Hollywood agent aimed at securing cameo roles in films, with a view to him switching more to that arena upon retirement. And of course there's the major meal replacement endorsement he signed about a month ago with the ads going live in a fortnight.'

Jess couldn't help but be impressed both with what James Garfield was on the cusp of and also how candid his agent was being. 'Sounds like sequins up to next Christmas then, and as if you had so many bases covered he was going to be extremely busy. So, a very lucrative client then?'

'Potentially, extremely,' agreed Kate Summers. 'There's still some value in James Garfield, which will go to his estate. My team are organising a vigil close to where he was brought off the mountain, and I'm waiting for a TV crew to arrive so that we can get material for a tribute documentary that I'll be able to sell. We'll go with that either tomorrow or the next day, depending on the weather, as we need to get in while he's still trending.'

'Would all of what you've just told me have meant he'd not have a lot of time to do what he was known for – the mountaineering and fell running?'

'It's a question of timing. I need to work at securing the big deals when clients are at peak performance, which is the stage James was at. But for athletes like him that stage doesn't last for ever, and we're all too aware they're at risk of a life-changing or career-ending injury at any time. So the plan is always to set enough up so at least some of it will carry through to the life they have after they have stopped competing or setting records. Punditry, say, or being a documentary presenter. Endorsements change too as time goes on. But it all begins with carefully strategising and placement when they're at their peak or, ideally, just about to reach their peak.'

'What about his peers? Would any one of them have hated or been so jealous of the opportunities you were creating that they wanted to do him serious harm?'

'It's possible,' the agent said. 'But I have no personal experience of this, and James never said anything like this was happening. Of course, the people who were his direct competitors will have their own agents who'll be busy creating opportunities for them.'

'Dog eat dog?'

'It can be,' admitted Kate Summers. 'But as I say, I wasn't aware of anything or anyone making our business strategy problematic.'

'When did you last have contact with Mr Garfield?'

'A few days ago. We had an online meeting with a charity local to here that James was quite interested in being an ambassador for. He was exactly as he usually was.'

'And what did you think about the charity thing? Presumably he would have been doing that for free?'

'Well, yes and no in terms of it being "free". There would have been no payment in monetary terms, but of course there's always value in a client being associated with the right charity, which drives up fees elsewhere. And there would have been a "payment" of sorts. James would have been driven around and generally made a fuss of, and his profile strengthened through the association. The further in their careers they go and the more success they have, the more clients become aware of having a long way to fall should things go awry, so a bit of personal spoiling is relaxing and doesn't cost anyone too much in the financial sense. Doing what I do gets one thinking differently about value; it's not just about cash.'

'What did you advise after the meeting?'

'I told him it wasn't the right charity, but he said he wanted to do it as it was close to his uncle's heart. And it reminded James of his childhood.'

'His uncle Bob Newman?'

'Yes,' said Kate Summers. 'James was keen, and then another opportunity came up and he decided to spend the time elsewhere, although nothing had been signed with any of the parties. Until a signature is on the dotted line, I always say to my clients it's not a deal but a suggestion.'

Jess took some details down, and then asked the question she was most interested in: 'And what did you think of James as a person – in a private capacity?'

'Emotionally greedy.'

'That's forthright, seeing as he was your client.'

'Emotional vampire would be more exact, actually. A total narcissist.'

'And that didn't put you off?'

'I believe that narcissism makes for an ideal client.'

'He was good-looking too?'

'Yes, extremely. And Teflon-coated when it came to lovers. He had no conscience.'

'Did his spurned lovers ever fling more at him than words?'

'Shouldn't think so. And if they had, I think he'd have been good at ducking out of the way.'

'You ever tempted?'

'Not for a moment.'

And there was something about the way she said this that made Jess sure that James Garfield's personal agent was telling the truth.

The interview came to an end with Jess thinking more favourably of Kate Summers than she'd expected.

Several hours later, Margot gave a formal version of the events of the previous day to Tony Peters. Returning to the waiting area after signing the statement, she saw Jess stuffing into her mouth the last of what looked like an egg mayonnaise sandwich as she walked towards her. Margot noted Jess looked very much at home in an office environment, in stark contrast to how discombobulated the detective had appeared when out on the fells the previous day.

Margot glanced down at her own clothes. The boot was on the other foot now, with Margot out of her comfort zone. She had come straight from the stable and could detect a faint whiff of horse wafting from her person. Her hair was all over the place and her fingernails weren't very clean at all.

'Happy to be back on firm ground?' Margot said, with a smile.

Jess forced down the last of the sandwich with a determined swallow. 'Well, I'm putting yesterday down to experience. Thank you for doing this, although before we leave I have to give you the ground rules: we won't be talking about yesterday, or anything to do with James Garfield. You're a witness, you've given a formal statement, and it's possible you will get called to give evidence at the inquest or at a criminal trial should any defendant plead not guilty. But we can talk about anything other than the case, James Garfield or what might have happened.'

'Understood loud and clear,' said Margot. 'Before we leave though, in case you decide not to go shopping with me, I think you should have a word with Tom Drake – he owns where I keep my horse. He knows everybody around here and all the gossip.'

'Noted,' said Jess. 'Now, in a very obvious attempt at changing the subject, what do you think I need clothes-wise?'

'I've made a list of basics,' Margot replied as she pulled a piece of paper from her pocket.

As they crossed the car park, Jess looked aghast at Margot's list. 'Basic?'

'Very basic.'

Jess was unable to decipher the tone of Margot's voice to decide if she was being ironic.

Fortunately Margot had called ahead as she knew the owner of the outdoor wear supplier in Carlisle, and a selection of clothes and equipment had already been put to one side, both for winter and also for warmer weather. This saved a lot of time.

Jess agreed to all the clothing, and the rucksack, and then it was on to boots and gaiters, and once these had been chosen, various socks and liners, and hats, gloves and so forth, although the jacket Margot said she really must have as it was suitable down to minus fifteen degrees wasn't in stock in her size, so that had to be ordered, Margot saying that Jess could continue to use the one that she had worn the day before until her new one arrived.

Margot added that Jess would need a longer version of the thigh-length coat she'd just ordered, one down to lower calf, as standing around in the Cumbrian midwinter, she would need all the coverage she could get. 'Assuming you have to do standing around. I like the length you've ordered for walking on the fell, but if I need to be waiting for any length of time, then I always wear the full-length version. In fact, I keep them both in the car; if it's totally arctic I wear the long one on top of the other.'

'I really hope I won't be out in that sort of weather,' said Jess.

'Maybe I've got police work wrong,' Margot said, 'but on telly there always seems to be a lot of people milling about at accidents or murders. The thing is that after Christmas the weather can be really atrocious, and you'll think global warming's a myth. Remember Scafell Pike yesterday and how you felt – that's November and relatively mild. Factor in a blizzard and a minus-ten wind chill, and you'll be really sorry you've not got what everyone else is wearing.'

'You're not wrong about standing about,' admitted Jess.

Along the way Jess mentioned that her running shoes hadn't been great earlier that morning, and so she was put on a running machine to check her stride. The shopkeeper then picked a pair that Jess tried on the machine. They were a revelation.

The whole process took what felt to Jess like for ever, and even included specialist non-slip goggles and sunglasses for all sorts of conditions, and maps and a compass as Jess was going to return what she had borrowed from Mountain Rescue. All this meant the shop stayed open just for them for a long while after the CLOSED sign was displayed on the door.

Jess had prepared herself for a muscular bill, but when it was presented at long last, not a total *that* big.

Margot had a quick peek over her shoulder. 'Ouch. You could buy my car four times over for that.'

Jess's voice was weak as she said, 'I'm sure you can think of a scenario when I'd need your car on the mountain, so why not add it to the bill?'

She scrutinised the list of what was now folded in the plethora of bags, but this was very likely the only time Jess would be persuaded to fit herself out properly, and so with a pointed sigh, she got out two credit cards, saying she'd need to split the bill.

Returning Jess's cards, the shopkeeper placed a tiny bar of Kendall mint cake in one of the bags and said, 'On the house.' Jess couldn't help laughing.

Juggling the bags, they stopped off at a pizza place. Jess said, 'With the rider that this is in no way any sort of bribery before any further formal interviews, have whatever you want, Margot. You didn't need to spend such an age with me, nor did you need to lend me your gear in the first place, so go wild. I might as well be killed for a sheep as a lamb, and I'm going to get the largest pizza I can, with *all* the toppings.'

'Fighting talk,' said Margot. She perused the menu, and then told Jess after they had ordered, 'I promise those new things will make all the difference, and you'll wonder in a week or two how they were never in your life before. You'll never regret having the proper trousers or the perfect boots or a warm coat. There's a saying that goes something like "There's never the wrong weather, just the wrong clothes." And if you don't dry everything properly, he's going to think you just wanted an excuse to see him again.'

'Mister "On The House", you mean?' said Jess. 'Honestly, for the amount I spent, he could at least have given me a bigger bar of mint cake.'

'He didn't want you to think he was flirting.'

Jess realised she was enjoying herself, even though normally she hated to spend money on clothes, and she wasn't big on going out for pizza at the best of times. And normally in the heat of an investigation she never took a moment for herself.

In fact Margot proved such easy company that Jess didn't glance at her messages or alerts for two hours, and so wouldn't have seen the excitement building online about the proposed tribute to James Garfield that Kate Summers was organising.

James Garfield might be dead, thought the stranger, but he was almost more irritating dead than alive. There was speculation building online, and tiresomely the detective inspector seemed reluctant to box-tick. And now this damn vigil. Maybe it hadn't been too easy after all . . .

DAY THREE

Jess was back at the police station by 6 a.m., her new boots and socks, and Margot's coat, now dry, neatly stashed in the bag-for-life in her car.

Not a lover of early starts, today was one of those days where Jess couldn't see how she would fit everything in if she got up at her normal time. However, she'd struggled to get out of bed and then was so dozy she had taken a while to find her phone and notes among all her new gear.

A cup of strong black coffee beside her, Jess emailed to make an appointment to visit Tom Drake for the gossip Margot had promised and then arranged to visit Bob and Reeny Newman, and asked Kate Summers for a breakdown of exactly what was being planned for the tribute. Then she emailed Tony Peters to chase up the forensic reports, especially the specialist who'd gone the previous afternoon to the spot that Rose Thorne had recommended, and asked him to check if there'd been any progress on finding the GoPro and any will. She also asked him to do background and alibi checks on Tom Drake and the Newmans. After she'd watched a short drone film of James setting out on the final run that had been posted late the previously evening on Instagram, Jess sent a second email to her sergeant asking a bit snippily whether they were any further forward on finding @FanBigRunClimb001.

It looked like noon when the inquest into the death of James Garfield would be opened, and then adjourned for more information, and Jess wanted to go to that, although there were a couple of other things that she wanted to do first, including visiting his home.

Although it was strictly against protocol, Jess texted Margot: 'An imposition, but would you come with me back to where you found JG? Now I've got some background, I could do with picking your fell-running brain on the spot.'

Although she was determined to keep Margot in the frame, Jess didn't feel as bound by the accepted way of doing things as she once had been. Thinking of Margot's open expression and serious answers, Jess couldn't square the idea of her as prime suspect with the woman who had been so helpful. And she didn't set off warning bells by trying to ingratiate her way into the investigation; Jess had experience of cases hampered by over-keen witnesses. And so Jess told herself that she was simply looking for an expert opinion on what might have happened out on the fell. And if Margot Voyce wasn't as innocent as she seemed, perhaps she would give herself away.

Despite it not yet being seven o'clock, immediately Margot replied: 'Meet you in twenty where the ambulance was waiting, us both booted and suited?'

It still wasn't wholly light when the women met, and wouldn't be so for another thirty minutes.

Jess looked a different woman to the one Margot had met two days earlier, not least as she appeared to have had breakfast and was wearing appropriate clothing with things hopefully of the useful variety in her new backpack.

'Such a shame I never got that sponsorship – it looks good, doesn't it?' said Margot as she appraised the jacket she'd loaned to Jess.

Jess thought the multicoloured jacket verged on the hideous with its clashing blocks of primary colours and that it was too ready to shout out its reflective strips in the beam of Margot's head torch, but she had noted in the outdoor wear shop the vogue for brightly coloured outer gear – in part, she'd been told, because shades such as Day-Glo orange made people easier to find in deep snow. And Margot's coat was warm and waterproof, but also enviably lightweight, indeed all the things a good top layer needed to be for heading back to Piers Gill.

'Very snug,' Jess replied.

The women began to climb, with Jess asking about the technicalities of running over the different sorts of rough terrain on Scafell Pike, and how fell runners typically dressed and how their clothes varied from someone doing mountaineering proper.

Margot was clear in her answers, and gave several demonstrations of the differences between uphill and downhill pacing techniques, as well as lots of background about the diet, nutrition and gym work that James would have done, and the finer points of rough-ground running footwear.

'Were you ever drawn to get an agent like James did?' Jess asked.

Margot guffawed. 'Chance would have been a fine thing! I'd have loved to, but I was never good enough, as witnessed by my prototype jacket remaining a prototype. Agents don't like small fry. The financial side is also riddled with sexism, although some women in the field undoubtedly are good at building their online profiles. But their followers tend to be mainly female, and for things like TV shows, say, the accepted thinking is – or at least was, as I could be out of touch these days – that male viewers aren't interested in female experts, and this can have an impact on advertising. This can be positive as they'll attract ads for menstrual products, pan-sexual make-up, woke advertisements with lesbian relationships, female-aimed alcohol, etc. from firms who might be prepared to pay a premium for placement around an extreme sport and/or fitness programme led by a woman presenter. On the other hand, high-end car brands will probably steer clear, for instance, as will the lucrative shaving and male fragrance markets. This all means it's nigh on impossible for a woman to have the earning clout of a man of the same level of skill and level of attractiveness. Show me a woman who honestly claims that it's now a level playing field between the sexes in terms of money, and I'll show you someone who's lying.'

'Strong,' commented Jess.

'Oh, believe me I'd like to think there isn't still a difference in the way the sexes are perceived. But somebody like James can seem aspirational even to the lumpiest male couch potato, while a woman at the same level will seem unfeminine somehow, too pushy, too awkward. And some women would go along with that view too,' Margot replied.

'Really?'

'Perhaps Generation Z are changing all this – I'd like to think so,' said Margot, and the two fell to talking about women's place in society.

Jess was surprised to look behind her a while later and see it was now fully light, with daybreak a distant memory. They were much nearer where James may have plunged into Piers Gill than she had realised, and she and Margot had got there more easily than she had expected.

'Can we go up further, more towards the summit? I need to see what James would have seen running down,' said Jess.

The two women resumed climbing. Shortly, Margot stopped and turned to look back down, and gave Jess an idea of just how limited the visibility would likely have been.

Jess now understood how easy it would have been for James to have made a terrible mistake, despite all his expertise and years of experience. Although she didn't say so to Margot, Jess concluded that he might well have had an unfortunate accident, and then been unlucky enough to have been victim of a flash flood once he was down in the depths of Piers Gill. It still didn't feel wholly right, but it felt more right than wrong. With a bit of luck, she and her team could be stood down before too long. She should get things wrapped up as quickly as possible, and all witness statements completed while events were still fresh in everybody's minds. Certainly she wasn't going to push the view that James had died at the hands of another, Jess decided. Mike Bowers had been right to advise caution.

And then she looked at Margot.

'This wasn't an accident. Even if he were disorientated, he'd have crouched down and studied what was at his feet. I know he would. And close up, the ground would have showed him the way to go.'

Jess looked up and down the terrain, and then leaned down for a better look at the ground around her new boots, muddy now. She walked up and down the lip of the gill. She groaned. Suddenly, she wanted this over.

But Margot was right. James Garfield hadn't simply run over the lip of Piers Gill in foggy weather. He might have stumbled, but there wasn't any sign of this, and nothing around that either of them could find which might have tripped him, and no slide marks towards the lip at the highest part.

Jess knew if she'd been there on her own, she'd have decided what had happened was an accident, and she wouldn't have continued the investigation. But Margot's conviction that something wasn't right made her study the location differently, more closely, with more understanding.

Now that she had, Jess knew she couldn't give up.

Margot led the way to Tom Drake's stables, with Jess following in her own car. Rather to her surprise, Margot discovered that she wanted to show off to the inspector the closeness of her friendship with Tom. This surprised her, as she'd never felt like this before about him.

As he slouched across the yard to greet them, Tom looked as scruffy as ever and announced he hadn't got much time. But then he fetched coffee and pastries, and the three of them went to sit in the seating area overlooking the outdoor school, where one of next season's trekking ponies was being broken in and was making rather a fuss about it.

Jess watched the way it bucked on the lunge rein and then said, 'That's why I don't trust horses.'

'Come next Easter; a two-year-old will be able to ride him,' said Tom. 'You'll see.'

Jess heard the sound of galloping hooves as the pony tried a different tactic, towing his handler across the arena, and shook her head.

'Moving on, I told Detective Inspector Chambers that you're the fount of all local knowledge, Tom,' said Margot.

'Don't know about that,' said Tom, 'but I take an interest in what goes on.'

'It's good to pick a local's brains,' said Jess.

In other circumstances she'd have wanted to talk to Tom without Margot present, but there was something about the dynamic between the two of them that wasn't easy to interpret and made Jess wonder if having them both there together would be more useful.

'What can you tell me about James Garfield, Mr Drake?' she asked.

'Tom. Well, not much, really. It's common knowledge James were close to Bob Newman once his own parents died,' said Tom. 'In fact, I think his house actually belongs to Bob. We attended the same school, as did this one –' Tom nodded in Margot's direction '– but we weren't in the same year. Among me and my friends, James didn't have that good a reputation – sorry, Margot – but he was never outright called out on it by us, probably as he was older and we thought it just part of school.

Suspicions at the time were he wasn't above dirty kicks during football – someone from another school ended up in hospital once at an inter-school game – or passing off people's homework as his own. And a rumour stuck that he'd been hauled over the coals in Year Seven for taking lunch money from some kids, so we tried to steer clear of him. He was a lone wolf, and an unhappy lad, now I think about it, but after we left school, there was a time he were a party boy, and into drugs, the story goes. The rumour is that Bob had to ask for a favour more than once to keep him out of trouble. More recently I got the impression some of what James was talking about was designed to big up Bob.'

'Were the drugs just school stuff, or more serious?'

'It's all just speculation,' chipped in Margot, but the look on both her and Tom's faces suggested neither disbelieved the gossip. 'I think it stopped at school level.'

'I never heard about the police being involved, and I know he went to the States last year, so there can't have been an actual drugs conviction,' pointed out Tom.

'How was James bigging up Bob?' Jess said.

'I never heard or saw it myself, but somebody told me down the pub that it was something to do with planning or licensing.' Tom scratched his head. 'Actually I can't really remember what it was, so that probably means it was dull. Parking, maybe, as that gets everyone excited.'

'Right,' said Jess.

She wanted to probe Margot on how she'd got involved with James, but as she wasn't quite sure of the relationship between Tom and Margot – they knew each other well and were close to each other to judge by their body language, yet neither seemed to be acting proprietorially as Jess had seen in some couples – she thought to stray into this area now probably wasn't the time. Jess wanted to keep them both onside.

'I suppose you're wondering how I came to be with James?' said Margot.

Jess thought the police were missing a trick by not employing Margot, who would have made an excellent interviewer.

Tom said, as if Margot's question had been directed towards him, 'Well, the thought has crossed my mind before now, Margot, seeing he were a right, er, twerp.'

Margot couldn't prevent a smile at the quaint "twerp" seeing as Tom wasn't yet thirty, but then she frowned.

'I suppose I felt like a country lass with zero sophistication and ordinary looks. And when James and I found ourselves together on that first training climb in the Sierra Madre, he seemed very glamorous, and he dazzled me by showing some interest. I didn't understand back then that as I was the only woman in the group, I stood out for him just by virtue of being there, and that would help the nights at camp. He gave me the impression that he was fun and smart, and he knew people I didn't, and of course we had our Lake District and school connections. Before I knew it, I felt that I belonged to an elite group, and it seemed that James had engineered this, just for me. For a while I felt we were good together.

'And then we weren't either good or together, and I realised it had all been in my imagination, and I had believed there was a relationship when there never had been. And James's lack of limits made him unattractive, and the fact that there were other people who felt about him as I did made things worse. I think he later cleaned up his act, but there was a time when anything went with him – and I mean anything, and that includes *anyone*.'

Tom looked uncomfortable, but Margot was staring at Jess and didn't see.

Tom cleared his throat. 'I hear he's got a large bill outstanding at a garage, and he got a friend of Bob's to rent a house to some people James recommended, and they left without paying and they'd damaged the property, after which James wasn't at all helpful in sorting that out, and neither was Bob, from what I hear. And there's more than one woman around here who's said to have got rid of his child, as well as a young man who suffered depression after James ghosted him. All rumour, you understand. James was good at wriggling away from things.'

'I didn't know about the abortions,' said Margot, a small stumble in her voice. 'That was the sort of thing James never talked about, at least to me.'

'You're surprised?' Jess asked.

'No,' admitted Margot. Jess thought she looked resigned.

Jess stood up, wondering if that was a further line of enquiry to follow, although the way Tom had spoken suggested it had happened a fair while previously. 'I've got to go,' she said. 'How much do I owe you for the second breakfast?'

'On the house,' said Tom.

'Oh! In that case I'll just pick up a few things from the shop before I leave,' said Jess.

'The chicken and mushroom puddings are delicious, and there's vegan pies too if that's your bag,' Margot called as Jess walked away, 'and the rhubarb crumble and custard is irresistible.'

100

Tom looked at Margot once Jess had gone into the farm shop. 'Was James killed, do you think? Or was it the accident your inspector seems to hope it was?'

'I'm pretty certain she's veering towards believing that what happened to him was an accident. But she seems thorough, so I don't think she'll go for that until she's done a bit more digging,' said Margot.

'I was asking what *you* think.'

'Oh, foul play of some sort, I'm sure. I thought as much before, but back up there today I just knew it was no accident. And I'd plump for a deliberate act designed to kill, as not calling for help suggests somebody knew a night out in that gully would be fatal, if James wasn't already dead. So murder, I'd say. James would never have lost his way and fallen into Piers Gill or tripped, no matter how foggy or wet the weather. He always concentrated on what he was doing when out on a run, no matter what was going on in his personal life.'

'Is that what you said to the inspector?'

Margot shook her head. 'It didn't seem appropriate. You know a bit too "the lady doth protest too much" and all that. You should've seen the way she looked at me when she and Bob arrived at the scene. I'm not involved in this and I don't want to be, and I didn't want to make it seem as if I am by suggesting anything. I just wish it hadn't been me who'd found him, but once I had, what else could I do but report it?'

Tom looked relieved, as if while he hadn't really thought that Margot was involved, it was comforting all the same to hear her state outright she hadn't.

Margot's thoughts were elsewhere.

She stared unseeing into the distance as she added, 'But the really interesting questions are why, and why *now*. With all his sponsorships and business opportunities, James would have made sure everything he touched was squeaky clean. Three or four years ago, he could well have really annoyed someone for a whole variety of reasons. Now, it's much harder to credit.'

'I've just had a thought too,' said Tom.

Margot turned towards him.

Forty-five minutes after Jess left Margot and Tom, she let herself into James Garfield's house just three miles away with the set of house keys retrieved from his car.

Jess had been delayed in Tom's farm shop. Several people were standing around waiting for someone to come to the till. One rang an old-fashioned school bell for attention and eventually a lad came out of the storage area next door, washing his hands at the outside tap.

Out of the four cars that had arrived while Jess was speaking to Margot and Tom, three were top end, and when Jess had a word with the drivers, it became clear they were the owners of second homes or staying in holiday rentals. None was aware of what had happened at Piers Gill, and they weren't particularly interested either. Jess could see that while their money helped the local economy, they didn't participate in the community.

The fourth car was more modest, and belonged to a man about James Garfield's age who spoke with a Cumbrian accent. 'Aye, I heard,' he said. 'I never met him, but my cousin knew him back in the day. They had a thing, but it ended poorly . . .'

'Ah,' said Jess, thinking this would be something to follow up.

'And then my cousin went to Seattle. He said James Garfield was a git, but he'd made the decision to take a job abroad very easy, and he's not been back to the UK since. James made an approach a while back about company sponsorship possibilities, and my cousin said he'd ignored him.'

Jess took details for Bill Harper to follow up.

She parked at James's home and looked at it from outside. It was small and the garden was unkempt.

With his six-figure income, she'd expected more, Jess thought as she stood in his kitchen a few moments later. It was quite shabby, and untidily grubby too, although then she told herself that maybe this made sense, seeing as the cottage was a rental belonging to Bob Newman. It felt and looked like a stopgap, the sort of place a person who wasn't at home much would put up with while they were on their way to something better. A bit like her own place really.

Jess had a good poke round, but she found nothing of interest other than a lot of condom foils under the bed. Jess presumed that James practised safe sex these days, given the rumours of aborted pregnancies. And what if they hadn't gone through with termination, but James had refused financial support for the children? And of course the condoms may not necessarily have been for male–female sex only. Ambushed suddenly by memories of an abortion she'd had as a junior police officer in uniform, and when she had wanted but failed to get pregnant a decade later, Jess shook her head and forced herself to concentrate.

Looking more closely at the wrappers, she saw they pretty

much all had a fine patina of dust. This might indicate either recent unsafe sex – less likely, Jess assumed, than it might once have been, as James didn't seem to have been at a stage in his life when he'd welcome being a father or catching an STD – or else a reduction in sexual partners.

She then walked around the house, trying to imagine how James would have used each room. Jess noted there was no sign of a desktop or a laptop, nor had there been a laptop in his car. There was however an extension lead with four empty sockets close to the coffee table in front of the sofa.

It was difficult to imagine James doing all his posting from just a telephone. While it wasn't impossible, Jess doubted that a person focused so heavily on growing a strong digital footprint would not have had more high-end technical equipment. Editing his films and photos and posts on a larger screen and with a proper keyboard made much more sense, especially given how professional the films he posted on his YouTube channel were. There wasn't even a decent television in the house, and only a very few personal papers and a well-stamped passport, which a gloved-up Jess slipped into a plastic evidence bag.

As was to be expected, there were a lot of trainers and running wear, mostly lying on the floor where they'd apparently been kicked off. There was little furniture and precious little in the way of comforts in the house, and only a very limited range of clothing that didn't have to do with running or climbing.

Jess wasn't thrilled with her cottage, but in comparison to this sea of inhospitality, it felt like a cosy home.

As she was checking the windows and discovering the

unlocked back door, she phoned DC Harper. 'Bill, how are you getting on with James Garfield's phone?'

He was non-committal, and she wondered if he'd even looked at it yet.

'Any sign that James was editing his videos on it?'

'Nope, so far. Anything else you want me to look out for?'

'Not sure. Anything you wouldn't expect to be there. Print off his calendar and contacts. And see if there are any angry women – I've heard rumours of pregnancies and abortions – or any regular child support payments.'

On her way back to the station, Jess took a detour to the Newmans' home in the market village of Hawkshead, which Bob had told her the first time he had driven her around the area had been voted one of the poshest places to live in the UK.

As she drove down its pretty main street, Jess could see why.

Reeny answered Jess's knock. 'Come in, Inspector Chambers. Bob's having a nap, so I'll just go and give him a nudge.'

'Actually, Mrs Newman, before you do that, I need a quick word. Do you know if James tended to leave his back door unlocked?'

'Aye, sometimes. Bob told him not to, of course, as burglaries have picked up locally. But I doubt he'd have listened if he wasn't in the mood. James liked to do things his way and was always talking about travelling light, or some such nonsense.'

'I got the impression yesterday that you weren't James's greatest fan, Mrs Newman. Am I wrong?'

'Reeny, please. One doesn't like to speak ill of the dead . . .'

'Of course not,' said Jess, adding, 'Reeny.'

'He were a reckless tyke when younger, and not much changed as far as I could see.' Reeny's voice dropped to a whisper. 'But Bob has always been in his corner and wouldn't hear a word against, and—'

Abruptly she stopped. There were sounds from the stairs.

Jess could have groaned out loud. Reeny had seemed on the point of saying something that may have been useful. She now seemed intent on feeding a miaowing cat so plump it was almost spherical when sitting down.

'How are you?' said Jess. She thought Bob Newman looked very peaky.

'Fair to middling, all things considered,' he said as he made his way to the other side of the kitchen table, sinking onto a chair with an audible clicking of his knee joints.

'Bob, you look awful,' said Jess. 'That was a lot of running around on Scafell Pike, and then you were up early yesterday too. Against all advice at the hospital.'

'See? I told you!' Reeny's voice was anxious.

Bob looked long-suffering.

'The inquest today is a formality, you know – it'll be opened and immediately adjourned. There are reports yet to come back from the PM and potentially other witness statements to take, and these may have a bearing on our investigation and could take weeks, or even months,' said Jess. 'Please don't make a special effort to be there, Bob; nothing of note will happen.'

'I need to show my face. What would James think if I wasn't there? Or my voters if a TV crew is filming and they can't see me?'

'Bob, are you listening?' said Jess. 'If James were here right

106

now, he'd be telling you to stay at home and get your strength back – your health has to be the priority. And your voters wouldn't want you to make yourself poorly. They know you'll make every effort to attend when it's necessary. But they won't want to think they've elected a councillor who's foolhardy, will they?'

'Precisely, Bob,' said Reeny, who turned to Jess and added, 'I've said as much already, but he's got cloth ears.'

'I do need to be there all the same.' Bob's voice was firm, and Jess knew he'd barely heard a word she'd said.

'Men!' sighed Reeny as she and Jess exchanged a look.

And it confirmed to Jess that if James had displayed the same blinkered and stubborn streak as his uncle, then he could have rubbed someone up the wrong way.

'After you left earlier, Tom and I spent some time going over James's own posts,' said Margot, her voice tinny on the car's speakers as Jess drove to the station.

'Go on,' said Jess, nevertheless catching the tentative note in Margot's voice.

'Well, I know many of the indications at the moment are that what happened was very likely an accident, but I – er, we, I should say, me and Tom – have gone over James's recent posts of training on that same route, and we thought you should know that if there was somebody else involved, it wouldn't have taken much if they were experienced on the peaks to work out pretty accurately when James would be making his way down near Piers Gill. They could just have waited for him there at the most lethal nip point.'

'You think?' said Jess. 'Wouldn't it have been suspicious if they were just standing around doing nothing? It's relatively open with views that stretch for miles. And in any case, wouldn't it have relied too much on chance?'

'Well, yes and no. You're half right and half wrong,' said Margot. 'Okay, look at this way: if anyone did plan to do James harm or play a prank that went wrong, they couldn't have relied on the bad weather or hardly anybody else being there, both of which were random events. But even without that, there would have been an element of surprise, and pushing him over the edge or whatever would only have taken a matter of seconds.'

'You think this is plausible?' said Jess.

'It's possible, I think. James had been banging on endlessly about his training plan, and anybody could have worked out pretty accurately how long it would take to get to the precise spot where they could do most damage to him. Although James played fast and loose with his personal life and enjoyed the element of chance – I think he was a natural gambler – this wasn't the case in terms of his training. He just wasn't like that. His posts make it clear he worked to a strict plan, doing set routes at the same time of day and giving times at various points in order to compete against himself in similar conditions and track minute improvements. He was very disciplined. He ate the same foods daily, took his supplements regularly, and all the rest. He'd even post his interval times on occasion.'

Jess turned on her windscreen wipers as she drove into a squall, and turned up the car's speakers as they squeaked back and forth over her windscreen to make sure she could hear.

Margot added, 'Where it becomes really interesting – Tom

pointed this out just after you'd gone – is that someone experienced on the Lake District fells could have assumed that on his descent James would have been concentrating on his foot placement in case there was debris underfoot, and so would not have been looking around him at other things.'

'Go on.'

'Well, this has implications, doesn't it? For instance, it's not hard to get outdoor clothing that would pretty much match the terrain, and if someone was wearing a balaclava and gloves too, they might not be immediately obvious if James was concentrating on his feet and they kept their body close to the ground. I was sceptical at first, but then we tried out some coats and whatnot out on the fell here, and when I was moving fast it was surprising what I didn't notice, and that was even when I knew exactly where Tom was crouching, which of course James wouldn't have if he wasn't expecting to see anyone.

'And James would have been intent anyway on his timings, and picking up his knees properly, as well as where to place his feet as he wouldn't have wanted a tumble, and looking at the ground, and so his brain would have been distracted by a lot of things at once. He'd have been noisy too, and somebody could have surprised him.

'The other thing is that although it looks open up there – your eye is continually taken to the horizon – in actual fact the terrain has nooks and bumps. The brain and the eye work together to see what they *expect* to see, remember, and not necessarily what is actually there. Tom told me about an experiment where students were told to watch a video and count passes of a basketball, then they were asked about the man in a gorilla suit, and most of them hadn't noticed him even though he walked right through the game.'

'Hold on. Don't go anywhere for a mo,' said Jess and she manoeuvred the car into a gateway. She put on her handbrake and found the clip on her phone's YouTube, and sure enough the gorilla was clear if one was expecting to see it.

'Okay, yes, I get what you're saying now,' said Jess. 'So what you're describing wouldn't have relied upon strength? If James had been taken by surprise?'

'I assume you're asking if a woman could have done it?'

Jess was watching the gorilla clip again and didn't answer.

'I think a woman could have wrong-footed James,' Margot said carefully, 'provided she made sure she had the element of surprise. She'd need to be bold though, as it could have gone terribly wrong, if James had got wind of what she intended. James might not have carried much weight or much obvious muscle, but he was strong, as well as flexible and very sure of himself physically. A woman would have needed to be very bold and confident, but she could have done it.'

'Would you describe yourself as bold? I know you're confident.'

Margot answered with what sounded to Jess like a natural laugh. 'These days I'm not bold at all, I'm afraid, nor confident. And if I had planned on harming James – which I hadn't and never have – I wouldn't have chosen a method like this, not least as it could have re-injured my back and left me in a wheel-chair. Sudden pushing movements are a no-no. And the uncertainty wouldn't have appealed when there would be much easier ways to get to him.'

Jess thought she should have a word with her superiors about whether there were enough grounds to get Margot's medical records to check whether this was in fact true. She wanted to believe her, but the fact that she had found the body and reported it, and now had initiated this conversation, had to raise suspicions. Jess knew that many killers liked to brag covertly about their expertise by doing something like 'finding' the body of their victim.

'I don't want to interfere, obviously,' said Margot. 'And I'm sure that me making this call doesn't scream "Not guilty" – assuming I'm right about what happened. But I thought it was worth telling you that you have to keep very focused when going steeply downhill at speed on a treacherous slope. The point I'm making is that the level of concentration this requires can reduce a person's other senses. And if you're going for a personal record, it's just not the same as doing something for leisure. And this got me thinking that maybe you needed to know that James would have been extremely focused, and I didn't know whether you appreciated this.'

'You're giving the benefit of your experience as an expert witness?' said Jess.

'That's overselling it,' Margot said. 'Would it help clear me if I emailed the information on my back injury and its initial treatment and prognosis, and also my most recent X-rays? These were taken only four or five weeks ago for insurance purposes for my walking guide job. I'd be happy to do this, and to give permission for you to double-check everything with my medical team. Only if it's helpful, of course.'

'That would cut down paperwork,' agreed Jess.

She'd been correct about Margot's ability to read both a situation as well as people; she really had the knack of anticipating what was about to be broached.

'How does horse riding fit in then?' Jess wanted to assess Margot's attitude to risk generally.

'I said I was cautious and averse to taking stupid risks, not that I wrapped myself in cotton wool. And I'm a competent rider, much more than I ever was a skilled mountaineer,' said Margot.

'Horses account for a lot of deaths and long-term injuries.'

'True. But probably not so many among people who know what they're doing. Although I suppose a counter-argument would be that experienced people try more challenging things, and so when things do go wrong, the consequences are likely to be more severe. Anyway, I can only speak for myself, and I'm careful to stick within my limits, both on horseback or out on the fell. And my horse is very sensible.'

'I know even less about horses than I do about mountaineering or fell running or fell walking,' said Jess, 'so I won't comment.'

'I daresay it all evens up. I know next to nothing about police investigations or murder,' answered Margot.

'Of course, if there was another person up at Piers Gill, it could be that James Garfield arranged to meet them there, so taking out the element of surprise.'

'Yeah, Tom and I talked about that, but we were totally unable to come up with a convincing scenario. If somebody asked to meet there, why would he agree? And the idea that James instigated such a meeting isn't credible. He wasn't wearing clothes that he'd be happy standing around in during November – he wouldn't have wanted his muscles to get cold.'

'I see.' So a planned meeting at that location made little sense.

Jess thanked Margot for getting in touch and gave her the email address to send her medical records, then started her car and a couple of minutes later was turning into the staff car park at the police station. But rather than getting out and making her way to the incident room, Jess remained where she was, deep in thought.

Although she had never experienced precisely what Margot had just described, Jess had often found she could hyper-focus when on her Northern Ireland operations. She remembered she had been shocked several times during debriefs by not being aware of some really glaring things that her fellow officers had reported.

Her phone alerted her to an email arriving, and Jess scrolled to see Margot had sent over a sheaf of documents and the telephone numbers and emails of various people who could corroborate the injuries she'd sustained.

Margot could still have taken a tremendous risk and given James a firm shove, but deep down Jess couldn't find it in her to believe she was guilty. She just didn't seem that foolish, if her back was as fragile as she said it was. And motive seemed lacking too. Although the relationship between James and Margot had ended unhappily, that had occurred five years earlier. Above all, there was still no absolutely clear and firm *evidence* of any wrongdoing in regard to James Garfield's demise.

It was all extremely frustrating. Jess knew she needed that light-bulb moment, an insight with which she could inspire her team. The problem was, she wasn't feeling inspired and had no new ideas.

A thorough study of James Garfield's laptop yielded results, and it had been sensible to work offline. It was clear James had died not a moment too soon. Even waiting a day could have proved disastrous. So now the question was, would it be a good idea or not to go to the inquest opening?

Tony Peters and Bill Harper looked very industrious when Jess came in, and Bill Harper held up a camcorder to indicate it was on charge, one of the things Jess had asked him to take care of.

'Ah, glad to see you, boss,' said Tony Peters after he hung up his phone. 'You'll be pleased to know that @FanBigRun-Climb001 is cooling his heels in Interview Room One, waiting just for you. I brought him in an hour ago, as I didn't trust him to come here on his own.'

'Ah.'

'You'll like this,' said Tony as they made their way down the corridor to the interview room a minute or two later. 'Not a lot, but you'll like it.'

Jess looked at her sergeant.

'Not a Paul Daniels fan?'

'Too young.'

'Ouch,' said Tony and then held the door open for Jess to go through.

'Trevor Walton,' said Jess. 'What a surprise, and you so quiet about your activities as @FanBigRunClimb001 on the occasions we've spoken . . .'

Trevor Walton slid his feet around on the floor in a way that signalled he felt uncomfortable, but he didn't say anything, although Jess hadn't expected him to, remembering how quiet he'd been.

She explained that he wasn't being interviewed under caution, which meant he could leave at any time, although that might not be a good idea if they decided to press charges against him further down the line.

Trevor Walton stared back, his enlarged pupils making his eyes look dark, and Jess noted the sheen of perspiration on his forehead.

'So will you confirm that you are the person who posts online as @FanBigRunClimb001, Mr Walton?'

Trevor Walton blinked in a way that made his eyes pop slightly, and then he nodded.

'You prefer to watch extreme sports than participate. Would that be correct?'

He glanced at his legs and nodded again. Jess remembered how carefully he had moved the first time she had seen him, as if he had painful knees. She scanned his fingers – pale and stiff-looking.

A rheumatoid arthritis sufferer, if she had to bet. Very painful, especially for someone as tall and broad as Trevor Walton, as he would be carrying a fair amount of weight on each joint.

'Do you post on anyone else besides James Garfield?'

'No.'

This confirmed their assumption that under the @FanBigRunClimb001 tag there had only been posts about James.

To clarify, she added, 'And if we get a forensic technician to look at your postings and all your electronic equipment, would we find other tags that you write and post under?'

'No.'

'And if the forensic technician studied your equipment, would we find anything sinister? Or threatening?'

'I should hope not.'

Jess thought this answer wasn't quite a no.

'Would it be fair of me to say that you posted obsessively about Mr Garfield?'

'I wouldn't say obsessively.'

'How would you describe your posts then?'

'I like him, and he likes me. James looks out for me.'

' "Liked" would be more accurate. You often used a drone to film him?'

'Sometimes.'

'A bit more than sometimes? All those times you filmed him, times you led me to believe you were simply there to wave him off, I'm sure you remember implying when we spoke in this very room.'

Trevor Walton declined to answer, but Jess took his pained sigh as affirmation. He was obviously finding the interview extremely awkward.

'What really interests me, Mr Walton –' Jess's voice was soft '– is why at this very police station when we spoke to you after you'd reported James Garfield potentially missing and I specifically asked whether there was anything else you needed to tell us, you *didn't* volunteer you were @FanBigRunClimb001. And nor did you mention your frequent drone filming of

Mr Garfield, even though what you had shot clearly might provide some sort of clue as to what had happened.'

The silence swirled between them as the sheen of sweat on Trevor Walton's brow grew to drops hanging from the outside ends of his eyebrows.

Jess suddenly felt rather sorry for him. She didn't think he'd withheld information with the intention of anything other than hoping to hide how obsessive he'd been about James Garfield.

Trevor Walton didn't seem to have a lot going for him in terms of looks, personality or fortune, and a major enthusiasm – James Garfield – had now been taken from him. Jess could imagine that all of that didn't make Trevor Walton particularly well placed to deal with the world about him in the way that others might. He looked panicky.

Jess told him to take it easy and to remember he wasn't under caution.

'However, I take it we'll have your full cooperation from now on, and you'll hand over all the digital footage you have of Mr Garfield,' Jess said quite gently as she stood up to show she was ending the interview.

'I'll make sure you have it all,' Trevor Walton croaked.

If Jess had had to come up with a word to describe the hasty nodding that accompanied Walton's reply to her last question, it would have been 'disturbed', or maybe 'cowed', she thought as she headed back to the incident room. She was planning to get Bill Harper to scour the parts of the films that Trevor Walton had shot over the last three months on his drone of James Garfield but hadn't posted, and then correlate any car registrations that appeared with the scant CCTV available locally. The posts themselves should already have been checked, but it wouldn't hurt if Bill double-checked them, she decided.

Jess thought Trevor's physique almost definitely indicated more an armchair enthusiast who had slightly stalkerish tendencies than someone able to race up a mountain with murder on their mind. He'd driven to various car parks around the Lake District in order to film James, but it seemed unlikely he'd ever strayed far, especially when he could cover such a lot of ground with a drone. He'd have struggled to get up to Piers Gill.

So while fixation could turn to hate and beyond that, Jess inclined towards Trevor Walton being an isolated and lonely man who lived vicariously through the odd nod or acknowledgment that James Garfield occasionally threw his way, rather than being in any way involved in his death. All the same, she sent Tony Peters back to Trevor's house with him, giving her sergeant strict instructions to give the place a good visual once-over, including any sheds and the garage.

'Be respectful though – it'll save time if Mr Walton agrees on a voluntary basis. If needed, we can think about getting a warrant and looking at his medical records, but that's time and expense we don't want to incur unless we have to. Tread carefully. Although you and I will probably never understand someone like him, Mr Walton doesn't need to be made to feel bad about himself. He doesn't seem to me like he has a whole lot going for him, and yesterday and today have probably made him feel important and needed just for a short while. It's possible he just wanted to eke out the experience for as long as possible by not saying anything earlier about his involvement. Do photograph his medication though.'

'Right. I'll make sure to be nice.'

'Oh, and ask him not to post today or for the next few days. See what his response is to that.'

'Got it, boss.'

Jess brought the policy book up to date and then reviewed Margot's medical notes and X-rays.

Her phone alarm beeped, and she realised it was nearing the time of the inquest, so she headed to the town hall.

Kate Summers, wearing a powder-blue trouser suit that looked identical to the cream one she'd sported the day before, was smoking a cigarette outside the town hall as Jess parked. She told Jess the vigil would take place at three o'clock that afternoon.

'You've got your skates on – I was expecting it to be tomorrow,' said Jess.

'I need to be back in London then,' said the agent as she ground the cigarette stub into dust on the pavement between them in spite of there being an ashtray in the top of the refuse receptacle she was standing beside adorned with a notice on it about the fine for casual littering. A lot of people were heading inside, both out-of-towners and locals, and Jess heard a woman who looked the sort who posted angry emails on nextdoor.com give a huff of disapproval.

Kate Summers gave her a withering look and said to Jess, 'My team moved heaven and earth to get the damn vigil sorted for today, and have been publicising it heavily for the last few hours. We'll do a decent memorial in London probably a few weeks after the funeral, of course, but the slant today is on local superfans honouring the final run of James Garfield, the man who broke all the records on these peaks.

'Tiresomely I had the Mountain Rescue stressing any gathering mustn't be too large, and it has to be in a car park because of the risk of injury in the dark. They don't want to get called out for anyone wandering off or falling into a lake. There'll be a couple of speakers and then, as the light dips below the horizon, we're going to light sky lanterns – people will have the chance previously to write personal messages on them to James – and release them en masse. It should make good footage for posting and for the documentary.'

On cue, Jess's phone received a message from Margot: 'Just seen the notification about the tribute to James at three. Me and Tom will be there.'

'OK,' Jess replied as she said to Summers, 'That's two people confirming they'll be there. I doubt anyone will wander off to a lake and throw themselves in.'

'I prefer to leave nothing to chance. People are idiots sometimes.'

Jess knew what she meant. 'Was James Garfield an idiot?'

'Yes, but not that way.'

'What way then?'

'Oh, the time-honoured tussle between ambition and conscience.'

'Conscience?' said Jess, unable to disguise the surprise in her voice as she stepped aside to let some people who looked like they were fell runners pass.

'Yes, I wasn't expecting that either,' said Kate Summers. 'At one time I'd thought he'd do anything to get to where he wanted to be.'

Jess frowned. 'Please elaborate.'

'Absolutely not. Client privilege.'

'Client privilege doesn't apply to your profession,' Jess said as patiently as she could.

Kate Summers looked genuinely amused at that and not in the slightest as if she was going to answer, and for a moment Jess felt naive. Then she felt a tap on the shoulder and turned to see Rose Thorne, Kate Summers taking the opportunity to make herself scarce.

'A quick word before we go in, please,' said the pathologist.

'Ah, Ms Thorne, just the person I needed to see,' said Jess, a trifle peeved about Kate Summers having bested her but needing to talk to Rose.

Jess and the pathologist walked a little away from those clustered around the doors.

'No steroids or anything suspicious through on toxicology yet. The report has just been released, and I'll send it on to you, although nothing yet from the firm testing for the newest sports toxes. And nothing back either on Mr Garfield's clothing,' whispered Rose. 'But there is something interesting. That blurry mark quite high on the victim's back has developed into something that looks much more like a contusion caused by the heel and fingers of a hand. Just before I left the mortuary, I checked the measurements on the contusion to see whether it had altered, and it was definitely clearer to the naked eye.'

She scrolled to a photo on her phone, which she then held for

Jess to see. The mark had an angled measure against it to give an idea of scale.

'I think it'll come through a little clearer yet. But if it was caused by a hand, it's a large hand,' added the pathologist as Jess stared intently at the image

'Are you saying that what I'm looking at definitely belongs to a man?' asked Jess as she continued to peer at the picture. It still looked to her like it could have been made by just about anything, but there was more contrast between the natural skin tone and the marks than she had seen the day before.

'I wouldn't want to swear to it under oath yet, but my best guess is that it was made by the hand of a tall man. I'll update you once I've studied the reflectance spectroscopy as this will show more of the structure of the tissues and the damage to the dermal layers of Mr Garfield's back. I haven't observed any abrasions caused by his clothing on the outer surface of the contusion, but I want to give this a closer analysis. I'm sorry not to have got to this before, but it's been chaotically busy and I've colleagues signed off sick. Anyway, you wanted to speak to me about something else?'

From her shoulder bag Jess retrieved the X-rays Margot had emailed. 'What do you think?'

Rose Thorne held them up to the light and studied them one by one for a minute, and then she said, 'Somebody has had a nasty injury.'

'If I email them and the medical reports over, can you have a closer look, please? What I need is verification that these belong to Margot Voyce and occurred when she claims. I'd be grateful for your opinion as to whether the injury would stop her – or make her think twice about – running up Scafell Pike or giving somebody a push into Piers Gill. Anything that could rule her out would be helpful.'

'Okay,' said Rose Thorne. 'Send them over. Is your Margot Voyce very tall for a woman?'

'About my frame and height. She's lent me a waterproof jacket until one I've ordered arrives, and it fits nicely. And I haven't noticed her having unnaturally large hands.'

The pathologist stood back and looked Jess up and down.

'If that's a handprint from a push hard enough to cause a contusion on James Garfield's back, I would say your woman is too short and likely has too-small hands. I suppose she could have been standing uphill from him, which might account for the height of the contusion, but in my professional opinion that doesn't get around the span of the potential handprint.'

The moment the inquest was over, the proceedings opened and adjourned with a minimum of fuss exactly as she had hoped, Mike Bowers leaned over from the seat behind Jess to give her the welcome news that her food and gas deliveries had both arrived safely.

'Thanks, Mike,' Jess said. 'Where would I be without you?'

'Cold and hungry,' he said, and Jess laughed.

She was heading for the station to collect Tony Peters and then going on to the vigil for James Garfield that Kate Summers had organised. She had sent an email to her sergeant as she waited for the inquest to begin to warn him to be ready to go.

As Jess walked to her car, she noticed Bob Newman standing

on the steps of the town hall talking to a reporter who'd shoved a microphone under his chin.

Gone was the grey-looking and frail older man of yesterday. Now, the councillor was dapper and rosy-cheeked, with his conker-brown leather brogues newly shined, altogether much more the robust and avuncular councillor Jess had met when she first came to the Lake District. Several people were standing watching, and he looked as if he was playing up to them.

Mike caught Jess's eye and raised a brow. He'd noticed the same thing.

In contrast, Reeny was tense and anxious, to judge by the white-knuckled manner she was holding on to her handbag as she watched her husband from a distance of about twenty feet, and Jess wondered if Bob was as all right as he seemed from a distance.

The councillor was an old warhorse who knew how to put on a show, and Jess thought he wouldn't be above taking a nip from a hip flask to bring the twinkle back to his eyes; he might even have given his cheeks a quick pinch before making his exit. He'd know all the tricks.

Jess felt a twinge of sympathy for what his wife had to put up with, and raised her hand to let Reeny know she had seen her. Reeny Newman gave the tiniest lift of her shoulders in response, and Jess sent her what she hoped came across as a supportive smile.

'First thing in the morning we need to get more info on that possible handprint bruise and double-check nothing has come back re DNA,' Jess said to Tony Peters as he drove them to the vigil. 'And if the bruise is clearer as a handprint then, I'll have to alert the CPS as we might need their input along the way over the clarity of the evidence, and the suspects – of which there aren't any as yet – and any realistic chance of conviction. What happens after that will come down to money.'

Tony's voice was downbeat as he said, 'Don't hold your breath on the response of our legal advisers. I don't know about your experience, but ours seem to go out of the way to make life difficult.'

'Surely they just want to remind us of the high burden of proof that's built into the legal system, and make us aware of the high cost of proceeding with futile cases in court?' said Jess.

'Just you wait and see,' said Tony Peters. 'It may just be our local people or even my dealings with them. But it seems to me that we could have a convicted psychopath come to us with a full confession of how he'd killed someone, and a whole lot of collaborating physical evidence, and witnesses all supporting his story, and they'll still say there's not enough for us to get a conviction. And then it's only a matter of time before the investigation is shelved, and we're left having uncomfortable conversations with relatives of the victim.'

'Unfair, surely. That can't be true – they'll have targets to meet just like we do.'

'In my experience, not so you'd notice.'

'Depress me, why don't you? Let's hope something comes up at the vigil that means we can put the whole thing to bed or move forward. That either knocks a criminal investigation on the head, incriminates someone or gives us a solid lead.'

'Like what?'

'No idea,' said Jess. 'But something's got to give, otherwise we'll just get bogged down. I don't think Bob Newman will settle for that, and as this is my first SIO here, it doesn't work for me either. Kate Summers hinted to me outside the inquest that James Garfield had had an attack of conscience, but then closed that down when I dug a little deeper. I haven't been able to think of a way of getting her to open up, and I don't think direct questioning is going to help. Have we discovered if there was a tracker on his laptop?'

'Typical . . . agent,' said Tony Peters. 'And nothing yet on the laptop.'

'Sure you weren't about to indulge in a touch of misogyny with a "woman" there, Tony?'

'Actually, I wasn't,' he answered in a way that convinced Jess he was telling the truth. 'It was more I was referring to how pushy she is, but I couldn't think of a word to describe that. I've no idea if all personal agents are like her, but I can see that she would have taken a lot of pressure off James Garfield and organised much of his professional life – possibly some of his personal life too. All he'd have to do is show up for the gigs they'd agreed, and concentrate on his fitness and completing his challenges. I could do with a personal agent to sort my life out.'

'I know what you mean. There've been moments when I'd have loved to have somebody like Kate Summers in my corner. With decent application you can be a good copper or good at being an adult, but to try and be good at both at the same time is where a lot of us come unstuck.'

They looked at each other and laughed. What Jess had just said was hard to argue with.

126

'Well, maybe that's what was happening with James. If he wanted to break agreements made a while back that weren't now suitable or when he didn't have as much nous about him as now, some people wouldn't have been best pleased.'

'To the point of harming him?'

'I don't know. But somebody had it in for him, it looks like.'

'You may be right. Margot Voyce and Tom Drake were pretty convincing about how somebody could have ambushed James Garfield out on the mountain. It would have needed audacity but not much skill or strength. Ask around whether there were signs of James having an attack of conscience that could have rattled someone.'

'That narrows the suspect we are looking for down?'

'If Rose Thorne confirms a handprint on James's back, it belongs to a tall person with a larger than average span, almost definitely a man,' said Jess. 'However, we should probably look at Kate Summers more seriously – her commission on the deals she was striking for him is sizeable, and she wouldn't want to hear any doubts from him, but I don't see how it would have suited her to actually harm her client. And you've seen her – she doesn't look like the sort of person who'd yomp up a mountain.'

'She could have paid for a hit.'

'I'm not seeing that,' said Jess. 'Too chancy for someone like Ms Summers – she'd hate the number of variables she couldn't control. And that's aside from the fact that if James Garfield was on the cusp of the big time, she'd never want him dead. And if she did need him out of the picture, I think she'd arrange something simple and effective. A meeting with a bank of expensive-looking lawyers behind her, say.'

'What about if *he* was intent on leaving *her*?' asked Tony. 'If he really was about to make megabucks, perhaps he was off to one of Kate Summers' competitors.'

'Have you come across anything to suggest that might be the case?'

'Well, no.'

'Keep digging. He might have taken pains to hide it, especially if he was going to one of Kate Summers' main competitors. Check his phone records don't show calls to other agents – they'll have had contact with him somehow,' said Jess. 'And tomorrow get on to some agents anyway. See if you can dig up anything else – it's an industry that thrives on gossip, and somebody may have got wind of something. Ask Bill to cross-reference their phone numbers and emails with Garfield's social media and the rest of his personal and business email accounts. Let's get a proper business picture, and not just Summers' version. Get Bill to see what he can find out about Summers' commercial insurance too – she may have some sort of cover for the death of a client or for a client terminating their agreement early. In fact see if Bill can discover the start and end dates of their contract of representation. Belt and braces, please.'

Using his dashboard help, Tony Peters compiled a verbal 'to do' list on his phone, Jess sneakily impressed that he remembered everything she had asked and in the same order she'd spoken.

'Also whether there were business firms he'd upset, or people in some official capacity. Perhaps James Garfield died because of threatening someone's interests commercially or over what they had going on in the public arena, and his death wasn't personal.'

'How will I do that, boss? These people play their cards very close to their chest.'

'Actually I have no idea how to narrow this down,' Jess admitted. 'I guess a start would be scanning stories in the local papers and on local websites, and looking at the minutes of meetings and public enquiries, and court cases – civil and criminal – and seeing if anything cross-references with James Garfield negatively. You could start with comments he's made to the press opposing someone or something.'

'It's a nice idea, boss, but it's surely a long shot and not practically viable.' Tony Peters sounded weary at the thought of the potential work required by what Jess had just said. 'You know how small the team is. We don't have the resources now, or enough probable cause for you to be able to get extra people or resources to do this effectively or in any way thoroughly. I don't want to be defeatist –'

'– but . . .' finished Jess. 'Yes, you're right, Tony. We'll keep it in mind, but back burner for now.'

There was a brief silence as they both went over things in their minds.

Then Jess said, 'I'm not sure any of this is bringing us closer to the *why*, if it is a suspicious death. And perhaps this is going be what we never quite get, even though really it is the most important cog in the whole damn wheel. Normally we'd have a clear why.'

'Yeah. I can't help thinking that too.'

'Keep open minds,' Jess said.

They drove on for a while, and then Jess asked, 'Anything unexpected on the stuff Trevor Walton gave you? Or suspicious in his home?'

'No joy there yet either. He did shoot a few minutes of James Garfield setting off on his final run though. But from what Bill and I could see, it's not helpful, and it got very wet about five minutes in and very blurry, and he stopped recording. I couldn't see anyone else around, and there weren't any other identifiable cars – other than his and Garfield's.'

'Have you sent to the electronics specialists, just in case?'

'It's with them now, skip. And I couldn't see anything out of the ordinary in Mr Walton's house, greenhouse, garden shed or garage, and I had a good poke about in his car too. All innocent from what I could see, although perhaps if we get a warrant, forensics would be able to pull something up. He didn't seem any more anxious at his home than when we had him in the station, and a man like him would get twitchy if I'd been getting close to anything dodgy. He could have a stash of weird stuff somewhere else of course, but he was happy to show me his bank and building society records and there was no standing order to a storage facility. I had a look at his bank accounts and he's actually quite wealthy. His lottery win was huge, but he seems to live very quietly, and his house and car are modest. Everything was incredibly clean and *very* neatly arranged though, so our Mr Walton may have had a tidy-up in the last couple of days, before we took him in.'

'Not house-proud yourself, Tony?'

'Ha ha. I'm more a beer-and-footie-on-the-telly sort of person than getting out the hoover.'

'Somehow I'm not surprised. That aside, I'm having a hard time thinking of Trevor Walton as anything other than sad and lonely – someone who never saw his life turning out this way,' said Jess. 'And I'm inclined to think much the same of Kate Summers too.'

'Or else they have Oscar-level acting skills,' said her DS.

Jess was glad that Tony Peters was driving, as although they didn't have to go a long way, the narrow lanes close to the vigil were crammed with cars and pedestrians. Most of the people were presumably fans wanting to pay their respects, although Jess also saw a local television news outside broadcast van in front of them in the queue of traffic. At one point Tony mentioned that the Lake District had over nineteen million visitors in 2018, after it was designated a World Heritage Site.

'It seems as if most of them are on the way to this damned vigil,' Jess muttered.

Tony Peters had to mount the verge more than once to allow large vehicles to join at junctions, and it was a relief to Jess when they finally arrived; she wasn't used to seeing drystone walls at such close quarters and hadn't enjoyed the experience.

Rather than being a grim gathering in a grotty car park, it turned out the event was taking place on an adjacent piece of land. There was proper lighting, and a stage had been rigged up with a large screen, speakers and a microphone on a stand.

Remembering Margot's advice, Jess made sure to lace her new boots firmly and pull on a hat and gloves as it was going to be a gusty, cold evening.

'Nice coat, boss. Very jaunty,' said Tony with a raised eyebrow at Margot's waterproof.

'It's not mine,' Jess replied curtly.

Jess was surprised when several people came up to say hello. She thought she'd probably met them when out and about with Bob Newman, but everyone was bundled up in scarves and hats and it was hard to be sure.

A hot-dog van was doing good business, and there was a wine and beer table too, and as a chilly blast of wind prompted her to zip up Margot's coat over her chin, Jess caught the smell of mulled wine.

'Shall we have a word? They won't have licences.'

'Don't worry about it, Tony. People will clam up if we draw attention to ourselves. I think let everyone get on with it. Keep them onside as I'm going to ask for help.'

They saw Bob and Reeny Newman arrive, and headed over to them, Jess thinking Bob was back to looking wan and old again.

'How are you both?' she said.

'Well enough,' said Reeny in a tone that suggested she was trying to keep up her husband's spirits.

Bob looked at Reeny and then at Jess as he said, 'I'm his closest relative and I'd like to be able to make a start on arranging his funeral.'

Jess assumed this was a continuation of a conversation that Bob and his wife had been having on the way to the ceremony, as Reeny now had an expression on her face as if she'd heard it all before.

'I understand, Bob,' Jess answered. 'But we've spoken of this before, and you know it might take a while. The coroner's office will give you an information pack and you'll get an interim death certificate so you can start dealing with James's personal affairs. You wouldn't like it if we rushed the investigation and then weren't able to convict – assuming we do make an arrest.'

Bob Newman sighed as if the delay was Jess's fault personally.

'Bob, my advice is not to rush around right now getting things sorted as it will just exhaust you. An option could be a small private funeral once James is released to you, and a bigger memorial service that maybe ties in with an event that marks the fell-running year,' said Jess, feeling sorry for the older man. She had thought of asking Bob for a copy of the will, as it might be helpful to see what James had wanted to happen to his estate, but decided not to do that now. 'You should speak to James's agent Kate Summers, as she's planning a memorial for him in London. If you're his executor, she'll be able to help you with his financial affairs.'

Jess knew money would probably be owed to the estate for several agreements James might have completed but not yet have been paid for, and it might amount to quite a large sum, but she didn't mention this to the Newmans as she didn't know how much they knew about James's finances. She really wanted to know but couldn't see a tactful way to ask them. Meanwhile Tom Drake had mentioned rumours of an unpaid bill, and if James had had one invoice outstanding, then there were likely to be more.

Bob Newman grunted impatiently, and Jess caught Reeny's

eye. She twigged and immediately diverted Bob's attention: 'Oh Bob, look, there's Alan Jones looking as if he wants a word – I bumped into him in the supermarket and he was talking about pollution. I said you were the person to speak to as I knew nothing about it.'

Reeny slipped her hand under Bob's elbow and guided him towards a cross-looking young man.

Jess and Tony watched them go.

'Knocked the stuffing out of him, hasn't it? Up close he looks a shadow of the man he used to.'

'You wait. In half an hour Bob Newman will be grandstanding on that stage, acting as if he's forty-five rather than pushing seventy,' said Jess. 'I'm sympathetic, but he's up against a system that there's no way he can buck, no matter how many favours he might have done for the coroner in the past.'

'The coroner is a Freemason?'

'No idea, so don't you go starting any rumours about the coroner and Freemasonry. Bob Newman being used to getting his way was the point I was making, but this time it's not going to work out for him like it usually does.'

Kate Summers, now in pillar-box red from head to toe, marched into the field, trailed by three or four frazzled minions each bearing a box of unlit lanterns that they began to hand out along with felt-tip pens and matchbooks. Meanwhile the documentary makers had begun filming on their expensive-looking handheld cameras.

'Looks like you have a good turnout, Ms Summers,' said Jess as the agent strode past. 'You must be pleased. I wonder if I might say a few words from the stage?'

Kate Summers frowned as she surveyed the gathering crowd. Jess noted that the agent's lipstick matched her suit exactly. It was possible to over-coordinate a look, although Jess could see that the suit would look striking on camera, which was presumably the effect intended.

'I should think there is a good turnout. I've made damn sure about that,' the agent snapped. 'Every member of the team has been on it – it's been sheer graft. Yes, you can go on before James's uncle, but keep it brief. I'll let the team know, but make sure you're ready when they indicate, and you're on stage as the other person is coming off. I don't want gaps.'

Jess didn't doubt for a second that the vigil had been hard work to arrange, although the brunt of the work had probably been borne more by those who worked for Summers than the agent herself.

'It's a good way of capitalising on what's happened, and we'll build on it with the event in London. I'm sure this is what James would have wanted.'

'Are you speaking tonight?' said Jess, less sure than his agent that James would have been delighted by being the subject of a vigil. She thought that he would much rather have been alive and preparing for another fell run.

'But of course,' Kate Summers said, before thrusting a couple of lanterns and pens into Jess and Tony's hands that she swiped from a passing box, then quickly stalking away with a cameraperson bunny-hopping in her wake in an attempt to catch up in order to get some film of the agent with Bob and Reeny Newman as this was clearly where Kate Summers was heading.

'Doesn't suffer fools then, that one,' said Tony Peters. 'Not that I'm suggesting for a moment you're a fool, skip.'

Jess laughed and then noticed Margot Voyce and Tom Drake heading across the field towards the crowd, Margot smiled and waved a hi, and Tom nodded that he'd clocked Jess. Jess watched as various people said hello to Margot and Tom. They were obviously popular, and Jess noticed that both looked relaxed and at home as they chatted.

'You like Margot Voyce, don't you?'

Jess realised her sergeant was more observant than she'd given him credit for.

'Yeah, I do,' she admitted. 'To the point that it's going to rankle if she turns out to be involved. Make sure you get some footage of them both, mind, and of Kate Summers and all of her team. I might like Margot Voyce and her friend, but if I have to go in hard on them at some point, I will.'

'Okay,' said Tony, and it was clear that he didn't doubt for a moment Jess would do exactly as she said should she have to.

It wasn't long before the vigil kicked off, and even though initially cynical about the event as it smacked of schmaltz to Jess, something that she was hard-wired to find abhorrent, it wasn't long before she had to admit that Summers and her team had done an amazing job in a very short time.

The speakers – several well known in endurance sport, to judge by the enthusiastic reception from the crowd – were slick, well prepared and generally professional in a way that suggested Kate Summers had drilled them over what they were each going to say. They spoke standing in front of a looping professionally edited photo and film montage of key moments in James's life, interspersed with press headlines, all designed to show what an affable, likeable man he'd been, what a superb role model for the upcoming generation of climbers, fell runners and extreme sports enthusiasts he was, and how great he'd been in a crisis. James looked strong and happy, capable and absolutely the last person who would have come to such an untimely end.

Jess remembered Margot's description of how James had reacted following the accident that had damaged her back so badly and thought James hadn't been exactly great in that crisis. She looked over to Margot, who was staring stonily straight ahead, ignoring those around her, and thought she had probably been transported back to that time. Whatever she was thinking about didn't look like it brought back happy memories.

Tony Peters was walking around with his phone set to video, but alongside the camera crew Kate Summers had brought in, the local news TV people and the host of other folk, including Tom Drake, who were busily recording the vigil on their phones, he didn't stand out. Jess also noticed Mike Bowers on the other side of the crowd, but he didn't acknowledge her, and she didn't him, although she could see Mike glancing about keenly. His impressions might prove useful.

At a signal from a harried minion, Jess climbed on to the stage to address the gathering.

'Good afternoon. I'm Detective Inspector Jess Chambers. I've recently moved to Cumbria, and I'm leading the police enquiry into what happened to Mr Garfield. It's good to see so many people who knew James here this afternoon.'

Jess didn't like the sound of her own voice or public speaking, but she couldn't pass up the opportunity to appeal to so many people directly, even though her throat felt tight under the scrutiny of the crowd.

'To explain the interest of the police: what has happened is so far being termed an unexplained death, and an inquest has been opened and adjourned into the passing of James Garfield to give us time for further reports and evidence to be prepared. It's not yet clear precisely what occurred, and so if any one of you has any information, please get in touch. I'll leave business cards beside the book of condolence. Please take one, as you might remember something later that we should know. Any detail, no matter how trivial it seems to you, could be immensely helpful, remember. I'm thinking of conversations you might have had with James, either face to face or via social media, over the last month, photographs or videos of him you may have taken, or any rumours you may have heard about him or his behaviour.

'Do know that we're absolutely not looking to lay blame on anyone if he died as a consequence of a simple accident and if no deliberate wrongdoing by a third party was involved, although if somebody hurt him, then that is a different matter. Aside from this, anything you say to us will be in confidence, and we will not pursue any offences that do not relate to James and his death. I say again – just so that we are all clear – that we are not interested in pursuing any other offences that come to our attention. So, as long as you didn't mean Mr Garfield physical or psychological harm, you are safe. Our *only* focus is establishing his cause of death and who, if anybody, was responsible.

'As we've heard, James Garfield was a man with a social conscience, to judge by the concerns he supported, and he was a staunch supporter of all things to do with the Lake District, as we've heard too. He grew up here, and loved these lakes and peaks. No one would disagree that he was too young to die. Let's work together to try and find out what happened to him. Thank you for listening.'

The stranger gauged the enthusiasm with which the audience clapped DI Chambers and tried to follow their lead. There was nothing in what she had said to suggest that the police were closing in on a person of interest, or even that they had any firm leads. And a casual-seeming scan of the audience didn't raise any red flags. Of course Chambers was too smart for her own good, it was easy to see, but a lot of what had happened had been designed to avoid firm assumptions. And the thing about smart people was that they usually forgot that simple could be remarkably effective. So far, so good . . .

As she stepped down on to the grass again, Jess was surprised by the enthusiasm of the applause; it seemed people very much did want to know how James had died, and were prepared to help her investigation.

Bob Newman replaced Jess on the stage as the twilight dipped towards darkness, and the sky took on tinges of inky velvet.

'Thank you, DI Chambers. I second her request; as the uncle of James Garfield, I won't rest until I know what happened, and so if you have information, please pass it to the police.

'Words can't express what I feel. James was the very best nephew a man could have, always up to something new and exciting. Indeed, only this week he told me he'd thought of something new I should hear about; sadly he didn't live long enough for us to have that chat. His death will always leave a hole in my heart and a huge sense of loss. I have no doubt it would have been an exciting new project, as he was one of those people who knew how to get what he wanted and how to persuade others to believe in him, and he loved coming up with new ideas.

'I know old fogeys like me are sometimes criticised for not appreciating the younger generations, but people like James showed us all how fantastic a young man can be, and his passing is a sadness for us all, especially when he had so much still to give.

'The book of condolence can be found on the table beside the hot-dog van, and so please do take a few seconds to write a sentence or two in tribute – I'd very much appreciate it. It's early days yet, but I intend to set up some sort of memorial in my nephew's memory, so do leave contact details so I can keep you abreast of this. Meanwhile, in a minute we'll light our lanterns after the final speaker, but before I finish, I'd just like to introduce one of the final pieces-to-camera that James shot.'

Jess watched the councillor. It was the first time she'd seen him up close speaking in public, and his years of experience stood out. She glanced at the audience. He had them in the palm of his hand.

Tony Peters mimed writing something to Jess, and she nodded back, understanding that he planned to photograph the pages of the book of condolence once everyone had signed.

On the screen James was wearing his running gear. He was talking about his forthcoming three-peak record attempt and how his preparations were going. The date and time stamps showed that he had recorded this just five days earlier.

He looked calm and confident, and very fit, Jess thought,

exactly like a man with no doubt in his mind that he would achieve all the objectives he was setting himself, or that sponsors and business opportunities were going to make him very rich in the near future. James Garfield certainly gave no indication that he thought he might die within the week.

Jess suddenly felt somebody's eyes upon at her, and she turned right and left. She could see at least ten people she didn't know looking at her with curiosity, as well as a couple she had seen before. She caught the eye of several of them. She noticed a person standing in shadow on the other side of the crowd. Even if she squinted, she couldn't see who it was, but for the first time in a long while she felt a tingle of attraction fire somewhere deep within her belly, and she missed the next few seconds of what James was saying in the video.

Jess forced herself to concentrate, and she turned her eyes back to the stage just in time to see and hear James add, 'I feel fortunate – a lucky person indeed – as I get to spend my time doing what I love to do. There's no better feeling than to run up a peak and then stand and look about you, and draw our clean, wonderful Cumbrian air deep into your lungs – it makes you feel, quite literally, on top of the world. And now it's time for me to head back once more to the top of the world. So long and speak soon, folks.'

James filmed his hand setting off the stopwatch on his wrist and on his phone, and the clip ended.

There was applause, and Jess sneaked another look towards the person in the shadows and for a moment thought it might be Mike Bowers, then felt a rush of shame as she'd never thought of him as anything other than a paternal mentor. She caught a glimpse of a hooded head angled her way, and her heart bumped. It was such a long time since anyone had shown an interest in her that she felt fizzy inside, a sensation she'd almost forgotten.

Jess immediately felt foolish and humiliated. *They were probably looking at someone else.* But when she leaned down to pretend-check on the bow on her bootlace and was able to snatch a quick look about her, it was to see she was standing quite alone, with nobody behind or to the side of her. Flushing – although that could have been because she had been bending down – Jess risked another peek as she straightened up. Yes, she was pretty certain she was being looked at.

Kate Summers had replaced Bob Newman on stage, explaining that now everyone had had the opportunity to write on their lantern some last thoughts to send to James, on her count they should light them with the matches provided, adding the lanterns were eco-friendly with no metal skeletons and no danger to wildlife.

Jess quickly wrote on her lantern, 'I <u>will</u> find out.'

Joining in with the vigil like this wasn't professional and something she'd never thought she'd do. Rituals such as lighting paper lanterns had always seemed to her silly and over-sentimental. But the atmosphere as they stood together on this November afternoon had got the better of her, and it felt the right thing to do. Jess told herself she was doing it only to show respect for a man who had died years too soon.

Kate Summers said, 'James and I had worked together for several years, and we had some projects in the pipeline that would kick off after the record attempt he was promoting had been completed. One of these was so secret that we were to explore it in depth later this week, and let me tell you, it would have shown him in a whole new, much more serious light. He also had a major television documentary series planned on a key streaming channel. I think the action man we all loved was paving the way for the metamorphosis of James Garfield into someone with a more serious agenda. And in tribute I'm going to try my level best to make sure that the docu-series happens in memory of this wonderful man: our friend, mentor and inspiration, James Garfield.'

She took a step back as the crowd responded enthusiastically.

Jess risked another glance, and in the dimness, although she didn't feel under scrutiny any longer, perhaps someone had edged closer to where she stood. It was hard to tell as the crowd wasn't stationary.

The lanterns were lit as the lighting rigs and the screen dimmed, and everyone joined in Kate Summers' countdown to letting them go. And as the final embers of daylight slipped away to the west, the indigo sky was ignited by hundreds of environment-friendly lanterns rising into the air. The breeze caught them, and Jess thought that for all the world the lanterns looked as if they were dancing in memory of James Garfield. It was surprisingly moving, and Jess felt a lump come to her throat.

Tearing her eyes away from the sky, Jess thought that the person who'd interested her had drifted even closer. And then Tony Peters reappeared. Blocking Jess's view, he said, 'Once we're done, fancy a hot dog from the van?'

When Jess leaned to look around her detective sergeant, there was nobody of interest where she'd hoped they would be, and she felt an intense pang of disappointment, a pang she masked by waving a twenty-pound note. 'Whatever you want, and extra onions and ketchup on mine. Please.'

Margot Voyce choked up when the lanterns were released. As she watched them drift up into the sky, she felt there was something much more significant about them than she'd thought there would be. Tom seemed to understand this without her saying anything, and she felt him move so close that the elbows of their coats almost touched.

'I hope that wherever James is right now, he can see this,' Margot said.

'Yes,' agreed Tom, adding after a while, 'He'd have made a meal of all this fuss and brouhaha though, wouldn't he?'

Margot turned to look at Tom. His expression was innocent, and she couldn't tell if he was being snide or not, but she felt raw all of a sudden, and too emotional to question him about what he'd meant.

She'd never asked herself whether Tom liked James, even though she knew there had been tensions when they were at school. But now it seemed as if perhaps Tom really hadn't, and this unsettled Margot, who wasn't sure if it was significant or not.

Margot had just experienced a deep sense of loss and regret, despite the sorry way that she and James Garfield had left each other's lives all those years before, their relationship dwindling to nothing in what felt like the blink of an eye. It meant Margot had felt overwhelmed at several points in the vigil, her feelings strong reminders of the helplessness she'd experienced in the immediate aftermath of her accident and how acutely she felt that James had let her down.

The maelstrom of negative memories jostled against the loss of James, who'd also given Margot at times a sense of excitement and self-worth, and Margot was cross with herself that she hadn't thought more deeply before attending the vigil how it might affect her when she heard strangers describing the James Garfield they knew. She hadn't expected it to be an uplifting experience, but neither had she expected watching the speakers on stage to leave her so disorientated.

She gave Tom a sideways look. For once his sturdy familiarity didn't offer her the sense of ease it usually did, and this spiralled Margot into unease, although she pulled herself back with a private instruction that she really must get a grip.

Margot wasn't sure why, but she sensed Jess was no stranger to experiencing diametrically opposed feelings at the same time. There was something resolute and dogged about the detective inspector, traits tempered with a sensitivity Margot felt was lacking in most people and which she hoped would rub off on her. But much as she wanted to, it wouldn't be appropriate for her to seek Jess Chambers out now, Margot decided.

'Pub?' said Tom after they had stood in silence for a time watching most of the crowd disperse and the headlights from the cars streaming away on the narrow road.

'Pub,' Margot agreed, although without the enthusiasm she would ordinarily feel if Tom suggested a drink. 'But I need to sign the book of condolence first,' she added.

Right at this moment spending time with Tom felt second best somehow, but then Margot reminded herself that second best with Tom was much better than a lot of the bests she'd experienced in her lifetime. There were many worse ways of spending the next couple of hours.

'I wonder what the more serious direction the woman in red thought James was heading towards actually was,' said Tom. 'Do you think she knew?'

'Well, she spoke with authority, but I assume that's how she normally speaks. I can't really see James as some sort of pioneer in terms of having a serious agenda, can you?' said Margot. 'I can't quite get my head around it.'

'No, me neither. And there was the documentary series. I wonder what that was going to cover. I guess James must have changed a lot in recent years.'

'Maybe.'

Margot was very thoughtful as they drove to the pub.

It went so much better than expected. Sometimes hasty plans really deliver. Admittedly, it would have been more efficient, in a sense, if the two women had been there together. But that would be truly suspicious, wouldn't it? With a bit of luck, maybe this will appear to be a second accident.

The temptation to stick around clawed at the stranger's skin. But that wouldn't have been sensible at all.

DAY FOUR

It was two minutes past midnight when Jess was woken by repeated pings from her phone, which was lying next to her on her pillow. She'd noticed before that when she was at home her emails sometimes arrived in a batch, despite her having forked out for a top-end router and internet connection so that she could be instantly contactable.

Her bedroom was pitch black, and Jess squinted at the screen to see the time while trying to ignore the notifications, and then closed her eyes without clicking on any of the emails. She saw from the phone's clock that she had only been asleep for a few minutes, which was why it felt brutally soon to have been wrenched awake.

Normally Jess went to sleep easily and promptly, something which had irked more than one of her partners. But that hadn't been the case this evening, despite her feeling worn out physically. Theories of what might have happened to James Garfield had crowded her head as she lay under the duvet, occasionally interspersed with thoughts of the mysterious figure at the vigil, thoughts Jess made sure quickly to suppress. After she had turned on a calming app on her phone, eventually she'd dropped off, still turning ideas over in her mind.

Jess knew she was letting this case get to her. There wasn't any concrete evidence either way as to an accident, a sudden death through natural causes or wrongdoing, but she was also sad about James Garfield's fate, although she knew this could be in part because she'd been exposed to Bob Newman such a lot in recent weeks, and so felt more connected to James Garfield than she had been to previous victims she'd dealt with.

And – Jess wasn't happy about this, as it suggested to her that she was the sort of woman she tried very hard not to be – she couldn't quite work out whether the discombobulated feeling she had as she lay in bed was partly due to a hormone rush at apparently catching the eye of someone who even in the merest shadowy glimpse she'd had didn't seem to be a gargoyle, her interest in anyone new being so rarely piqued these days it felt unfamiliar territory.

There were another two *dings* from the pillow beside her.

Jess gave up trying to sleep and sat up in bed.

From the email headings she could see Bill Harper had emailed about the drone footage and then had sent a second message to say the GoPro looked to have turned up, unless somebody had lost a second one in Piers Gill. Jess then scrolled down to the previous messages to see one from Rose Thorne saying further forensic reports had come in.

She was just about to open the first email when the phone rang, making her jump.

It was Tony Peters. 'Boss, are you up still? If not, I'm afraid you're about to be.'

Jess made a non-committal sound before rubbing her eyes and then said, unable to mask the reluctance in her voice as it was obvious her sergeant wasn't calling with good news, 'What's happened?'

'There's been a fatal car accident, and I think you're going to want to visit the scene. In fact, there's no *think* about it – you need to be here. You wanted something to give in the investigation, and now it has.'

Jess found it hard to believe that a modern luxury car with all its safety features could be reduced to such a tangle of metal. What she was seeing must be testament to the speed the car had been travelling as it crashed down the hill. Whatever had happened, the once sleek silver-grey body of Kate Summers' Audi Q7 now bore little resemblance to a car.

There were deep gashes on one side of the vehicle where it had somehow rolled over an unforgiving drystone wall before ricocheting down a steep incline. The wrecked boot had been wrenched open; the bonnet had sheered clean away, and two wheels had lost their tyres, while the windows on the other side of the car were shattered. Kate Summers' bloodied body was half in the driver's seat and half hanging through the now glassless window. No internal or external lights were showing, suggesting the car's electronics had most likely been annihilated, assuming nobody had switched the car's engine off.

Jess scanned the surroundings with her torch, and even though the beam wasn't as powerful as she really needed – she'd get something better from the outdoor shop when she went in to pick up her jackets, she decided – she could see the agent's possessions were scattered over a wide area. Her Louis Vuitton travelling bag had ripped open, leaving the trousers from the cream suit hanging out of one rear window like some sort of pennant.

Although it was approaching one o'clock in the morning, a police specialist from the Serious Injury Collision Unit was busy taking measurements and tapping them into a touchscreen tablet. Jess heard him murmur to himself he'd never seen the like before.

'Something unusual?' she asked.

'You could say that. It'll be clearer once it's daylight, but right now it's not looking good.'

Putting it mildly.

Up close to the car, it was a horrific sight. Kate Summers had sustained devastating injuries nobody could have survived.

'I'd stake my reputation on it that the car rolled downhill at an increasing speed after the point of initial impact, that impact causing the vehicle to mount and then tip over the wall. The air bag deployed in the impact as there's glass up there too – could be when the windows broke. I don't necessarily think the car was going at a huge speed when it went over the wall – but it could have been, and I should be able to clarify that when it's light. But I would think the power of the air bag emerging, which probably happened at that point, plus the centrifugal force of the rolls, combined to partially eject the driver through the window. Those head injuries mean she wouldn't have stood a chance.'

Jess looked at the pulpy mass above Kate Summer's shoulders and the agent's curiously unbloody neck, on which right behind an ear she could see two tiny and unblemished Sailor

Jerry-style tattoos, one of a lipstick and the other of a high-heeled shoe.

The contrast between the injury above and the smooth skin of the agent's neck was extreme, and Jess couldn't prevent a shudder pass through her before she had to turn away. She'd seen dead bodies with hideous injures before, but without a doubt this was the worst.

'Why did the car roll so fast? How do you know it did?'

'I'm not sure I can say precisely why at the moment.' The officer beckoned Jess up the incline, showing her deep indentations in the ground. 'But I can say categorically that once the car was over the wall, then it picked up speed. Look here, and here.' He shone a heavy-duty torch at the furrows the accident had scarred across the grass. 'These are the marks the wheels made during the rotations of the rolling car, and the distance between them grows, which suggests an increase in speed, with the depth of the marks suggesting the vehicle was rolling so fast it bounced. The trajectory of the roll was nearside, top, offside and bottom for at least six revolutions from what I can tell at the moment, as opposed to top, back, bottom, front.'

Jess struggled to picture this for a while and then said, 'So would the car have needed to be travelling fast for it to mount and go over the wall? And you mean it rolled sideways rather than somersaulting end to end?'

'You're correct about the rolling. But your question about the speed the car might have been going previous to that is not as easy to answer. Coming into the corner on the road above, it looks as if the car might have been going too fast and clipped the wall, causing it to go over. But there are many films of stunt drivers traversing all sorts of obstacles at quite low speeds, so it's not a given that this car was going fast prior to the impact. Having said that, I expect that we'll find out tomorrow that the car was probably moving at a speed too high for the conditions. In addition, there are marks on the car's right-hand side that suggest there could have been a collision with a third party, or a ricochet on the car's offside, probably with the stone wall on the opposite side of the road.'

'Paint from another vehicle would be too much to hope for, I suppose?' said Jess. 'Or else something that would indicate it hit the wall?'

'There's nothing apparent in terms of paint or transfer markings from anything else, but bear in mind I'm looking in the dark, and we might be able to find something once it's daylight and we can survey the whole scene better. There nearly is always transfer of material in a collision, but if there was a collision on the road, it's possible that the evidence has been massively compromised by what happened to the car on this side of the wall.

'And of course, if somebody else was involved, then it could have been a large farm vehicle, although that might yield, say, sample soil material from someone's tyres or a sample of the tyre rubber,' the officer said, running through his notes on the tablet to make sure he wasn't missing anything.

'Anyway,' he added, 'Forensics will check once the car is with them in a controlled environment. If it was a farm vehicle, there's an upside as there are fewer for you to check, although agricultural tyres are probably purchased from a very limited number of suppliers, so you could find all relevant vehicles have tyres made from the same compounds. There could be soil samples, but they might not stand up in court; the land here has a lot of history, and can yield many different readings within a small area. It's child's play for a good expert witness to introduce a reasonable element of doubt that leads to an automatic acquittal when soil analysis is used as a component of the prosecution's case.'

Jess let out a mighty sigh of frustration.

'I feel your pain. If you're really lucky and a farm vehicle was involved, there's a chance. Some tyre manufacturers include the date of production on the side of the tyre along with load and speed indexes, and this would definitely narrow your search.'

Rain began to fall heavily.

'Well, bang goes some of your forensics,' the officer added, looking up with a scowl.

'These roads are difficult at the best of times,' said Jess. 'Would you be able to determine whether it was driver error? A strange suicide attempt, perhaps? Or do we think the driver had been pursued?'

'I hear what you're asking, but I wouldn't hold your breath,' the officer told her. 'There's no sign so far that anyone else was in the car. All the doors were locked shut electronically, and the blood marks show the body is unlikely to have been disturbed by anyone climbing over the fatality, while although the boot was open, the back seat was also jammed in position through the roll cage wedging it. And without a witness any case is likely to fail. You need a witness who saw the car on the road prior to the accident, and who can say also if there were any other vehicles in the vicinity and then identify for certain any such vehicles. But these roads are quiet once it's dark. There are few houses around, while the dog walkers you might get late at night in a town are non-existent. This high up, there aren't even poachers. Your best bet is to find someone returning from the pub, but I doubt you'll have any luck as this isn't a direct route to any houses.'

Jess looked down towards the car. From this angle it looked like Kate Summers had lost her left arm from the elbow down, while the rain was clumping what was left of her hair, and Jess could see how little of her scalp was left. Dizzy for a moment, she had to close her eyes and hug her arms to her chest.

The traffic accident expert didn't say anything but waited for Jess to compose herself. She was grateful that he hadn't tried to make her feel better. What had happened to Kate Summers was horrible. Nothing anyone could have said during training could have prepared an officer for anything like this. She knew she'd be thinking about it for quite some time.

Jess felt she owed it to Kate Summers not to try to feel better about how she had died. Instead, she needed to gather herself and concentrate with every ounce of her being.

'What time do you think it happened?'

'Early evening, probably. I would estimate about six hours ago. She didn't make a rendezvous with colleagues for an early supper before they all returned to London, and they got worried when they couldn't raise her by phone – very out of character apparently for the deceased not to be available – and so they called it in, although at that point there wasn't anything suspicious and the accident wasn't reported until gone ten o'clock.'

Jess nodded. In the short time Jess had known the agent, she had never not had her mobile phone in her hand.

'By chance a farmer on his way back from attending to some sheep noticed the damage to the wall. He stopped and investigated, and saw the car. It's lucky he looked as the damage isn't very noticeable from the road. And although I'll check this in daylight, I think the fact that the car ended up in a gully might have made it difficult to spot even in broad daylight. It would be clear enough from a helicopter, but we don't send them up if we can avoid it. The car registration suggests it belongs to—'

'Oh, I know who the victim is, thank you,' Jess interrupted. 'She's called Kate Summers and she is – was – from London. She was here to organise a vigil to mark the death of her client, the fell runner James Garfield, who died in Piers Gill several days back. She could have borrowed the car, or rented it for all I know, but right now I'm more interested in what happened to her in the last hour or so of her life. Ironically, I saw her very much alive at five thirty, when she was in her element, thriving on bossing everyone around.'

'When you say fell runner, you mean the man who was found strung up on the rock face in Piers Gill on Scafell Pike?'

Jess nodded.

'Odd,' said the traffic officer, apparently to himself. 'Two strange deaths with people connected to each other.'

Jess nodded once more. 'Exactly.'

Forensic pathologist Rose Thorne arrived along with an assistant, and Jess went with them to the car, the downhill walk being slippery now in the wet weather.

'Not a pretty sight,' said Rose Thorne as she stood surveying the scene after sending her assistant back up to the road for a tent. 'This is going to be a bitch to deal with.'

Jess was trying not to look too closely at the body of Kate Summers, which looked worse the second time around, and couldn't for the moment think of anything to say.

Rose Thorne noticed and said gently, 'My assistant will take some photographs in a minute, and then I'll take the dead woman's liver temperature. You might not want to stay for that bit, as she's going to be awkward and messy to deal with.'

Ordinarily Jess would have remained at the side of the pathologist come what may, but it was a completely different experience having had previous contact with the victim. She hadn't much taken to Kate Summers but this was a particularly foul end.

'Thanks, Rose. I really don't think I do want to see what you have to do.'

She plodded back up the slope to where Bill Harper was using the team's camcorder to film the wall where the car looked to have gone over so that they would have a visual record for their own purposes.

'Bill, I know the weather isn't helping, but make sure to get a good look at the road up there, then ask uniform to do a house-to-house first thing to check security camera footage and doorbell cameras,' Jess said, pointing each way along the tarmac. 'Three miles around on all roads, I would think. And get a good torch and go back about half a mile, then film from there up to where the car left the road – it might be useful to have a view in the dark of what Kate Summers would have seen. Also, see if we have any tents or gazebos to hand to put over the car to see if we can try to preserve at least some of the evidence. And find out what the latest is on versions of recognition software at our disposal.'

Jess went to stand by Tony Peters, who had just arrived and was now acting as scene coordinator.

'Good call, Tony, asking Rose Thorne to attend the scene here,' said Jess. 'I think it's wise we have continuity.'

'What do you think?' he asked. 'Our mate from SICU isn't exactly known for his optimistic outlook.'

'So I gathered. He's definitely lowered my expectations about our chances of getting decent evidence from the scene, and I can't say the pathologist was overly enthusiastic either. And in answer to what I think, one strange death is peculiar at the best of times,' said Jess. 'Two – and from victims closely connected – is beyond coincidence.'

'Agreed,' said Tony Peters.

'What I suspect we're dealing with is somebody wanting to close things, or just a single thing, down. It will be something that links James Garfield and Kate Summers, which means we know now that we have, almost definitely, two murders on our hands, and probably both committed by the same perp. Even though death couldn't be guaranteed through a car accident, I think the killer gambled on Kate Summers sustaining a serious enough injury to remove her until Garfield's death was ruled accidental at the inquest. Take a statement first thing from the farmer who reported the accident. Check timings and ask if he noticed any other vehicles or anyone looking over the wall. The usual drill.'

'Will do. Talking of timings, I've just done a recce between the vigil site and here. Driving normally, it was eighteen minutes from here to there, and driving like the clappers from there to here, it was fourteen, and don't forget I'm used to these roads, while I assume Ms Summers was not. No idea if that is helpful, but it will go towards the timeline. And I think you're right that now it's murder in both cases,' said Tony Peters. 'Well, you wanted something that was going to bust the case open or put it to bed. Looks like you got your wish big time on the bust option.'

'I didn't see this coming though,' said Jess.

'No one could.'

'I'd better check what the overtime situation looks like, and I need to make sure the coroner is alerted,' added Jess wearily. 'This isn't good, and I'm just about to make the DCS really cross by waking him in the middle of the night and calling both deaths murders, and he'll be thinking CPS, with both of us knowing we don't have a clue what the Crown Prosecution is going to like. And what the bloke from SICU said won't cheer him up either. It would help if we had a suspect, which of course we don't. Meanwhile take a list of anyone up on the road. I would think that late and filthy as it is, there'll be gawpers.'

Jess and Tony looked down the hill at the sorry sight of the car.

Then Tony said, 'I won't be looking to put myself forward for promotion any time soon. Life's too short for the amount of stress of your call, boss.'

Margot couldn't sleep. She got out of bed and pulled on a Fair Isle woolly and some fleece-lined tracksuit bottoms over the top of her pyjamas and then went to make herself a hot drink and find some paracetamol. The emotional turmoil provoked by the vigil was taking longer to get over than she had expected, and she had had far too much to drink at the pub. The result was a thumping headache.

As she waited for the kettle to boil she took the painkillers and gulped down a pint of water, followed by a second pint. Then with a steaming mug in her hand, Margot went into the generous conservatory on the side of her parents' house, their pride and joy, where she stood and stared out of one of the banks of windows, watching the drips of rain make their way down the outside of the glass.

She had been back in her old childhood home since returning to Cumbria, although both she and her parents took great care to talk about this as 'a temporary arrangement'. Depressingly, the longer Margot was back in the Lake District, with its limited options for her to earn decent money, the less the arrangement seemed in any way temporary, which was something she tried hard not to think about. Finding herself at getting on for thirty in more or less the same position she had been at eighteen was frankly not what she'd signed up for.

Catching her reflection in the glass, she looked away. She really didn't want to compare how she was now with how she'd been when she and James were together or when she and Tom were at school together. Moving to the far end of the conservatory where it was dark, she peered out. The view during the day was amazing as the house was high up, but outside was black, making it impossible to appreciate the dramatic views on three sides that made the conservatory so special.

Then she noticed something flickering against the opaque

blackness. Moving to the window closest to the blinking lights, she looked around for the binoculars kept in the conservatory for bird watching and general snooping. When she had found them and got the focus right, Margot realised that what she was looking at were arc lights and the repeated blue flashes from the emergency warning bars of several police vehicles and a larger vehicle that she thought was probably an ambulance. They were all on the remote road high up on the opposite side of the valley.

Margot scanned around and thought, although she wasn't certain, that she could see fainter lights zigzagging around lower down the hill. *People on foot with torches?* she wondered. She kept the binoculars to her eyes and pressed speed-dial on her phone with her free hand, and then held it to her ear.

There was no reply the first time she rang, but she tried again and her call was answered immediately.

'Tom,' Margot said. 'Sorry to disturb.'

He grunted.

'Are you up? Have you seen what's going on? Something's happened across the way from ours, and the emergency services are there, so I guess it's not looking good for somebody.'

Thirty minutes later, Margot's parents had joined her at the conservatory windows, and then a rather damp Tom arrived, holding aloft a bag containing a bottle of whisky, several pairs of binoculars and his laptop.

'Grim weather,' he said as Margot's father poured the whisky.

Tom passed around his spare binoculars as Margot's mother found a selection of tartan picnic rugs. It was chilly in the conservatory as the underfloor heating wasn't on. Soon everyone had a wool blanket draped over their shoulders, making Margot think they looked like a band of raggedy druids.

'Cheers,' said Margot as she lifted her glass. They all toasted her back and took a sip, and then she added, 'Tom, any idea what the hell is going on?'

'Not at the moment. But as I was setting out, I saw Bob Newman on his way to have a nose about, so I suppose somebody rang him. We stopped for a quick word – he thought there had been some sort of accident.'

'I don't know,' said Margot, 'but there looks a lot of police activity if somebody has just wrapped themselves around a gate post or something. Maybe there were several vehicles involved.'

'It does seem odd. Shall we go and see if we can get a closer look?' suggested Tom.

'Nosey,' said Margot.

Tom laughed. 'Nosiness has always been my best quality.'

'Me too. Give me a minute to get something warmer on.'

Margot gulped back the rest of her whisky, and then as her mother and father told her to say that anybody could come back to the house if they needed to, Margot went to get dressed in appropriate clothing for post-midnight on a wet Cumbrian November night.

It was fascinating to watch the police at the accident scene. And interesting to see the people in the conservatory watching the police. There was that man too, also very interested in what had gone on. Best not to draw attention to oneself, as at this time of night one risked being remembered.

*

The road was closed to vehicles a fair way back from where the police were parked, so Margot and Tom turned around in a gateway and drove back the way they had come, not noticing Trevor Walton watching from inside a field, sheltering from the worst of the rain in a dip by a wall. Finding somewhere to park that wouldn't blook the road for the emergency vehicles, Tom and Margot got out, turned on their camping lanterns and head torches and trekked back along the road towards the scene of all the activity. It was still bucketing down.

It wasn't long before they found Mike Bowers on the verge, peering intently over the wall towards where the activity was.

Mike said hello first; he recognised Margot Voyce from Jess's description of her. Then the trio introduced themselves, saying they'd seen each other at the vigil. Mike explained that he and Jess had worked together in a professional capacity and known each other for years. Now he had a house two miles away, and had found Jess her cottage.

'Ah, Inspector Chambers,' said Margot. 'We've met; she's interviewed me, and she came out to have a word with Tom. I assumed she'd be here. Tom and I are just rubbernecking, but it seems a lot of activity, doesn't it? I live across the valley and the flashing lights made it hard not to be intrigued.'

'I'm retired now,' said Mike, 'so I'm rubbernecking too and most definitely here in a non-official capacity. There were lots of vehicles going past my gate late at night, which I've not had before, and I got curious.'

'So you can take the copper out of his job, but you can't take the job out of the copper?' said Tom.

'About sums it up. Shall we see if we can get closer?' said Mike.

Margot and Tom didn't need asking twice.

A few minutes later they came across Bill Harper camcording in the lane. He didn't recognise the two men, but thought Jess Chambers might be interested that Margot Voyce had turned up, and so he allowed them to go past without saying anything. He texted Jess's phone, but the message didn't get through.

Margot, Tom and Mike got as far the flashing lights of the first parked police car, which was unmanned. They stopped to survey the scene. There was a small section of the wall on the corner in front of them that was lower than the rest.

'If a car did go over, that looks like where it happened,' said Tom as he indicated the wall and some displaced stones on the grass verge.

'I was thinking just that,' said Mike.

Suddenly Jess's head appeared from the other side of the wall. She didn't look best pleased to see them, but nor did she look particularly surprised either.

'Thought I heard something, but it must have been the sound of bad pennies turning up,' she said. 'What on earth are you all doing here? And where's my DC? He should have headed you off.'

'He was concentrating very hard on his filming back down the road,' said Mike soothingly, 'so probably doing exactly what you asked him to. He'll have been thinking about priorities, Jess, with what you asked him to do being top priority. There's only the three of us, after all – it's not exactly a stampede, not by any stretch of the imagination.'

'Potentially you risk corrupting evidence, which I'm sure

that none of you want to do. Mike, I thought you at least would have known better.'

The twinkle in Mike Bowers' eyes told Jess he knew she was putting on an act for the benefit of the other two, and she had to make sure to keep a straight face so as not to give the game away. And having Margot Voyce here, Jess thought, could turn out to be a blessing in disguise.

'Corrupting evidence! Have you noticed the weather, Jess? Your evidence will be washed away whether we're here or not, while we've been very careful not to disturb anything,' Mike said. 'And who knows, one of us might have spotted something.'

'And have any of you noticed anything?' asked Jess.

'Well, no,' admitted Mike, as Margot and Tom shook their heads.

Jess looked at Margot, her brows raised.

'My parents' house is across the valley,' said Margot. 'I couldn't sleep after the pub, and I saw all the lights. And then I called Tom, who came to mine, and then we headed over here as we thought we would have a scout around, and then we met Mike. And actually I've been told to say if anybody needs anything, they can go to my parents' house.'

'Snooping. Yes, I can see that,' said Jess.

Margot gambled that Jess wasn't really grumpy with them by asking, 'Are you able to say what happened?'

Jess weighed up the benefits of saying nothing.

If James Garfield and Margot had still been involved with each other, then perhaps she had a motive for killing him, but as there were no indications that they were, and because Tom's alibi for the day James had died checked out – there was a clear image of him driving miles away on a traffic camera – Jess had also just about removed Tom Drake from the equation. He'd been at a dog trainer's nearly all afternoon way across Yorkshire near Scarborough, where he'd gone to drop off a couple of young collies for basic training as sheepdogs. And of course Mike Bowers didn't need thinking about.

'The indications are that there has been an RTA with one fatality, with the vehicle leaving the road and going over the wall,' Jess said as the rain began to ease slightly. 'It seems likely the fatality is Kate Summers, James Garfield's business agent. No formal identification as yet and the family has not been told, so you are to keep this information to yourselves and not speak about it with anyone else or put it on social media.'

Apart from the rain there was silence as the three in the road took in what Jess had said. Mike seemed as if he wanted to say something but Jess gave him a look, and he took the hint.

Margot's brow crinkled as she broke the silence. 'You mean the woman in red who was on stage at the vigil earlier? Why would anyone do that? It probably doesn't move things along for you, but I said to Tom yesterday, or maybe it was the day before, that I was pretty sure James was killed. I guess this accident – or whatever it is – confirms that.'

Jess thought that the tone of Margot's voice very much suggested the naming of the victim was a surprise to her.

'You need to tell me why you think that,' said Jess.

'Isn't it obvious?' said Margot, but then she stopped. 'Actually, it might not be obvious. I wasn't certain when I said that to Tom; James's death just felt malicious and not an accident. But now his agent has come to a sticky end too, so . . . Did she have much contact with anyone while she was here?'

Jess was torn between protocol and wanting to open up avenues for further investigation, eventually saying, 'Kate Summers seemed more the sort to sit on her phone pulling strings, getting others to do the actual donkey work. As far as I know, this was her first visit here, and she intended it to be brief, so I wouldn't imagine there'd have been time for a lot of contact with local people, at least face to face.'

Jess realised she'd been so busy she hadn't checked whether this really was the first time Kate Summers had visited the Lake District.

'A bit like the wizard in *The Wizard of Oz* then, orchestrating it all from behind a curtain and allowing everyone to think it all very mysterious and clever,' said Margot.

'Something like that,' said Jess. 'Not sure it ended brilliantly for the wizard though.'

'Well, there has to be somebody behind what's going on, somebody who wanted both James and his agent out of the way,' said Margot, and Tom nodded agreement.

Jess glanced at Mike, but he was looking at Bill Harper, who was now close.

'Maybe James Garfield was a bit of a wizard himself; he certainly liked to control things.'

It was Margot's turn to say 'Something like that.'

Standing on either side of the drystone wall, the two women stared at each other in silence, with neither Tom nor Mike daring to do anything to risk breaking the moment.

★

The stranger tried to work out what was going on between the detective and the people she was talking to. The body language was interesting. It didn't quite feel official, but it wasn't matey either. But other people were starting to congregate at the scene, and it definitely wasn't time to make a fuss.

Back at Margot's childhood home an hour later, the house in darkness other than the outside lights at the front of the house. Her parents had gone back to bed.

Margot and Tom stayed up well into the small hours, Mike Bowers remaining for quite a while to watch the videos on Margot's laptop that Tom had shot on his phone to see if he could spot anything suspicious at the vigil. Mike, after saying that they'd need to hand the recordings from the vigil over to Jess and her team, was largely silent as he concentrated on the images, leaning forward with his elbows on his knees. The way he held his breath at times as Margot and Tom pointed out to each other people they recognised, with Margot compiling these names into a list, showed that Mike was paying close attention to all that was said.

Margot and Tom also noticed that Mike seemed to be appraising them with the same care. It didn't feel awkward or offensive though, more like a thorough man doing a thorough job.

Mike wasn't above accepting a tot of the whisky that Tom had brought over, saying he'd take a risk on not getting stopped, as a taxi would have to come miles to pick him up, even if he could get one to come out at this time. After he had gone, Margot and Tom agreed that he had played his cards closer to his chest than they had. Nevertheless, it had been companionable having him there.

'At the vigil, I couldn't see anything or anyone odd standing out in the crowd.' Tom divvied up the last of the whisky between himself and Margot as they sat close together on the sofa and then gulped his in a single slug. 'I reckon you and I could put names to the vast majority who were there. It's hard to imagine any of them having murder on their mind.'

'Nobody obviously looked like a killer, you mean?' said Margot. 'Wouldn't it make it so much easier if that was the case? But chances are that something was said or happened there that led to Kate Summers getting killed, as otherwise why would anyone take the risk and not just let her disappear back to London? I can't help feeling that forcing her car over a wall or whatever looks like something improvised very quickly, which brings us back to the vigil. A spur-of-the-moment decision, I'd say.'

Margot took a sip of her drink, and then said, 'Tom, what on earth is going on, do you think? This all feels very, very wrong for around here. To me, where we've grown up and sown our wild oats is quiet and out of the way, and what's happened to James and his agent feels like something alien, something dark and malevolent. Don't you agree?'

Tom didn't answer, and when Margot looked at her friend, it was to see that his eyes were closed and he'd dozed off.

Slowly Margot stood up and then gently manoeuvred Tom so that he was lying on the sofa with his head on a cushion. Margot was pleased she hadn't woken him. She arranged a couple of the tartan blankets over him, and put a glass of water on the coffee table where he could find it.

She went to bed, remembering to set her alarm for five thirty so that she could wake Tom. He kept early hours and there were animals to feed, she knew.

Before Mike Bowers drove home, he sent Jess a text: 'Just watched videos at Margot Voyce's which her boyfriend took of the audience at the vigil. He was very through. Couldn't see anything of note, but they seemed to know almost everybody there.'

Jess texted back immediately, 'Not sure they are a couple . . .'

Mike ignored this, replying, 'If helpful, didn't get any sense of either being other than bystanders to the two deaths. You're going to be stretched tomorrow – today more accurately. Do you want me to see if they were in the pub for as long as they say? I know the landlady.'

Jess responded with a string of texts.

'Good to know, and yes.'

Jess pressed Send too soon, so immediately followed this up with a slew of texts, 'Of course you know the landlady, Mike. Wouldn't expect anything less!!'

Then, 'The pub has probably got CCTV inside and outside. Ask her to email it, pl.'

'CCTV from 5 p.m. until 1 a.m.'

'Thanks, Mike. Gotta run.'

There was a pause, and then a final message arrived on Mike's phone. 'Just a thought, but was the pub where Margot and Tom were the same place Kate Summers' team were waiting for her? I need to establish where everyone in her team was too.'

Mike chuckled at the battery of texts. Typical of Jess. Actually, typical of Northern Ireland Jess, when she'd always had a liveliness about her. Not so typical of the much more sombre and quiet Jess he'd been dealing with since she'd moved to the Lake District.

There had been moments when he'd wondered if he'd done the wrong thing in encouraging her to move. But it had seemed a good thing for her career. Now she had something to get her teeth into, but he hoped she wouldn't become *too* obsessive.

As Mike made his way home, Jess gave final instructions to those still at the crash site and then got into her car to drive to the police station.

For the first time since she had arrived in Cumbria Jess felt sure of what she was doing. She'd had hardly any sleep – a matter of a very few minutes only before the incoming messages had woken her – but she felt alert and as if she were firing on all cylinders. Jess knew that she could keep going on this rush of adrenaline for the next forty-eight hours should the investigation require it. She'd always thought of this ability as something to be proud of.

Jess smiled to herself in the darkness.

She could *feel* the perpetrator in a way she hadn't been able to previously; she was convinced that they were part of this community, perhaps even a pillar of local society. She didn't know yet who the perpetrator was, but she could definitely feel them nearby, thinking about her every bit as much as she was thinking about them. It was a good feeling, an exciting one. The chase was now properly on, and Jess hoped whoever she was seeking was frightened, very frightened. They didn't know what she was capable of, but Jess knew herself inside out, and thought the killer should be very worried indeed.

By the time Jess was ready to take the morning meeting, she was on top of her paperwork, with the policy book brought up to date, and she had a thorough picture in her mind of where the investigation currently stood.

Unfortunately, the information that had come in since she was last in the office hadn't yielded anything game-changing. Trevor Walton's drone footage from the day James Garfield died contained nothing of interest, other than a second or two in the car park as Trevor Walton brought the drone back to him of something that could have been an SUV, although nobody could say for certain that it even was a vehicle. The footage had been forwarded to a specialist team in London. There was nothing suspicious in the rest of the footage other than its slightly creepy feel.

And, although it was James's GoPro that had been found a long way down Piers Gill by an enthusiastic metal detectorist, who had defied the instructions of the local Mountain Rescue to keep out for safety reasons, what could be retrieved from it was at first glance next to useless. It had been repeatedly smashed against the rocks, immersed during the flash flood and then spent several days in icy water. There was a tiny bit of something blurry that might just be salvageable, and it had been sent to the same specialist team to see if anything could be enhanced.

Rose Thorne's forensic reports on James's clothes had arrived with an email: 'Nothing of much use has come back, I'm afraid, though we almost definitely have a handprint on JG's back.

173

When we spoke previously the odds in favour of that were about 75%, and I'd now go to 85%, but that's likely to be insufficient for proof of a push, as there's a reasonable element of doubt. No usable forensics and/or DNA on the back of his waterproof running jacket either. What you might be able to work with is that JG had recently waterproofed it with what seems to have been a homemade concoction as it's not matching anything on any database that I can find, so any transfer could be victim to perpetrator, rather than the more usual other way round. If you can find out exactly when he waterproofed his coat and send me gloves and outer wear and boots from a suspect, I might be able to do a conclusive match.'

This was reasonably encouraging as it might help to build a case in court, but it relied on variables – the waterproof concoction and a witness timing for the waterproofing, plus the clothing the perpetrator had worn, which might have been disposed of by now – that might be impossible to obtain.

There was a detective constable at the Carlisle station with forensic accountancy experience. Jess had been allocated a day of his time, and she'd asked him to look into the finances of James, Bob and Reeny Newman, Trevor Walton and Margot Voyce. The officer's report confirmed that they all seemed above board with relatively simple finances. Trevor Walton hadn't done much with his winnings; he still had a huge sum sitting in his current account – he clearly wasn't using it for nefarious purposes. But Bob Newman's financial arrangements were very complex and quite hazy – according to the Carlisle DC 'impossible for me to unravel in the time you've allocated' – with his tax returns showing a smaller income than his and Reeny's quite lavish lifestyle suggested. Yet there were no obvious sources of alternative income and no property port-folio on the Land Registry in either of the Newmans' names, other than the house the couple occupied and the cottage Bob had let James live in. And as they had driven around the Lake District together, Bob had boasted to Jess more than once that he and Reeny both came from very modest backgrounds and had left school at fifteen.

Jess made a call, got authorisation for another day of the Carlisle DC's time, and then emailed him to request he spend three quarters of it delving further into Bob Newman's finances and a quarter examining the financial affairs of Kate Summers and James Garfield.

Jess ended her email to the DC: 'Btw, Bob Newman is heav-ily involved in charity organisations locally, presumably in a fund-raising capacity. He has mentioned the Rotary Club to me and I would expect him to be a Freemason. See what you can dig up, and also see what the Chamber of Commerce has to say about his business dealings. Does he belong to the Lions Club, or Odd Fellows, or other similar organisation? Check out too schools, hospitals and libraries, scholarships and prizes – Bob Newman is the sort of man who would love to have something named after him. He's proud of his connections at the local golf club. The local press could be helpful – see if you can find a friendly local journalist?'

Then Jess studied a spreadsheet that a member of Kate Sum-mers' team had supplied first thing, which displayed all the work that she had been setting up for her clients. Kate had been incredibly organised, with contact names plus telephone and email details beside each entry.

Jess checked that next of kin had been informed of Kate's death, which they had. Now she knew they knew, Jess felt able to phone the television company to see if she could find out more about the proposed docu-series James had been involved in. She was passed from person to person and then told what she was asking was market-sensitive information and without a warrant no further information would be supplied, although the negotiations had been at a very early stage and nobody had yet signed on any dotted line.

As she finished the call she glanced up to see the last member of the team arrive in the office. This was Tony Peters, who had detoured on his way to work to take the statement from the farmer who had called in the accident. He shook his head at Jess's look, so she took it that nothing startling had come up during the interview that they hadn't already known about when they were at the scene of the crash.

Jess got up, went to the front of the room and stood there quietly until everyone was looking at her. She had been allocated several other officers for her exclusive use for several days.

'Right, we'll do a recap as we have new people here. We're running two investigations concurrently into two unexpected deaths, with our suspicions now further raised about the first death. Our rationale for connecting the deaths is the working relationship between the two victims. I am the SIO of both cases.

'We'll keep this meeting brief as I have to go to the mortuary, then I want to speak to Margot Voyce and Tom Drake about getting names put to as many faces from the vigil as we can, which we can then compare with the intel Tony has already, or will have by then. After which I'm going over to Legal, and at some point I'll need to speak to the parents of Kate Summers.

'The good news is that I've just heard the car in the RTA yesterday evening has been retrieved from halfway down the hillside. It pitched over a wall and rolled down, coming to rest a fair distance down. I'd estimate the distance from wall to car is in excess of two hundred metres, but there will be accurate measurements in the report from SICU. The car is awaiting forensic testing. Having said that, the investigating officer said we shouldn't hold our breath for forensic evidence that will help a conviction.

'The other piece of positive news, from my perspective at least, is that photographs of the two tattoos on Kate Summers' neck will be shown to her parents in London by a pathologist local to them who will also take DNA samples from them, saving them having to come all the way here for a formal identification. Of course they might come here at some point anyway, but they will be told this morning that if they do ask for a visit in person they are advised not to ask for the cover to be removed from the body. I'm hoping they decide to stay in London and I can speak to them on the phone. The path department moved heaven and earth to get overnight medical and dental records for Ms Summers.

'Bearing in mind the strangeness of these two deaths, no offensive jokes or gallows humour, please, now or at any other time. What I saw last night was a terrible way to die. If I get wind of anybody not being completely respectful about the deaths of Ms Summers or Mr Garfield, then I will go straight to HR and ask for a formal warning. Am I crystal clear about this? I don't care if it's meant in a jokey way or not, or you don't mean any harm. And I hope it goes without saying: absolutely no photographs or posting on social media.'

The mood in the room was serious and there were nods from everyone. As Jess looked around, she noted how the whole team seemed alert, efficient and keen to begin. It wasn't that Jess necessarily thought that any of them would behave poorly, but she still had little idea of the prevailing culture in the station, and she was keen to nip any problems in the bud.

'Now, before everyone gets to work, Bill, keep on top of the RTA. See where the report is from that officer last night, log all your material and collate what the house-to-house people are doing. Let me know if we get decent security camera footage, or CCTV – we want sightings of Ms Summers' Audi and all other vehicles or pedestrians in the area. There should be dash-cam footage from her Audi, so keep on to that. While you're about it, check also for CCTV to see if there's corroboration on the possible SUV leaving the car park on the day James Garfield died that appeared on Trevor Walton's drone footage. Don't forget to check with Walton over how accurate his date and time stamps are. Everyone else note that anything odd that comes up to do with the RTA must be fed through to Bill, who's also going to keep chasing the forensics team examining the car to hurry up their report.'

Everyone nodded. Bill had squared his shoulders in a way that told Jess he was pleased at the responsibility she had given him.

Jess wasn't finished. 'Tony is in charge while I'm out of the office, so anything that doesn't concern the RTA, you need to tell him. Anything on James Garfield, or arising from the vigil for him that Ms Summers organised, that's Tony's bag today. Tony, stay at your desk so you can keep an eye on information from members of the public, either from the vigil –' Jess read out the email address on the cards she'd left beside the book of condolence '– or from concerned people who may have been witnesses to the Kate Summers RTA and who come to us of their own volition, this information to be shared with Bill as relating to the RTA. Collate as much as you can, and work on that timeline too.

'Tony, with what you shot at the vigil, see if you can add names to faces and prepare a rough plan of where people were, and check the condolences book to see if there's anything interesting there. And don't forget the hot-dog guy and the two selling the beer and wine, as we daren't rule out anybody just yet. Tom Drake has vigil footage too, and I've made an appointment to visit later – he and Margot Voyce are compiling a list of names and marking the times they appear on their footage, and so can you cross-reference, firstly to make sure they haven't missed anybody Tom filmed, and then with your information to see if the two versions accord. Look for anyone we can't name. Oh, I nearly forgot, check into the will and insurance situation for both of the deceased. I've a feeling that we might not have seen this through yet for James Garfield, and we should have. We need to know who benefits in terms of possessions, money and business interests with these two deaths.'

Tony Peters nodded.

As a few queries were called out, Jess added, 'Tony and Bill will answer anything you want to know.'

Jess sat down for a moment, scanned her notes to make sure she had all the bases covered that she needed to, and then grabbed her shoulder bag and car keys.

As she left the room, she heard someone whisper, 'Perhaps she's not so bad after all.' She stopped and pretended to check her pockets in order to hear the reply, 'You're about to say she's growing on you, aren't you?' 'Oh, I wouldn't go as far as that – she'll never be one of us. But she sure can compile a list.'

As she inserted her key into the ignition, Jess tried to decide whether she had been supposed to hear. Were the comments intended to make some sort of point? If they were trying to rattle her, then they'd need to try much harder.

Rose Thorne looked weary when Jess walked into the PM examination room, but everything was ready and Kate Summers' body was prepped and had been placed on a metal autopsy table. Next to it was a trolley on which were the instruments needed for the procedure. You didn't have to be any sort of expert to see that Kate Summers had sustained multiple traumatic injuries the length and breadth of her body.

Jess couldn't prevent a shudder when she caught sight of the severed arm on another metal trolley.

The pathologist had waited for Jess to arrive, using the time to compare the X-rays she'd taken with the medical and dental records she'd had sent from London.

'Thanks for waiting, Rose,' said Jess. 'I apologise.'

'No problem as far as you're concerned. But we had the devil's own job removing the body from the car, not helped by the jammed door locks. The steering wheel had crushed the ribs of the victim as the car rolled and it was all meshed together. I'll spare you the details of how we got it out, but it wasn't pretty.'

'Poor Ms Summers,' said Jess. 'All glossy and bossing everyone around right in front of me one minute, and unrecognisable the next.'

'I'll get on, then. Make sure before you go that I show you that possible handprint contusion on Mr Garfield's back – I don't think that will get any clearer.'

Jess watched carefully as Rose Thorne carried out the post-mortem.

There were several times when the dissection or the close-up video showing on a screen were too much for Jess, who distracted herself by examining the X-rays taken that morning. These weren't much better, showing how many of the victim's bones had fragmented into multiple sharp-looking shards.

Rose Thorne was unable to pinpoint exactly what had killed Kate Summers, who had sustained a number of injuries so severe that each one on their own would have proved fatal. These included the chest injury caused by the steering wheel annihilating the front of her ribcage; the head injury resulting from her upper body exiting the driver's door window, which had led to a bleed on the brain and a badly fractured skull; the break in her neck vertebrae that had snapped her spinal cord; the loss of her arm, which would have caused a severe loss of blood, and the SCAD in her heart.

Jess queried the acronym SCAD. The letters, Rose Thorne

told her, stood for 'spontaneous coronary artery dissection', a blanket term for a tear in a blood vessel in the heart. 'In this case there's not so much a tear as a rupture across the whole of the blood vessel,' said Rose. 'It's a catastrophic injury.'

'The poor woman,' Jess said softly.

'Indeed, although she would have died very quickly, which has to be some sort of blessing, I suppose, so more prompt and therefore less agonising than James Garfield,' said Rose after a few moments. 'There are no indications of alcohol or drugs in the victim's system, and her stomach was empty, so she'd not eaten for a while, in fact probably not since the previous evening. Time of death is between 6.30 p.m. and 7.30 last night; the car's electrics jammed at 6.42, which is also the time on the smashed face of Ms Summers' rather expensive wristwatch and the time the activity tracker on the same wrist stopped logging, which accords with the tracker app on her phone. By the way, her phone, which was in a pocket, doesn't have a security lock on it.'

'She was hardly ever off the phone from what I could see, so maybe it was just annoying having to keep doing facial recognition.'

Rose Thorne passed Jess Kate Summers' phone and activity tracker in two small plastic evidence bags, and then her expensive handbag and laptop in a pair of larger bags, as she said, 'I can confirm too that the dental and medical records I've been sent match up with the body. Ms Summers was very healthy, although a trifle underweight, and she had a great dentist – her veneers were excellent. She had a mole on her thigh, and the two tattoos. She'd never been pregnant, and she hadn't recently been sexually active.'

'Right,' said Jess. 'Now you'd better show me that bruise on Garfield's back.'

A minute later Jess was staring once more at the contusion, but she still couldn't make out a definite handprint, and if she couldn't, then she suspected that jurors would struggle too, should it come to court.

Rose Thorne smiled and said, 'I think your best bet is matching a suspect's clothing to the waterproofing Mr Garfield used, and proving that there wasn't an opportunity for the transfer to have happened innocently prior to his death. There's only so much a prosecution barrister could do in court with a photograph of this contusion and comparative photos of others that have been definitely made by handprints – and that's assuming the judge deemed photos of comp pics admissible.'

'If that's my best bet . . .' said Jess.

Margot and Tom were in Tom's kitchen, sitting companionably shoulder to shoulder on one side of his sturdy table as he fiddled with the phone videos from the previous afternoon that he'd transferred to the larger screen, while Margot filled in a spreadsheet on her laptop.

There was a tray in front of them with several mugs on it, a jug of milk, a cafetière and a teapot.

Tom didn't live in the farmhouse belonging to the farm as his parents still resided there, although these days they had stepped back from farming and instead ran a large portfolio of rental properties, many of which they had hoovered up when houses in Cumbria were cheap. In fact they still went to auctions seeking out run-down properties as renovation and investment opportunities, and quite often were the winning bidders.

Mr and Mrs Drake were good landlords who let well renovated homes to locals – often those working in low-paying jobs, ex-offenders and single-parent families. This wasn't a particularly common business strategy; Margot knew they could achieve a much better rental yield on the homes they owned by concentrating on holiday or short-term lets.

There had never been any question that Tom, an only child, would not inherit the farm. He'd left school at eighteen and not gone to university even though he had been quite academic, and within a few years he had taken over the day-to-day running of the business, with its smiley-faced Herdwick sheep grazing on common fell land. Margot was fascinated by the fact that Tom's sheep 'hefted' – they stayed together by choice on a particular area of fell – even though they and other flocks were free to wander and mix with other sheep.

Traditional methods of Cumbrian sheep farming with native breeds weren't as profitable as they had once been, and so not long after he took over, Tom diversified into other areas including the farm shop and the livery yard. For his twenty-first-birthday present, Tom had asked his parents for a plot of land on the farm, rather than the grand party or gap year of travel they had offered. Full of her own plans for worldwide travel and climbing, Margot had thought Tom was making the wrong choice when he'd proudly showed her the small and wonky piece of remote land down an unmade track his parents had given him. Now she wasn't so sure. Her own twenty-first-birthday present from her parents had been a climb in Yosemite, which had given her good memories but nothing tangible to show for it nearly a decade later.

She couldn't imagine earning enough money to be able to buy her own home in the foreseeable future, and her parents had warned her that she shouldn't bank on inheriting their house. If they ended up in a full-time care home, the house would have to be sold.

But Tom was a very different type of person to Margot, and all those years ago he had told her that he'd said to his parents he was happy to have any piece of land they chose to give him, no matter how oddly shaped or unusable for farming. She'd been shocked at the plot they gave him, even though he explained it had good access and didn't compromise any of the grazing the farm needed in harsh winters when the sheep were brought down from the fells to the fields.

It had taken a total of eight years to get planning permission for a house. There had been a lot of toing and froing between the architect and the council planning department, and then costly complications with levelling the ground, but Tom had a clear vision of what he was trying to achieve, and eventually he was able to move into a home that although modest in size was all sleek lines and impressively big windows.

Margot had actually only been inside a couple of times previously, but now she looked about her carefully. It was very comfortable in a non-show-offy, quietly confident way. It was toasty too, with underfloor heating and a minimalist, open-plan interior that made the most of local wood and stone. His collie obviously appreciated the floor, lying flopped out deeply asleep.

Margot knew Tom had been keen that everything about the house, with its lightwells and circulating air pumped soundlessly around, was sustainable, and so it had been designed to take advantage of the hillside it stood on, which enveloped the whole of the back of the house and about half of each side, the sloping ground an integral part of the insulation, while the light-reflecting-inward glass in the front windows helped maintain a constant inside temperature no matter what the season. All the power needed for the appliances came from solar panels, and Tom told her he was even able to sell surplus electricity back to the National Grid.

Margot tried hard, but it was nigh on impossible not to be a little bit jealous of what Tom had achieved. But she would have died rather than tell him.

'Okay,' said Tom, after he had fast-forwarded through a couple of minutes of the latest video until he reached people in the audience that Margot hadn't yet logged. 'At 4.37.07 there's a couple – she's wearing a pink bobble hat, and he's got on a tartan fleece. This is Ann and Martin Jessop.'

Margot entered these details into her spreadsheet, including where Tom had told her the Jessops lived and what make of car they drove, and then she peered at the image, which Tom had paused on. 'Don't feel I'm nitpicking, but I think you'll find the hat is fuchsia, and his fleece is actually a shacket,' she said.

'Whatever. Moving on, 4.37.59, and it's Jim Billings and brother Tim – floppy mud-coloured hat for Jim, and green tracksuit under a denim jacket for Tim,' said Tom.

'You mean brown slouch beanie for Jim and green hoodie for Tim.' Margot tapped furiously on her keyboard.

'If you say so,' said Tom. 'Anyway, 5.10.09, and a mad-cow coat on Emma Bunce and something patterned on her friend. I don't know the friend, do you?'

'No, I don't.' Margot peered at the woman, sounding affronted at not knowing this person. 'Aztec blanket coat on unknown woman with ombré hair then, standing beside Emma Bunce, who's in a white faux-fur coat with large black patches.'

There was a tap at the back door, and Tom got up to let Jess in, who'd just dropped off Kate Summers' phone and activity tracker at the police station with instructions that they be immediately taken to Tony Peters, and then had driven over.

Tom told Jess to join them at the table and help herself to some coffee.

'How's the list of people going?' said Jess as she reached for the cafetière.

Margot and Tom both rolled their eyes.

'That well?'

'We've got about six or seven surely wonderful minutes of video left to look through,' said Margot, 'but I'd only expect maybe two or three names still to go on the spreadsheet. I think we've got just about everyone already.'

'May I see?' said Jess.

Margot passed her laptop over.

'Thorough,' said Jess as she rolled her finger around the laptop's trackpad. 'Obviously I've not checked it against the video to see if you've got everyone, but we'll go over it. Very useful, and your inclusion of where people live, and their cars, is a bonus.'

Margot and Tom looked pleased and nudged each other.

Tom said, 'I may be a bit hit and miss on the cars, but a lot of the same people use the farm shop car park. If you need to check the CCTV there, we keep that for twelve months.'

'Helpful,' said Jess.

Then Tom said with a significant look at Margot, 'Inspector, have you heard of a skort?'

'Don't think so,' answered Jess cautiously.

Margot laughed. 'A skort looks as if it's a skirt from the front, with a kilt flap that crosses over the lower belly and usually does up with a buckle on the hip, but from the back it's clear that it's really short-shorts. I thought they were a bit passé now, but Pippa Harris is wearing one over thick tights at 4.10.20, with a sheepskin bomber jacket.'

'All business at the front, but a party going on behind?' said Jess.

Margot gave a tiny snort, and added, 'We've looked at where Kate Summers pops up as she was walking around. Other than her staff, who were all wearing neon tabards on top of their coats, the only people we saw her speak to were you and your sergeant, and the Newmans. Nobody else seemed to be paying her any attention that we could see, and then she got up on the stage.'

'I didn't go on filming after the paper lanterns had been lit and let go, and it all wrapped up,' Tom added. 'But we stood there for a quite a while, and I remember Kate Summers remaining on stage for most of that time, talking again to her staff. Certainly we don't have film of anything else.'

Jess topped up her coffee and then said as casually as she could, 'There was somebody, I think a man, in dark clothes

188

standing on his own, youngish or early middle age maybe – I didn't see him up close – and then he was wandering about on the outer edges of the audience, on the other side to the hot dogs. Do you have him?'

Jess meant the person she had seen looking at her.

'Funny you should mention that one. We think it's most likely a him too,' said Margot as she slightly emphasised the 'funny', which passed over the top of Tom's head but told Jess she'd not carried off being casual. 'Actually Tom got bits of him, but there's no clear shot we can find that's in focus, and nothing of the face, and we can't work out who it is. It's just a bit of elbow here and a shadow there.'

'No worries,' said Jess. 'With a bit of luck my DS or the documentary crew will have got something.'

Jess's phone pinged.

The text was from Tony: 'Somebody has left a voicemail alleging they saw James Garfield and Bob Newman having a humdinger of a shouting match about a month ago in a pub car park. I'm going over to see the person who left the message at two – here's the address if you can join. Peculiar BN never mentioned?'

Jess pinged back a thumbs-up emoji to the Maps link he'd sent.

'I need to go. The moment you've finished, send your collation over, and the videos. And thanks,' she said, leaving a card, even though she'd given them the email address previously. 'Thank you for the coffee, Mr Drake – very nice.'

'I'll walk you to your car,' said Margot. Outside she said, 'That person you asked about.'

'Yes?'

'At the time I didn't really notice him, to be honest, and neither did Tom. But there are hints of *somebody* there in the videos, even if there's no clear shot. Tom said it made him think of a poem we did at school: "I met a man who wasn't there, He wasn't there again today." ' Margot stopped. 'I'm sorry, Inspector,' she said.

'When this is all put to bed, plain "Jess" will be fine. What are you sorry about?'

Margot smiled, but then her expression flipped to thoughtful. 'I'm not sure why I told you about the poem. It just feels as if you should know. It seems now and again I'm groping towards something, and then it slips away again. A bit like the person in the video.'

'Agreed,' said Jess. 'Something seems just out of reach. Meanwhile, you two have put yourselves out adding names to faces, and your efforts are appreciated.'

'Well, fingers crossed it's of some help.'

'Ms Voyce—'

'Even though the case *isn't* over, "Margot" is fine.'

'Margot,' said Jess. 'You and Tom Drake look like very good friends, I was thinking as we were all sitting in his nice warm kitchen just now . . .'

'Yes?' said Margot, her voice guarded.

'I'm wondering exactly how close. I'm not sure how it might be relevant, but somebody is going to ask me, and I need to know what to say.'

'Tom and I kissed once at primary school. It was a quick peck and I would guess we were seven or eight, playing kiss-chase,' Margot answered. 'And that's it. As far as I know Tom is single and straight, and obviously eligible, but we don't speak to each other about that sort of thing. I'm sure there have been girlfriends, but I've not heard about or seen anybody with him since I've been back.'

'Not friends with benefits then?'

'Um, no.' Margot's expression was inscrutable.

'Is there a chance Mr Drake and Mr Garfield were involved?'

Margot looked taken aback, but Jess waited her out. She was short of suspects and perhaps clutching at straws, but watching Kate Summers' post-mortem had aroused something in her that was making her review some past assumptions.

At last Margot said, 'Well, I don't think James was picky – I think a pulse might have been enough – and he was probably pansexual before it was fashionable. But I've never felt a same-sex vibe coming off Tom, and he didn't like or respect James. He's had a couple of digs at him, but in such a way I couldn't really be sure they were digs. But sex is odd and does strange things to us all. Even if Tom is straight and didn't like James, that doesn't necessarily mean they never had sex, I suppose. I would be surprised though. But what do I know? I don't really do relationships these days, so I'm unqualified to judge.'

'Me neither,' Jess replied, the words out of her mouth before she could stop them. She could have kicked herself and quickly got into her car. 'I'm running late.' She felt rattled and uncomfortable. Talking or even thinking about herself was something she never did.

Mike Bowers had told her this wasn't good for her, on several occasions. Jess was inclined to agree, but at this minute she didn't have time to think, not while running two investigations.

What was it about Margot Voyce? Jess wondered, momentarily feeling irked by the woman. But at the back of her mind she knew Margot wasn't the problem. Jess had shown a moment of weakness by daring to insert the mysterious man from the vigil into the conversation. She felt her heart jump as his image flashed before her eyes. Maybe it was just the strength of Tom Drake's coffee, she half-reasoned, but she knew this was nonsense.

As Jess put the car into gear, Margot tapped at the window.

Jess wound down the window, and Margot said, 'Look, I wasn't going to say anything, and I know what I'm about to say is probably well out of order. But have you thought about Mike Bowers as part of this?' Margot looked extremely uncomfortable.

Jess didn't for a moment suspect Mike. 'What makes you say that?'

'I don't know,' admitted Margot. 'But it feels peculiar that we came across him in the road last night. And he was very keen to latch on to us. I didn't think so at the time, but it seems strange today. I don't know, but he feels a bit weird to me.'

'I've never had cause to distrust him,' Jess said neutrally.

'Yes, he told us you two went back a long way. Look, I'm sorry. I shouldn't have said anything,' Margot backtracked. 'Of course you know him best. Forget it – I'm probably just tired.' Margot stood back to allow Jess to drive away.

Jess frowned as she drove. She'd been quick to defend Mike. But was this a mistake?

Now she thought about it, Jess realised that Mike had been giving her prompts for a long while that she'd not noticed, or if she had she'd put down to him looking out for her. And why was he in Cumbria, in that grand house of his that seemed beyond a chief superintendent's salary?

Jess stiffened as she remembered that Mike had a key to her home. That morning she'd had trouble finding her phone; could he have crept in to see where she was with the investigation? She didn't really think he had, but Jess couldn't help a twinge of suspicion. Mike was making himself so available to her. What was that all about? Should he be involved, it had to be something to do with money. And how might that work? If there was something going on, Mike would be very difficult to expose, Jess knew.

With a sinking heart Jess thought she would have to check him out. And she'd have to do this surreptitiously, as people like Mike were very good at covering their backs and making useful friends. Rather like Bob Newman really. Then she wondered if Mike and Bob were close in ways she didn't know about. Bob's house was in a prime location and would be worth a fortune, and the same was true of Mike's. She was pretty certain he'd bought it as he'd sent her a photo of the day he got the keys, the SOLD sign hoisted aloft in one hand as he stood at the garden gate. *Who'd taken that picture?* He always seemed so solitary.

The more she thought about him, the more Jess was convinced there were unanswered questions to do with her old boss. She didn't like it, but it was true.

As Jess drove, she thought of what they knew about both deaths, and then about the investigation in terms of Mike and what she had said to him. Yes, he had definitely been around a bit too much for her to be able to discount him. Had Margot done her a favour by mentioning Mike? Jess wasn't sure, but she knew that if he was innocent and she played this wrong, from this moment on she would have a powerful enemy. Before doing anything further, Jess decided to review what she knew and try to tie everything to suspects.

While Jess drove to Carlisle deep in thought pondering the case, the stranger was giving her every bit as much attention. Was it best to step forward now, or step back? Not an easy decision.

Before Jess could go with Tony to see the witness who had come forward about the argument between Bob Newman and James Garfield, she had had to make a late-morning appointment at the Crown Prosecution Service offices in Carlisle. As far as Jess was concerned this was a courtesy visit; she was keen to be very obviously seen asking for advice from the CPS during the early stages of the investigation. She wasn't expecting to learn anything but knew the visit could be hugely helpful to her if the investigation went wrong.

If that were to happen, then somebody would be expected to take the blame, and Jess as SIO would be the obvious scapegoat. Only a fool wouldn't take measures to protect themself, and whatever Jess was, she thought of herself as certainly not a fool.

In Carlisle the CPS office was busy with people bustling about or sitting at paper-strewn desks, and Jess couldn't easily distinguish between the senior legal staff or their assistants.

She was taken to a small side room, where she ran through the various charges that could theoretically be brought against the perpetrators in the cases of James Garfield and Kate

Summers with a representative of the service. Murder was the most serious charge in terms of sentencing; then there various scenarios that could instead lead to the CPS deciding on a lesser charge of manslaughter; and in Kate Summers' case the women discussed two further possible charges of causing death by reckless or careless driving.

Jess took notes, more to be seen to be doing so than because she needed to. There were no surprises, and the CPS representative went out of her way to be helpful, especially when describing how a plaintiff might try to show justification for committing the crime, and the ways Jess could mitigate through the evidence she obtained against the various defences that might be used in court. This all depended on the CPS deeming there was a reasonable chance of securing a conviction in the case of each death, and also in part on the final findings of the inquests.

The representative then went through causation, reminding Jess that the police must be able to link what the suspect did and the death, that this must be a 'substantial cause' of the death, and what this meant in legal terms. She thought the investigation didn't look at the moment as if it were likely to end up in court any time soon in the case of either victim, as causation was likely to be impossible to prove. Jess understood this clearly. A lot was going to have to go right for her and her team before that could happen.

The stance of the CPS over the high standard of evidence they'd require wasn't a surprise, but it felt to Jess almost impossible to achieve when laid out like this. And if it turned out Mike Bowers was involved, she was pretty certain it would never come to court. She'd so wanted her first case in Cumbria to be a triumph, but there was an evasive quality about this investigation that made it seem as if each new piece of the puzzle actually pushed the solution further away.

Jess must have looked downcast, as the CPS representative added, 'Give us sufficient evidence and reliable witnesses, and we'll get a result. Public interest in murder and/or manslaughter cases is high because the harm caused to the victims is of the utmost seriousness, and we do *have* to bear that in mind.

'And there would need to be agreement between the CPS and counsel, and the police, along with consultation with the victim's family, before a guilty plea to manslaughter could be accepted. So in a case of unlawful killing we will seek a conviction on a charge of murder if we possibly can, rather than cutting our losses by looking at a manslaughter charge instead with a lesser sentence. Our role is to help those cases most likely to get guilty verdicts on not-guilty pleas come to court. The police's responsibilities are naturally to the Home Office, and the prison and probation services, and not the CPS. But if you help us, then we'll help you.'

Box-ticking. By her and me, Jess thought as she stood up to go. *And we both know it's unlikely I'll be back in this office having a serious discussions about a court case any time soon.*

As she strode down the stairs from the meeting, Jess decided that although some things had been tough to hear, the legal feedback she'd been given was fair, and Tony Peters had been unnecessarily negative about the CPS.

Having to balance her own departmental budget, Jess was

aware as never before of the need for all the components of the judicial system to work within their financial limits, with everyone taking into account the expense of court time and prosecutions. Her heart went out to those who were let down by the system, but the present reality was that they all had to choose their battles. Perhaps she'd change her mind when she went back with a different case, but she felt today's had been a reasonable meeting.

Jess's stomach gave a dramatic rumble, and after glancing at her watch, she headed to a café she'd noticed earlier, where she ordered a mug of tea and a toasted cheese and tomato sandwich. She allowed herself to be talked into a touch of kimchee as an additional filling, and then sat down at a table in a bay window overlooking the street. The last thing she'd eaten was the hot dog at the vigil the previous afternoon.

Soon she was staring sightlessly out of the café's window as she considered the cases, and then she thought about how even a life sentence for murder could sometimes, with good behaviour, mean that the actual time served in prison was only a few years, with a significant proportion of it spent in an open prison where inmates were allowed out. And a conviction for manslaughter didn't necessarily even mean a custodial sentence at all, something which the families of victims often found very difficult to understand. Jess then couldn't help wondering how many convicted killers were walking around outside in a fifty-mile radius of where she was at that moment. Quite a few, she suspected.

Jess jumped as a male voice broke into her musings: 'Excuse me, do you mind if I join you?'

She looked up at the speaker. She glanced around and sure enough the early lunchtime rush was under way, with seating now at a premium.

Quickly she removed her bag from the chair opposite her. 'No, of course not.'

He sat down, and then as several people came across to say hello to him as they left and just as Jess began to wonder if he might be a local celebrity, he told Jess that this was his normal lunchtime place and it had a loyal clientele of office workers. Jess nodded at this to show that she'd noticed. But he'd not seen her in here before, he said, and he was in most days.

'It's my second time in Carlisle, and this place is a lucky find,' Jess said. 'My first visit I spent a ridiculous amount on outdoor clothing.'

'Yeah, good gear will punch big holes in a wallet,' he said, and took a bite of his sandwich after asking, 'Worth it?'

Jess shrugged. 'Two things are on order, and so far I've only worn the boots, gloves and hat. They seem, um . . . serviceable.'

He laughed, adding, 'The shop would be bowled over by your ringing endorsement.'

'I'm sure real fell-walking buffs love to boast about the clever features of their gear. All I want is dry feet and hair not blowing all over the place and no wind in my ears, and that's what I got.'

'You were talked into buying quality stuff?'

'Absolutely.' Jess thought of Margot. 'I was told it would last me a lifetime.'

He smiled. 'Exorbitant?'

'And then some' Jess said. And she found herself smiling too. They ate in silence for a moment.

'You go out on the fells much?' asked Jess.

'Not as often as I'd like. Good intentions and all that, but laziness often wins.'

'Well, life has a habit of slapping good intentions in the chops, or at least my life does.' Jess was pleased to see that he grinned again at this. 'Anyway, I've got to go – I need to be somewhere at two the other side of Keswick.'

Jess stood up, and then was slightly surprised that he half stood up too, and leaning over the table he stuck out his right hand for her to shake as he said, 'Simon.'

'Oh,' said the slightly surprised Jess. She found his hand felt strong and pleasantly dry. 'Jess.'

As she walked to her car, she tried to work out if they'd flirted or not. She decided they hadn't, even though she'd noticed he wasn't wearing a wedding ring.

'How's the morning been?' said Jess as she walked over to her sergeant.

While she was parking at their rendezvous, Tony Peters had got out of his car and was standing beside it.

'Don't ask – there's a mountain of work. Margot Voyce sent over her videos and spreadsheet – Bill's spending his lunchtime matching her images to mine, and I'll go back and check all the names. What's a skor—?'

'Don't ask,' interrupted Jess.

'Are you thinking those two are out of the equation?'

'Well, Mike Bowers was a bit sceptical when they turned up at the RTA – I'll have a word to see what he thought – and they've inserted themselves into the investigation. But it would take an awful lot of nerve for one or both of them to have been involved in the RTA and then risk returning to the scene, no?' said Jess, who'd decided not to voice any suspicions concerning Mike until she knew more, in part as she didn't know if he had a contact in her team. 'Also, why? No sign of a convincing motive,' she added.

'The pathologist's initial report on last night has arrived, and that's given us a conclusive time of death for Kate Summers.'

'That PM – I saw things that I'll never be able to unsee. I don't know how Rose Thorne does it day after day,' Jess said with a small shudder.

'Well, I guess the Summers death was extreme even by her standards,' said Tony.

'Moving on, anything striking on Kate Summers' phone or laptop?'

'Not that I've seen yet, although I've only dipped in. By the way, there's a backlog at the coroner's office as they've just had transferred to them some cases from another office with a bigger backlog, so the Summers inquest is unlikely to open until after the weekend; they know it'll be a quick open-and-adjourn.'

Although she didn't say anything, Jess was pleased the inquest into the death of James Garfield's agent opening was moving back, as she wanted some time at her desk. There were getting to be a lot of threads that she needed to pull together. And even though the inquest opening would not take long, it would mean time out of the office and a break in her train of thought just when she wanted to think through everything she knew.

'What about the RTA investigator – anything useful from him?' Jess asked.

'Not really,' said Tony. 'No forensics yet on transfer from another vehicle, or the victim's car to someone else's. He's a bit of a jobsworth.'

'I can't believe that with these cases so much can happen to each victim, yet we end up with so little concrete evidence,' said Jess, staring off into the distance. 'A nightmare if this ever comes to court.'

'How was Carlisle?'

'As expected. Going through the motions for when Bob Newman publicly calls us to account. Talking of Bob Newman, tell me about this witness we're about to speak to.'

'I don't have much to add to what I told you,' Tony said. 'A voicemail left late last night alerted us to an alleged argument between uncle and nephew – you pretty much had all the details in my message. I didn't go into anything on the phone when I arranged the interview. The witness is called David Smith, and he's a building labourer. I did however phone the landlord of the pub where the argument is supposed to have taken place, and while he can't swear to the date, several weeks ago Bob Newman and James Garfield did come in for supper – he remembers as he knows them and they both had the steak and kidney pie. They went outside right after they'd finished their mains, which he thought was odd as they quite often ate there and usually had pudding and coffee, and in any case their wine glasses were still quite full when they left. Then a flurried-seeming Mr Newman came back and asked at the bar for a treble brandy, after which he paid the tab by using the wallet function on his phone, which the landlord remembered as Mr Newman nearly always paid cash.

'It might not stand up in court if David Smith can't confirm the date when he was there, but the pub's going to email the bill and Bob's payment details over. There's CCTV in the car park with sound, although the camera wasn't pointed where they were standing, but the landlord has sent that over, and I've passed it on to the sound techs, in case it picked up something I couldn't hear.'

'I like this landlord,' said Jess as the alarm on Tony's phone signalled it was two o'clock. She added, 'You'd better come with me to see Bob Newman after this. I haven't warned him of a visit, but I've checked the council meetings and there's nothing on there that he needs to be at. And I think Reeny will insist on him resting if she can, so with a bit of luck we'll catch him off guard.'

David Smith had the slightly bulbous and purplish nose that suggested somebody who spent a lot of time in pubs. He was hobbling with a surgical boot on one foot and supporting himself with a stick.

'Injured your foot there, Mr Smith?' said Jess, even though he obviously had.

'Accident at work last week, and I've been signed off,' he answered as he led them to the lounge in his narrow terraced house, 'otherwise you wouldn't have caught me at home at this time of day. Not my fault, and it were caught on a doorbell camera so I'm hoping there'll be compensation. A duff wheelbarrow tipped over and dumped a load of hard core on my ankle.'

It was useful if a camera did indeed bear out David Smith's story of a recent injury at work, as there wouldn't be the opportunity for any defence counsel to allege he was a fall-down drunk. Should that happen, it would be child's play to instil in the minds of the jury that he was an unreliable witness.

Jess caught the eye of Tony Peters who double-blinked to let her know that he understood the situation and would check out what was on film.

'Mr Smith, why don't you tell us what you saw concerning James Garfield and Bob Newman?' said Jess.

'It were four weeks or so back – I know this as I was at the pub with my daughter and her husband, with the rest of the family, and it were my daughter's wedding anniversary and we were having a celebration,' David Smith said.

'Was it her actual anniversary that day?'

'It was, and it were a family do as she's been poorly and so it was to celebrate her being given the all-clear too. Anyways I quite often pop in there for a drink, and I've seen Bob Newman and his nephew in there more than once. I'd gone outside for a cigarette – I know it was about twenty to eight, as we'd had our starters but not yet our steaks – and I heard raised voices. I looked through the trellis that blocks off the smokers' area from the car park, and I could see Bob and his nephew standing as if they were squaring up to each other. My hearing's not so good as it was, so I couldn't quite make out what they were saying, but it were definitely an argument, and then I saw Bob look around, although I doubt he saw me, and then he seemed as if he were trying to quieten it all down. Then his nephew shouted, "It's got to stop, Bob. I mean it, you're just not being fair. I thought we'd dealt with this way back," or words to that effect, and then he pushed past his uncle and got into his car. He reversed out of his parking space so fast he almost knocked Bob over. I'd finished my cigarette and was going back inside when Bob rushed past me. He went to the bar, and I went to the Gents, then back to the family and told them what I'd seen.'

'And you're absolutely certain it was Bob Newman you saw arguing out in the car park, and his nephew James Garfield?' said Jess.

'Yes. I've worked for Bob, and I know him. And I helped get the house ready for his nephew, and then went back to sort out the guttering and so I've met James Garfield too.'

Jess was cautious how she worded her next question. 'Now Mr Smith, you mentioned you "quite often" drink at the pub. We need to know if you *really* like a drink, sometimes quite a few. Because if you do, perhaps you were a bit the worse for wear when you went out for your cigarette and heard the shouting, and got confused. If asked that question in court, what would be your answer?'

David Smith sniffed in a vaguely offended way and said, 'I was at work all that day, and then as I was close to where my daughter and her husband live, I went to theirs to shower and get ready, and then we drove to the pub to meet the rest of the family for seven o'clock. I was on antibiotics for a chest infection so I wasn't drinking alcohol. I think I told you that I quite like to go to that pub for "a drink", and that's exactly what I mean – I can't afford more than the one pint at a time, now or for a long time past. Unfortunately. And the landlord and my wife will say the same.'

Jess and Tony returned to their respective cars. They would drive to Bob Newman's home separately in case either of them needed to go on elsewhere.

As they'd left David Smith's home they'd agreed he was a solid potential witness. They'd asked him to go into the station the next day to give a formal statement and he'd readily agreed.

Jess had just got into her car and was reaching for her seat belt when she received a text: 'Hi Jess, Simon here – we met at the café earlier. I liked you, and I guessed the outdoor wear shop. It's owned by a good friend. I begged for your number. No pressure but a quick drink later? You may think this is too much, or you might be a married mum of six. If so, block my number! Simon.'

Jess was stunned.

Then she felt a wave of panic.

She watched Tony drive off and went hot and cold. Then she dialled a number.

'Mike, something very strange has happened,' Jess began. She really wanted Margot's opinion, but that wouldn't be appropriate. And so, even though she was concerned about Mike, she felt on this he would be a good sounding board.

'What is it now?' he said, a trifle wearily.

'Bob, we need a word, please,' Jess said when her knock on the front door was answered by him ten minutes later.

His smile quickly fading at her serious expression, the councillor stared at her in silence, and then his gaze moved to Tony Peters standing at her shoulder, after which he looked Jess in the eye again.

'This feels official, Inspector,' he said.

'It's just a couple of informal questions, Mr Newman.'

The councillor let out a tetchy sigh, and then stood aside so they could pass. Jess thought the sight of his well-worn checked wool slippers oddly touching, and for a moment she was reminded of seeing her grandfather in his slippers and shirt-sleeves when she was a child. She was sure Bob, who prided himself on being dapper, didn't appreciate her catching him in wind-down mode like this.

'Where's Reeny?' asked Jess.

'Hairdresser.'

Bob told them to go through to the kitchen, where he offered them tea or 'something stronger'.

Jess made an effort to be friendly, 'We're fine, Bob, but thank you.'

The councillor sat down opposite Jess. He looked wary.

Jess got to the point. 'Last night a voicemail was left at the station alleging you and James had a verbal disagreement in a pub car park that ended with your nephew driving off in a temper, him leaving you in the car park without so much as a goodbye. Is that true?'

Bob asked for clarification of date, time and location, which Tony gave him.

'Never happened. I was nowhere near. James and I never argued.'

Tony explained he had obtained confirmation from the pub landlord that both of them were at the establishment on the night in question, and there were electronic records of both the bill and funds transfer that could verify this.

Bob raised his eyebrows in a 'you're going to have to do better than that' manner, but he didn't speak.

Jess said, 'As I've said, this is an informal discussion, Bob, and you can ask us to leave at any time. If necessary, we can continue this at a later date at the station, and of course you're welcome to have a solicitor with you. But you should know that we have a witness to what went on in the car park, and I'm sure that if we speak to other people in the pub, they will confirm you and James left your table and went outside. It's very likely there's CCTV of the pair of you together too, and possibly other witnesses will come forward.'

'I'm not saying another word,' said Bob Newman. There was now zero hint of the fatherly, slightly patronising tone he usually adopted when talking to Jess.

'Bob, the question that really interests me comes in two parts: why didn't you mention this previously? And what is it that that you'd like to avoid speaking about?'

'Solicitor.' Bob stood up, indicating he wanted them to leave. As they stepped past him at the front door, he added, 'I'm sure I don't need to remind you, Ms Chambers, that you have never before asked me about the cordiality or not of my personal dealings with my nephew, nor the extent of our dealings lately with one another.'

Jess stopped at the bottom of the steps up to the door to look back up at him, and Bob Newman responded by closing the door in her face.

'Hell, he's right,' said Jess to Tony Peters a few moments later, as they headed down the drive towards their cars, which they'd parked on the road. 'I've spent so much time with Bob. I was with him when the first body was found and then at the mortuary and the coffee shop and the inquest and the vigil, and I just never got round to putting to him the obvious. Well, that stops a formal interview until we know more.'

'Well, maybe the Carlisle DC with the forensic accountancy background will come up with something,' said Tony, who didn't seem particularly perturbed. But Jess was most definitely knocked off balance, as an avalanche of thoughts raced through her head.

'I *was* going to ask Bob more about James as a person, and whether the two of them got on, and of course later Kate Summers went on to mention them in the same breath. But the time I meant to do it originally was when we were having coffee after the confirmation of identity, but I had to leave to go to the PM before I'd finished questioning him, and that Trevor Walton was hovering,' Jess was unable to prevent a whine creeping in to her tone. 'I think in my head I put to bed that I'd done it, and it's been so busy since that I never really thought about their relationship. Sod it.'

With irritating calmness, Tony replied, 'Let's get this in proportion, remembering that Bob Newman is the sort of old-fashioned player who will always deliberately blur the lines between the professional and the personal, and isn't averse to a bit of bluster either. He strikes me as the sort who likes to feel someone owes him a favour. That's why he invested time and effort in showing you around. No disrespect to you, as you wanted to bring yourself up to speed about the local area.' Jess didn't say anything at this point although Tony gave her the opportunity, so he went on, 'But with this all now, do you think for a moment that Councillor Bob Newman was actively involved in his nephew's death?'

'Put like that, no,' admitted Jess, as she tried to ignore the small stab of humiliation at the mention of how much time she had spent with Bob Newman, before adding, 'but something feels off.'

'Maybe. It's hard to tell with someone as wily as Newman. But fishy isn't necessarily illegal, and it almost always stops short of murder. Let's look at it another way. Do you believe Bob Newman was actively involved in the death of Kate Summers?'

'No,' Jess replied immediately. 'I can't see that. What on earth would the motive *there* be?'

'So, assuming that's the case and the murders were committed by the same person, he's probably off the hook as a killer, although we may find he's guilty of something. But to be sure, let's go back to the office and I can double-check the esteemed councillor's alibis for both fatalities,' said Tony Peters.

'Whatever we find out about the alibis, this is going to end up as the stick that Bob Newman uses to beat me,' said Jess.

'Not if you make sure to keep several steps ahead of him. I'll look over the council minutes of his meetings again over the last two years to see if anything seems odd. Bill had a trawl through, but I think that was before Kate Summers died, so he might have been looking for different things than we are now.'

'Let me know if anything stands out.' Jess gave her sergeant a weak smile. She was surprised by what a reassuring and encouraging presence she found him. 'I'm pretty certain that the Bob Newman I saw looking at James Garfield's body was totally thunderstruck, and that it really was a huge shock,' she said as Tony unlocked his car door.

'That's a positive,' answered Tony.

'Nice to think so,' said Jess as she got into her own car. But all the same, she was uneasy about how she had mishandled the conversation with the councillor. And she'd never had that feeling in other investigations without it coming back to bite her on the behind.

Mike Bowers had urged Jess to meet Simon, reminding her that being a police officer made people too suspicious for their own good. Why shouldn't an apparently available man find Jess attractive and want to spend time with her? Some women would find the effort Simon had made to track her down flattering. Jess could only grunt sceptically, and Mike continued that she should have more faith in herself.

Jess phoned the shop from the station. The owner was sheepish, apologising for passing her number on, but he said that he and Simon Lindsey had lived on the same street as kids and he could vouch for him. While not close friends, they had kept in touch over the years.

Simon had been married, but that had ended years ago, leaving him and his ex-wife to co-parent very happily a daughter of about twelve. As far as the shop owner was aware, there hadn't been anyone serious in his life since, and while Simon might not have lived like a total monk since his divorce and had spent a couple of years living abroad, he seemed okay – and he was solvent and enjoyed his job as a civil servant.

The shopkeeper apologised again, and as Jess cut him short, she was left with the impression that he was telling the truth as he saw it, not parroting a line Simon had drilled into him. She didn't mention at any time that she was a police officer or that he had broken data protection laws. And her job hadn't come up either when she and Margot had been in his shop, so Jess could only wonder how abject his apologies would have been if he'd known what she did for a living. All the same, she didn't think he'd be passing on anyone's number in the future.

Jess decided she would introduce an element of chance into whether she went for the drink or not. If Bob Newman's alibis checked out, she would take Simon Lindsey up on his offer of a date; if either or both of the alibis disappeared in a puff of smoke, then she wouldn't go.

Tony walked up to her desk as if on cue and said very quietly into her ear, 'Bob Newman was busy all day when James Garfield died, escorting a group of Japanese businessmen to various places, and in the evening he attended a civic reception for them at six. From seven thirty he was in a council meeting that went on until gone ten thirty, raising a point during AOB that is minuted. So his movements are accounted for from early morning until late at night.

'And at the vigil there is film of Bob Newman being whisked away in a taxi at just gone five p.m., and then of him appearing in a live television studio debate at six thirty. I checked with the taxi firm, and the cab to collect him was pre-booked by the studio. Bob asked for a taxi because Reeny needed the car to get home after the vigil. The taxi driver confirms Bob was taken directly to the television studio and delivered into the studio manager's hands.

'The taxi firm controller said that after Bob made his appearance on the telly panel, he went to the green room for a few bevvies along with the other panellists. The taxi took him home at just gone eleven, getting him there at eleven thirty.

The taxi firm has a contract with the studio and they know Bob well, apparently.

'So he looks to be in the clear personally for both deaths. That doesn't preclude a hit, but somehow I don't see Bob Newman hiring a contract killer, do you?' finished Tony.

'Right,' said Jess, who didn't know whether to be pleased or not that fate seemed to want her to see Simon. 'No, I can't think of any reason why Bob would want either of them out of the way. I just wish we knew why he is being so cagey.'

'Bob is a dinosaur of the sexist old-git variety. Having to answer to a younger woman isn't easy for him,' said Tony Peters. 'The most likely explanation is that he disliked being put on the spot by you, especially in front of someone like me. He's much more used to lording it over the police than being questioned by them. There probably is something Bob Newman doesn't want coming out, but it will be incidental to this investigation. I'm wondering if perhaps he's been seeing another woman, and the argument was James Garfield taking Reeny's side. Or something that he'd find embarrassing in the personal arena, perhaps something to do with his health that he's not told Reeny about.'

Jess frowned. While she did see that the alibis proved Bob couldn't have actually taken part in causing either of the deaths – not that she'd ever really thought he had – that didn't mean he was completely innocent, and because he was a public figure, she assumed that he could be slippery when required. The fact that he had remained influential locally for so many years almost definitely bore this out, as he would have had to do a lot of ducking and diving. Not that this necessarily implicated him in murder of course, but it was something to bear in mind.

But what Jess couldn't deny was that her relationship with Bob Newman had turned sour, or that Bob, if so inclined, could be a powerful enemy. Nor could she see any immediate way to repair that relationship. And if her investigation went pear-shaped, it wasn't going to help her in the slightest if Bob was already spitting feathers.

It wasn't that she'd handled Bob Newman terribly badly – she'd seen many colleagues do things to witnesses that were much, much worse. And Jess had no doubt Mike Bowers would just tell her to buckle her belt a notch tighter, get over herself and move on without giving Councillor Newman's ruffled feelings a second thought. It was more that she hadn't thought about Bob Newman as a possible suspect with the same serious-ness that she had just about everyone else that was irking Jess. And then she had made matters worse by being clumsy, racing off to Bob after they had talked to David Smith without ade-quately considering all the implications, or even whether she had followed protocol in all her earlier dealings with the councillor.

As Jess had already admitted to Tony Peters, it wasn't her finest hour. And she couldn't help feeling she had made another mistake that she couldn't quite pin down, and she hated making mistakes.

Stop beating yourself up. Move on. She was over-thinking the business with Bob to avoid dealing with Simon. Her stomach flipped at the thought. *A date.* It had literally been years since she was last on a date.

'I've had a word with your friend at the shop,' Jess messaged.

'So a single drink in Keswick would work. Jess.' She pressed Send before she had the chance to dither further.

Simon messaged back instantly with a website link to a pub and '7 p.m.?'

Jess drove to meet Simon. She was so out of practice that she felt queasy.

When Jess walked into the pub, she made sure not to catch the eye of Mike Bowers, who was sitting against the wall nursing a pint as he watched sport on a television high on a nearby wall. He'd offered to come for an hour to make sure Simon was kosher.

Jess almost walked past Simon. She was thinking she'd failed to ask Mike whether he'd confirmed that Margot and Tom had been at the pub at roughly the time Kate Summers went over the wall, or if it was the pub where Kate's team had waited for her.

Hopeless. At this rate I deserve to be removed as SIO, Jess berated herself.

And then she told herself that Mike's silence was actually confirmation that Margot and Tom had been at the pub, meaning they couldn't have been involved in what happened to Kate Summers, and that it had also been where the agent's team had been waiting. Mike would have been in touch if he had discovered anything untoward or if either of those assumptions hadn't been true. Sometimes the truth lay in what wasn't said.

There was a touch on her arm and she jumped.

'Forgotten me already?' Simon grinned, and Jess was struck

by how presentable he was, attractive but not obnoxious about it. He was managing to strike that difficult balance with his clothes – looking just trendy enough, but not embarrassingly so for a man close to forty, and he certainly wasn't emitting any signals suggesting a dating-app man who liked to pose shirtless and ideally holding a very large fish. This was a relief.

Jess thought quickly about the vehicles in the car park. She hadn't noticed any sports cars or powerful motorbikes that suggested a mid-life crisis.

'Sorry, Simon. Work things. Miles away,' said Jess, and with her heart thumping almost painfully, she tried a small smile.

'Shall we start again? I'll begin,' said Simon. 'Thank you for coming, Jess. I've never done anything like that before – go Sherlock Holmes, I mean. I feel a bit daft, but the minute you'd gone I kicked myself for not being braver and just asking for your number.'

'Hello there, Simon. Daft is almost my middle name.'

Mike Bowers was behind Simon. He widened his eyes at her in a mock-exasperated way.

'Actually, I am sorry, Simon. I don't go for many drinks with men who are not my colleagues. Well, I don't often go for drinks even with my colleagues. Now I'm over-explaining.' Simon stood in front of her, looking amused. 'But I should calm down in a moment with a bit of luck,' she finished lamely.

'Glass of red?' he said. 'I hear it's very soothing.'

'Actually, let me,' said Jess, 'then if I leave right after, I won't feel so bad.'

Perhaps it wouldn't be a disaster after all, she thought as she stood at the bar sneaking the occasional surreptitious glance at

Simon in the mirror behind the optics. She could see he'd caught the eye of several women in the pub, and she rather liked that he had. But she wasn't going to let Simon anywhere near her drink if she wasn't there too. While Mike Bowers might have told her to take things at face value, Jess felt she had dealt with too many cases of date rape when Rohypnol had been illicitly slipped into drinks, not to be cautious around a man she didn't know.

Still, Simon caught her eye in the mirror and grinned once more at her in a very open way, and Jess couldn't help flashing a genuine smile back that stayed on her face as she paid the barman.

'Tom,' Margot called from inside a loose box as she watched Trojan bury his muzzle deep in his supper bucket. She'd caught sight of him walking past out of the corner of her eye. 'Have you got a mo?'

Tom came over and rested his elbows on the half door.

'Putting on a bit of weight,' he said, indicating with a toss of his head he was speaking about Trojan, although Margot thought the same probably applied to her now that she was so much less active, not that she particularly cared. 'What can I help you with?'

She had always thought she could talk to her friend about anything, but Margot suddenly got cold feet, so she said, 'Oh, I don't know, Tom. Forget it – it's not important.'

He looked at her and scratched his head. 'Margot, everything you say is important.'

Margot told herself he was being ironic, but said anyway, 'Well, all right then. It was something Inspector Chambers asked as I walked her to the car. It was about you, and it's got me thinking.'

'About me? Why didn't she just go to the horse's mouth, seeing as she was sitting at his kitchen table drinking his coffee?'

'No idea, Tom, but don't shoot the messenger. She probably just thought I was a softer touch.'

'Softer touch? Doesn't know you then.' Tom's aimable expression morphed into something more guarded.

'Well, my reading was that she was on a fishing expedition for what you thought of James,' said Margot carefully.

'Fishing as general background, or as me potentially being more involved?'

'Well, that's the thing,' said Margot. 'I couldn't tell.'

'Ah.'

Tom's voice was, Margot felt, so non-committal as to be suspicious. 'Now you're making *me* wonder,' she said after he didn't go on to clarify.

'Are you sure you want to know what I really think about James sodding Garfield, Margot? Seeing how *you* and James were once together, and seeing how it was *you* who found him hanging from the pitch?'

'You think *I* had something to do with his death?' Margot had found his question offensive. She knew she was being prickly, and she didn't like how the pitch and volume of her voice had risen. She hadn't meant to sound so aggressive.

'Calm down, Margot. That's not what I accused you of, and it's not what I think. I only wanted to point out how quickly things can change. You went up Scafell Pike on a walking-route recce, and came down with a body and a detective inspector in tow.'

217

'Not sure I see what you're driving at.'

'Margot, it's all a matter of perception, surely. Nobody knows that James didn't just stumble and fall into the gully, or that his agent's accident wasn't a simple coincidence.'

'You don't believe that, do you, Tom? Not really?'

'Truthfully, I don't know what I believe, other than racing to conclusions and suspecting everyone isn't helping. Especially not you, or me.'

'I'm not sure what you're telling me, or why you don't just tell me what you think about James. I've always thought of you as so open, and now you're not being that way at all,' said Margot.

'How am I being?'

'Evasive, Tom. You're being evasive. And you're trying to distract me by responding to whatever I say with a bloody question. And I don't understand why.'

'I really didn't like anything about James Garfield, if you must know. I didn't respect him, which I've told you already, and I didn't like the way he used people and made everything about himself. I never really believed in what he said he was trying to do, and from all accounts it seems as if he treated you like rubbish. Now, does that make you happy?'

Margot realised that this didn't make her happy, not at all, and this made her want to irritate Tom so that he would feel as bad as she did. 'Well, Jess Chambers was also wondering how much you'd had to do with him recently.'

'Was she then? What was she getting at?'

'I don't know for certain, but I think she wanted to know if there had been any friction between you. Well, that was one thing she was interested—' Margot stopped in mid-sentence.

'And what was the second thing your inspector was wondering about?' Tom sounded really put out now.

'Um, whether you'd ever been up close and personal together. And Jess Chambers isn't *my* inspector, as you well know.'

'Do I know, Margot? Up close and fucking personal?' Tom's voice had risen too. 'And what does *that* mean?'

'I imagine whether you were, or had been, having sex or something approaching sex with him. It's common knowledge that James was pretty free like that.'

'And what do you believe, Margot?'

'No judgement, but it doesn't matter what I think, does it? It's what Inspector Chambers thinks that really counts, surely?'

'Well, I might be interested in what you think. You're supposed to be a mate, and now you're sounding like I'm being accused of something, and you're thinking the inspector could be right about me having hidden motives. No judgement is so far from the truth as to be laughable – you're *really* judging.' Tom stood glowering at Margot.

'I don't see why you're acting like this, Tom. I wouldn't be shocked if you'd been with him – well, I would, but only because you haven't said anything, not by you being together.'

'Fuck off, Margot. You're missing the point.'

'I'm not sure right now what the point is, Tom. I just get the sense you're holding back something.'

Tom let out a sharp *huff.*

Margot added, 'Look Tom, I think the inspector was also trying to test out the ground over whether you and I could be working together in a malicious way. I mean, I didn't sense she was massively suspicious of us, more that she wanted to establish we had nothing to hide.'

'Working together? Us? Are you fucking joking?'

'Are we about to argue, Tom?' Margot asked, her voice shaky now, not much more than a whisper. They had never previously shared a cross word, and suddenly Margot felt the atmosphere between them was nothing short of perilous.

They looked away from each other.

'How can you even ask any of this?' said Tom sadly. 'Don't you know me at all?'

And then he pushed himself away from the half door to the stable, causing it to rattle in a way that made Trojan throw up his head and whinny.

Tom stomped across the yard as Margot leaned out of the stable door and yelled across the yard at him, 'No, I don't think I fucking know you, Tom. Not fucking at all.'

He didn't look back and gave no sign of whether he had heard Margot, who was now more furious with herself than she was with Tom. She stood there quaking with emotion as she watched him fling himself into his Land Rover and drive off without putting on his seat belt. In fact he was still closing the door as the car barrelled out of sight, leaving Margot reflecting that she and Tom had just had a fight, although she couldn't have said exactly what about.

She patted Trojan to reassure him. He had stuck his nose back into his feeding tub, but his ears were still flickering back and forth with anxiety. And then she made sure his stable door was shut securely before driving slowly home, a maelstrom of doubts assaulting her, the biggest one of all concerning Tom and why he had been so sensitive. He had been nothing like the Tom she had known all these years.

Margot racked her brains and couldn't come up with a scenario in which the two men could ever have been involved with each other either personally or professionally. Tom and James were chalk and cheese. She'd thought for a long time that Tom was all about low-key kindness and community-minded decency, treating everyone he came across with fairness and respect. In contrast, James had grown into the very definition of self-interest and self-aggrandisement. The seeds of this had always been there, evident even when he was a schoolboy, but with social media and the business opportunities that had afforded, James had developed into a monster.

She was sure that they hadn't understood or respected what made the other tick, so couldn't have worked together under any circumstances. Or at least that was what she would have said an hour ago. As to whether they could have been drawn to each other, Margot couldn't really imagine that either. Neither man was the sort to hang out in pubs or clubs, and they were unlikely to have been part of the same social set. And she couldn't picture them being attracted to each other physically.

Margot had never seen any sign of Tom being homophobic – in fact he employed a number of non-straight people – but then neither had she spotted any indication that he had relationships or flings with his own sex. And if he had, he didn't strike her as the sort who would be in any way embarrassed or apologetic about it; it would simply be part of who he was, and Tom had always seemed content with himself as a person.

Actually, the more she thought about it, the more she

realised that she'd never noticed him talk about relationships of any sort, even flings or one-night stands, which might say something else. But if Tom was asexual, which wasn't a crime or anything to be awkward about, why had he been so touchy just now? Perhaps there was history between him and James in another way, but as she couldn't see them ever being in either a business or personal relationship. it was hard to imagine how they could have rubbed each other up the wrong way.

Margot thought she wouldn't get to the bottom of this unless Tom told her what was going on, but she also wished she had left well alone and not raised any of it at all. The thought of losing Tom as a friend was dreadful. And even if they made up, she wasn't sure they'd ever be able to get back to the easy friendship she so valued.

She slammed her car into a lower gear as she drove up the hill to her parents' house, firmly laying the blame for the discord between herself and Tom at James Garfield's door. If he hadn't already been dead, Margot felt she could have strangled him right there and then. James Garfield was more annoying now he was no longer around than he ever had been when he was alive, and that was really saying a lot, Margot thought.

DAY FIVE

The next morning the first hour or two in the incident room was almost wholly focused on digital images or feedback from external sources, and the team became increasingly excited as suddenly it seemed as if they were getting somewhere.

All the team except Jess, that is, who struggled to maintain focus and felt curiously disengaged. In part this was because she had ended up having a surprisingly enjoyable time with Simon, indeed much better than she'd banked on. She caught herself daydreaming more than once, although she tried very hard not to give in to ridiculously teenagerish sensations. In part her distraction was because not much of real use had come in, despite the volume of information, but Jess took care not to show this as she didn't want to dampen the biggest buzz of energy she'd experienced since she'd joined the police station.

The evening before, Simon had been endlessly charming, and had seemed genuinely interested in what she had to say in a way that Jess really wasn't used to. There was something about the way he spoke that carried through to how he held her gaze and concentrated with his head slightly angled to one side that made Jess feel funny and smart. She was flattered by his attention and a part of her whispered that she was punching above her weight; judging by how many women in the pub kept their eye on Simon, he was someone who effortlessly appealed to the opposite sex. Still, *she* was sitting across the table from him, Jess reminded herself

They'd decided they would stay and have something to eat, at which point Mike Bowers made himself scarce as he was obviously needed no longer. Jess and Simon kept the conversation light, speaking mainly about books and films, and other safe topics such as favourite foods or amusing stories about pets they'd had as children, or what they felt about keeping fit (not very much in Jess's case, confessing that these days she had become quite lazy; but reasonably enthusiastic in Simon's, being much more outdoorsy than he'd led her to believe when they'd first spoken, as long as it wasn't anything to do with teams, Jess shaking her head with mock horror at the word 'outdoors' but nodding agreement to his dislike of participating in team sports).

'No surprise there then,' said Simon.

'I'm not totally hopeless,' Jess replied. 'I can do a sprint to the fridge.'

And she liked it that Simon let out a bark of laughter.

Jess made sure to steer the conversation away from anything to do with work, as it was nice to have a night off from thinking about the two murders dominating her life, but also because revealing her job could really mess up a date. Potential love interests were either too fascinated by her being a detective inspector and would immediately urge her to dish the dirt on really gory cases – which Jess would never do, as from there it was only a short step to seeing what she had said appearing online – or else they were put off or even hostile. Jess had found it was almost impossible to tell which way someone would jump, so once she'd decided she liked Simon she kept well clear of what she did for a living. And the fact that Simon seemed happy to enjoy a general chat, and didn't delve too deeply into personal details such as previous relationships or possible children, made Jess take to him even more.

It was gone ten o'clock when they got up to leave, having meticulously split the bill down the middle. Out in the car park they leaned in to give each other a quick peck on the cheek as they said goodbye, which Jess thought seemed exactly right for the evening they'd had. She had spent the last part of the meal rather dreading this bit, as she'd always found saying goodnight to a new man awkward. Although she was attracted to Simon, she needed to take things slowly. Jess wanted to communicate to Simon that she was interested but needed more time to get used to the idea of a relationship, but hoped he wouldn't give her the brush-off for being buttoned up.

As Jess got into her car and waited for him to leave first so that she could see what he drove and make sure he didn't follow her home, she told herself to prepare for Simon to be thinking something along the line of 'thanks but no thanks'. She'd already decided that should anything untoward happen, she'd drive straight to Mike Bowers' home and then together they could deal with it. But she was calmed and reassured when she received a message from Simon before she'd even turned on her engine: 'Fun evening – our first and, I hope, not our last, S.'

Jess replied, 'Yes, good evening – thank you.'

He didn't respond, and Jess wasn't clear whether that was now the expected thing or not. It was exhausting trying to decode this sort of thing, Jess decided as she headed home, realising how on edge she was these days and unused to having a relaxed and pleasant time. But tired as she was, later that night Jess couldn't sleep even though she'd pretty much been awake for the last forty hours. She had lain in bed listening to the wind pick up outside her remote cottage, buffeting the slate roof and small-paned windows, and decided that the excitement of being involved in such a challenging case for the first time in well over a year had charged her with adrenaline, and in turn the adrenaline rush had tweaked her hormones.

The more Jess went over it, the more this spike of interest in the opposite sex – which Jess didn't for a moment believe would last – seemed inextricably linked in a subtle but complicated way with her arrival in the Lake District. There was, she concluded, something empowering about the majestic landscape, and this was seeping into her work life.

Margot Voyce – or to be precise her pragmatism – seemed somehow a cog in the wheel of Jess's psychological evolution too. And so did the workmanlike but amiable Tony Peters and Bill Harper, both of whom had come to feel like potentially staunch supports now they were all actually working together on two investigations with an objective obvious to everybody. And although the investigations were stuttering, she had definitely recovered something of her old energy, as well as a pragmatism that had seemed just a few months ago to have been wrenched out of her and stamped into the dust.

The next day, a cup of strong coffee in her hand as dust motes shimmered in the early-morning sunlight shining through the incident-room window, Jess attempted to take on board the various emails that had come in overnight. But despite her good intentions, she didn't feel that she was making much headway, so she asked Tony and Bill to give the team an update. She needed a general perspective on where they stood.

Margot had had a restless night too. The memory of Tom's face looking at her over the stable door and its shift from warmth to confusion to anger still felt too raw for her to be able to relax.

She sat up in bed, and sent Tom a message even though it was well past midnight: 'I'm sorry we ended up on the wrong foot earlier – I think we found ourselves at cross purposes, and just didn't know how to deal with it. Am I wrong?' There was no reply, and this made Margot feel worse. It seemed Tom was angry with her and, just as bad, wanted her to know this.

In the morning she kept checking her phone, but her apprehension only grew with Tom's radio silence, as did the niggling worry that perhaps he wasn't the genuinely good person she had long believed him to be. She hoped vehemently she was wrong about this, but it was impossible not to wonder. And Margot knew that should she have seen a side of Tom she hadn't believed possible, she would find it devastating.

'Bingo,' announced Tony Peters to the room as he stood by the whiteboard, a tablet in his hand. 'The specialist digital analyst people have got back to us. They've enhanced the tiny amount of retrievable data they've been able to get from what we are

229

assuming is Mr Garfield's GoPro, and just here –' Tony paused the video on the screen in front of them '– there looks to be the toecap of a walking boot, which looks like it's made of scalloped grey rubber with some sort of small reflective flash inserted into it. There's no picture immediately before or following, but there is a second of audio immediately afterwards. It's very muffled, but it's there. The experts say that it is most probably a scream or cry from the person whose mouth was closest to the microphone on the GoPro, and so probably James Garfield himself. We're just checking that the serial number of the GoPro links to the one he purchased – we're fortunate that he kept meticulous records that are with his accountant of everything he bought for tax purposes.

'Anyway, assuming the audio is from his GoPro and not one belonging to a random person who recently lost their own in the same place, when coupled with the image of the boot, it suggests the material is very probably a record of the precise moment of James Garfield going over the lip and down into Piers Gill. The recording ends at that point, and the boot is seen from the front as if directly level with the GoPro, which we know from various posts Mr Garfield habitually wore on a chest harness. This points to the boot belonging to Mr Garfield's assailant and the digital fragment being the immediate aftermath of an attack, when he could have twisted his body around as he went over into the gully. There is only one voice, according to the tech guys, and they think the distance from the boot toe to the mouth of the speaker probably means the cry did not come from that person. I've done a check on boot toecaps and it looks quite distinctive, although I haven't yet found a match.'

'Good,' said Jess. 'That gives us something to work with.'

'The other thing they found,' Tony Peters continued, 'is that although a lot of Trevor Walton's drone footage from the car park is useless because of rain on the lens, the section in the dry weather as Mr Garfield set off shows nobody else in the vicinity. More interesting is that when Mr Walton brought the drone back, there is the outline of what seems likely to be a dark SUV moving past in the car park. It's unclear whether this vehicle is arriving or leaving. But the weather was so foul by then people had gone home, and there was no sign of an SUV in the car park earlier when James Garfield began his run and the drone first went up, so we do now have a bit of a time window, and can incline just slightly towards this being a shot of the vehicle arriving. This was about twenty minutes after Mr Garfield set off, so it gives us a clearer timeline for checking adjacent roads for CCTV, doorbell films and witnesses. It might provoke a memory with Mr Walton too. No numberplate though. Whoever was in this SUV might have witnessed what went on, so we really need to find him or her.'

'Okay, as Trevor Walton knows you, make him a priority, Tony. Do it face to face at his house, with no prior warning. Is it suspicious, do you think, that he didn't mention this vehicle to us?' said Jess.

'I don't think so. Trevor Walton seems to have a one-track mind. He'd have been concentrating on his drone and annoyed about not getting more of his hero's run and so he might simply not have noticed another vehicle. Nothing useful was on his dashcam, by the way. He was in a spot at the edge of the car park, and his car wasn't facing the right way even with the engine on – I noticed when I checked his car he didn't have the sort that works twenty-four hours.'

Although Simon had displaced the mysterious person at the vigil in Jess's thoughts, she hated loose ends and so she said, 'Anyone have any luck identifying that person – I'm assuming a man – on his own in dark clothing at the vigil yet? Do we have names yet for everyone there?'

The team all looked towards Bill Harper, who said, 'I'd say I've got about ninety per cent of those at the vigil identified now. People have been very helpful and most put their details in the book of condolence. I've asked for anyone to send in any footage they took, which should help further once it's all in. But nothing yet other than glimpses of the man, who's just elusive or else was taking great care not to be photographed. Still, somebody must have caught him, so I'll keep trying. What you will like though is that the forensic accountant DC over in Carlisle has come up with something.'

Bill explained the officer had uncovered several apparently carefully concealed financial exchanges involving Bob Newman and at least two third parties. Bill was now cross-referencing them with council contracts. The DC had stressed that there was nothing obviously suspicious about these transactions other than the fact they had been hidden. He had however come across some uncorroborated gossip that he wasn't yet willing to share that suggested James Garfield had been on the periphery of this.

'Keep on top of that too, Bill, and tell the Carlisle DC to keep on it for another half-day. Let me know anything relevant,' said Jess. 'Finally, any forensics from Kate Summers' RTA?'

'Not yet – they're very busy apparently,' said Bill. There were a few ironic groans. 'And on that other angle you asked me to look into, skip, there's so far nothing either way on rumours of abortions or children born with Mr Garfield as the father. But it may help to know that the financial DC hasn't found any one-off payments from Mr Garfield to any woman, and there are no direct debits or standing orders either, from either his business or current accounts. There's also no sign of any woman having paid Mr Garfield money, incidentally, so nothing to indicate he was a kept man. There's not been any suggestion of this, but I mention it just in case it's helpful.'

'Okay, we'll downgrade that line of enquiry, Bill, for now. Meanwhile, everyone, keep sifting that information, and concrete developments via Bill,' said Jess. 'The fact we have been at this now for getting on for a week with so few pointers suggests a perpetrator with high intelligence and somebody who merges into everyone else, so bear this in mind. Everyone okay for now?'

Jess's session with her supervising officer went relatively smoothly. She set out where they were currently and asked if she needed to speak again to the CPS, which she didn't. She then telephoned the parents of Kate Summers, who had been too upset to speak to her the day before.

'I'm sorry for your loss,' Jess began. 'I worked with your daughter briefly this week, and it was clear she was exceptionally talented.'

She let the parents, who were on two extensions of an old-fashioned landline at their home so that they could both listen in and speak, tell her about their daughter and what she'd been like as a girl. They were clearly deeply shocked and very tired, and couldn't really take in what had happened, and so Jess decided to keep the conversation brief.

She explained that they still didn't know quite what had happened to their daughter but they were doing their best to find out. She didn't mention murder or give any hint that this was what the investigation was leaning towards, or even raise the possibility of death by dangerous driving, but said that the inquest would be opened in a few days. Unfortunately, she added, there would be a delay after that before the cause of death could be determined as official enquires were continuing.

'But I can see that your daughter would have been the sort of person to make her parents very proud. Did she ever talk to you about her clients?' said Jess.

'Not really,' her father said.

Jess hadn't really expected Kate Summers to have done this as it seemed out of character, but had to check. Then she asked if their daughter had ever mentioned the name James Garfield to them. Both replied that they were pretty sure she hadn't.

Jess didn't explain the context and quickly moved the conversation on. They sounded quite elderly, and Jess was pretty certain they wouldn't be au fait with the fell-running world or social media.

'And, last questions, did Kate ever mention anybody who'd threatened her? Or a boyfriend she was worried about?'

There was another no from both Mr and Mrs Summers.

'Can either of you think of anyone who might have wished her harm?'

The couple both sounded as if they were gulping back sobs as they said no once more.

Jess gave them her contact details, said once more she was sorry over what had happened, and then rang off. She stared at her phone. She hated intruding into someone's private grief. Mr and Mrs Summers had got to her. It was easy to get fixated on solving a death and to forget the personal cost to friends and family that a murder caused. Kate Summers' parents had sounded like salt-of-the-earth people who worked hard and lived within the law. Just two people who had very much loved their daughter.

Jess knew they'd never really get over what had happened, but if she could catch the perpetrator it might bring a sense of closure to Mr and Mrs Summers. This was why she did the job. It couldn't bring their daughter back, of course, but at least they would feel that Kate's story had come to some sort of conclusion.

Her thoughts were interrupted by the sound of a GIF arriving on her work phone. Jess activated it and saw a dancing Pikachu gyrating above the words 'Come outside'. She didn't recognise the number and couldn't think for the life of her who would send her this sort of thing or how they could have come by the number. She just wasn't the sort of person who'd appreciate such a message, and she thought that everyone who knew her was aware of this.

It was old-fashioned and childish, and she'd never been a fan of anime; in fact even over twenty years earlier she had thoroughly detested the yellow creature. Just as Jess was convincing herself that someone had sent it to her by mistake and it was meant for somebody else, another Pikachu GIF appeared, with a different dance and this time the word 'Now!' insistently flashing on and off. There was a hand-drawn squiggle above Pikachu's head that Jess realised was meant to be a policeman's helmet, and also a magnifying glass near its paw.

Clearly she was the intended recipient after all. She was bemused and irritated in equal measure.

A third GIF came through, with Pikachu's face filling the box and a tear sliding from an eye down its face. 'Pretty please' was the latest entreaty. Pikachu was wearing a giant medallion around its neck on which Jess's face had been superimposed. Somebody must have done a Google search as the hairstyle came from her time in Northern Ireland.

Jess googled the phone number the GIFs had come from, but nothing came up.

She went and stood at the nearest window, but all she could see was a low office block backing on to the police station, which really wasn't helpful at all. She heard the sound of a fourth GIF arriving on her phone, which she had left on her desk across the room.

'Right. Enough is enough.' She marched from the room having snatched up Margot's coat from beside the door, determined to put an end to this. Her colleagues were so busy nobody noticed her go.

It was still early when Margot went over to the stables, but there wasn't any sign of Tom, and nobody seemed to have seen him that morning.

She saddled Trojan and went for a ride, but being on horseback didn't make her feel calm in the way it normally did, and so she distracted herself by trying to name the birds she saw, but her heart wasn't in it. Trojan picked up her bad mood and began to snatch at the reins, and this dispirited Margot even more as it made her back twinge.

After a very unsatisfactory hour during which she headed to Tom's house and found no sign of him or his collie, Margot turned Trojan for home. As she rode back into the yard she was pleased to see Tom's Land Rover parked in its usual spot.

Ten minutes later she found him in the staffroom, where he was clearing out the fridge. This was a job everyone hated, as usually there were forgotten half-used cartons of milk and ancient tubs of yoghurt that had turned rancid and smelly.

'Tom,' said Margot. She noticed his shoulders stiffen at the sound of her voice.

He stood up and turned towards her. He looked very pale, as if he was nursing a hangover.

They looked at each other very seriously for a long moment.

Margot broke the silence: 'I'm sorry, Tom. I didn't mean for a moment to upset you.' She wasn't quite certain what she was apologising for, but she felt this needed to be said.

'I know, Margot,' Tom replied. 'It took me by surprise, that's all. And I'm sorry too.'

'What took you by surprise?'

'That you could think of me like that.'

'Don't read too much into my thoughts. I didn't know what to think, Tom. I asked what felt like simple questions and it seemed as if you gaslit me. It's so unlike you. Whatever you were avoiding saying couldn't be as shocking as what I began to wonder about.'

Tom stared at the floor and then he took a deep breath. 'I was avoiding telling you how I felt. You're important to me, Margot, and I—'

He stopped abruptly as one of the stable lads walked into the room and began rooting around in the cupboard where Tom put packets of biscuits from the farm shop that were close to their sell-by date or had been broken.

But Margot had heard enough. She smiled at Tom, who was standing there awkwardly.

'Anyway,' said Tom in a quite different tone of voice, 'I heard something at the pub that your inspector should know.'

And when Margot heard what it was and then tried to contact Jess on the phone, she thought it strange that no matter how often she called or sent a message, it went straight through to voicemail, or the ticks denoting whether a message had been read or not remained elephant-grey instead of the chirpy turquoise that showed the message had been picked up.

It felt odd. Jess had always either answered Margot immediately or had got back to her in a matter of minutes. It wasn't long before Margot grew increasingly uneasy. And she didn't like the feeling.

In the incident room both Tony Peters and Bill Harper were also surprised that Jess suddenly seemed to have gone completely off-grid. In the month they'd worked together she had never done this, and it seemed particularly peculiar at this stage of the investigation, when things were suddenly starting to make more sense, and when Jess's instruction they should keep her informed of developments was still ringing in their ears.

Bill Harper especially wanted to talk to Jess as he'd now managed to dry out James Garfield's phone and charge it up, and he'd just discovered hidden away on an email James had written to his uncle several years previously a PDF attachment of some council minutes, with the terse comment in the mail 'We need to talk.'

Tony Peters asked, 'What was the meeting?'

'Planning. Not sure though if it's relevant or moves us along, but it's something Bob Newman has been cagey about.'

'He'll say he hasn't been cagey because we didn't ask him about it, and we haven't directly,' sighed Tony Peters.

'Maybe not. But it's the only example on record I can find of James Garfield being grouchy to his uncle.'

'Yes, put like that, the boss should know.'

Their wonderings about where Jess could be were interrupted by the arrival of the transcript of the conversation David Smith had overheard between Bob Newman and his uncle in the pub car park. The techies had enhanced a fragment of audio which revealed that James had shouted at his uncle, '[inaudible] . . . can't believe you and that twat are still doing that, and after you telling me it was finished. It ends now, or . . . [inaudible verbal sounds] . . .promised . . . [sound of vehicle engine and squeal of brakes].'

It was only a scrap but pretty much accorded with what David Smith had told them, but what was new to the team was a sliver of a phone conversation with an unknown that Bob Newman had had as James exited the car park which had been picked up by the same outside camera: '[probable footsteps] . . . Linno, we have to speak. The shit's about to hit the f— [speaker moves out of range].'

'Would this be enough for us to get authorisation to seize Bob Newman's phone?' asked Tony Peters.

'Doubt it.'

He went over to Jess's desk, where he found her work phone. He rang her personal mobile, and immediately heard the ringtone nearby. Wherever Jess was, she hadn't got either device with her. He looked around and found her personal phone under her scarf. This was incredibly unlike their boss.

Indeed there was no sign of Jess anywhere in the police station and no one could remember seeing her recently.

Just at that minute Margot phoned to say she couldn't raise Jess, which she felt was a little peculiar, and could he pass along that she needed to speak to her urgently? Tony asked if he could help, and Margot said no disrespect but she'd rather have an off-the-record word with Jess directly, in case she was making a mountain out of a molehill.

As Margot rang off, concern became full-blown worry.

'Nothing about this feels right,' said Bill Harper.

'Agreed,' said Tony Peters.

They looked at each other for what felt like a very long few seconds, before Tony Peters said, 'I don't like it, and I don't think we should hang around. I'll give her a couple more minutes.' Tony stared at his phone deep in thought for a full five minutes, then he picked up the phone and asked to speak to Jess's superior over at Division.

Jess came to.

She was on the floor of an SUV, at best guess, lying on her side and stretched out almost full length. It was dark, her face covered. There was something under her back. Jess went to touch her face and discovered her hands were immovable behind her back; she quickly established that her wrists were secured together by a cable tie.

She was probably under a blanket, tiny chinks of light in the darkness peeking through the fabric. There was a faint doggy smell, which she tried her best to ignore.

The vehicle's engine was running, so they were clearly moving. She didn't know how long she had been unconscious; it could have been just a minute or an hour. She tried to concentrate on her surroundings, what little she could make out, but her brain felt strange and stodgy. Then, over the sound of the engine, she heard something else: someone breathing above her.

Her kidnapper.

For a while Jess lost herself in panic as she desperately tried to free her hands, but the cable tie was unyielding, and even as she scrabbled around with her fingers she knew that she was never going to be able to muster enough strength to break it. Calming slightly, she made herself stop; she knew she needed to conserve energy. She established that the tie seemed to be double-looped around the base of the driver's seat.

A fresh wave of panic hit her, and it was all she could do not to scream as she realised the full extent of her predicament. Then she told herself very firmly that she would surely die if she didn't calm down and think rationally. Well, she might die anyway, but she wasn't going to make it easy for whoever was doing this.

Jess closed her eyes and spent several minutes concentrating on her breathing, taking a breath in for a slow count of five, holding it for the same count, and then releasing it for a final slow beat of five. After a while she felt a bit better, although she could feel the adrenaline pumping through what seemed like every cell of her body.

She opened her eyes and looked around to take careful stock, but she had very little to go on. The blanket obscured her vision, while she had a splitting headache from whatever she'd been drugged with. Jess remembered taking poppers on a visit to a club in London when she was much younger and long before she joined the police force. Although at first she'd loved the heady sensation, surging heart rate and euphoria the amyl nitrate provoked as she danced, before long a thick and painful headache was insinuating itself into every crevice of her brain. That was more or less what she was feeling now.

Jess pressed the side of her head against the floor as an experiment. She couldn't detect anywhere on her skull the localised pain that would indicate she'd been whacked unconscious with something, while her face wasn't smarting in the way it would have if she had been knocked out with a punch. She ran her tongue around her mouth and was pretty certain the last thing she'd drunk had been her morning coffee; the fact that she could still taste this suggested she hadn't been out cold for too long, so a few minutes rather than hours, she guessed.

Although she had no memory of what had happened, everything she'd discovered about her predicament so far, coupled with her muzzy head, suggested to Jess that she had inhaled some sort of anaesthetic, something like ketamine.

She heard a sticky sound from behind and above her. Jess was sure she knew what it was – the sound of latex gloves moving to a new position on the steering wheel. This told her that her assailant had at least basic forensic nous.

Next she did a careful stocktake in her mind of the rest of her body to assess any injuries and to try to work out precisely how she was being held down as firmly as she was. Her ankles were also cable-tied and connected almost definitely to the passenger seat, she thought.

She made sure she didn't tug or wrench at her hands or kick her feet as she didn't want to alert the driver to the fact that she was no longer unconscious. She also didn't know if there was a passenger. It would be useful to know if there was more than one person involved, but she didn't want to invite their attention yet. While she might be able to outwit or escape a single person, Jess knew the chances of being able to get away from two people were slight unless she was incredibly well prepared.

As quietly as she could, Jess softly rubbed the toes of her lace-up brogue shoes against one another and eventually was able to hook between her feet a bit of the blanket that covered her. Manoeuvring slowly, she pulled it down from her face, until she could see. She blinked in the daylight, but her eyes quickly became accustomed to the light.

As she had thought, she was in the footwell and facing the rear seat. She tried to turn her head towards the front of the vehicle, but lying as she was she couldn't angle her head far enough around to see anything. The vehicle felt powerful, large and heavy, and the purr of its engine suggested it was probably high end. Jess thought there would likely be another row of seats behind those she was facing. She could see from the small area of paintwork around the internal door panel nearest to her the vehicle was black.

She strained to hear more. However intently she listened, she could only detect the sound of one person, and from their breathing surmised they had a deviated septum. Jess tried to get some sense of the driver, their sex or size, but she couldn't come up with anything useful. The twists and turns the vehicle made suggested they were on one of Cumbria's many narrow country roads, and the lack of gear changes meant it was an automatic, so that was something.

Nonetheless, Jess knew there wasn't much she could do to help herself at that moment – aside from leaving as much physical evidence as she could. If she was about to die, she was going to make damn sure it was obvious to a forensic team that she had been in the car. She looked at the carpet. It was very clean and had the chemical scent of a vehicle that was regularly valeted. That was to her advantage, as there was less likely to be traces of other people which would compromise what she was about to leave as forensic evidence.

Jess allowed saliva to pool in her mouth and then dribbled it on to the floor. Then, achingly slowly so as not to make too much noise, she rubbed her head back and forth across the carpet to dislodge some hair. She blew her nose as quietly as she could, forcing her nostril right against the carpet. It was all disgusting, but better than letting whoever had taken her get away with it. She thought about urinating too, but she'd been to the Ladies on her way out of the station. Then she remembered the used tissue she had balled into the sleeve of her woolly, managed to ease that out and very gently pushed it into a crevice in the underside of the driver's seat. She fiddled with her nails, pulling any bits off that she could, pushing them down into the carpet behind her so they wouldn't be obvious when she was taken out of the vehicle.

Finally she pushed her bottom against the front passenger seat for purchase and wriggled her shoulders forward as much as she could so that her mouth was close to the leather of the rear seat. Jess bit the leather, counting to fifty as she clenched her jaw as hard as she could. When she opened her mouth she saw down near the base of the seat wonderfully clear indentations of her top and bottom front teeth. Her attacker might be able to explain away the other forensic evidence by saying he had given Jess a lift, but tooth impressions would be much harder to discount.

As she pulled her head back from the seat, Jess heard a faint snapping sound close to her underside ear. It was the lanyard her police identity pass was attached to, and the sound was its clip snapping closed. She grabbed the nylon strap in her teeth and took several goes to slide it over her shoulder. Eventually she was able to push the strap and her pass behind her head, and then she spent a while wriggling her head and shoulders in an attempt to nudge it all under the driver's seat. She didn't think it was completely hidden, but the strap was black, as was its plastic holder, and so with a bit of luck it wouldn't be immediately obvious to her attacker when she was removed from the vehicle.

Exhausted by the efforts she had made since regaining consciousness, Jess told herself she had done all she could to connect herself with this vehicle. There wasn't anything else she could do until the car stopped. But the pounding in her head intensified now she was still, and Jess was reminded of how the first time she had met Margot her ears had hurt a lot more once she was sitting in her car and out of the rain and wind.

At the memory of Margot, Jess smiled. She wondered what Margot would have done in this situation and decided it was pretty much what she had managed to do. Jess tried to think of something else Margot might try, but couldn't come up with anything. What she could imagine though was Margot saying to her, 'Don't you dare give up, don't you *dare!*'

This picture in her mind seemed very real, and as Jess closed her eyes, she felt a tear slide from her eye and to the vehicle's floor.

There was a lurch, and the vehicle pitched slightly. The engine stopped and through her shoulder and pelvis Jess felt the catch of the parking brake. The stopped engine and brake suggested she wasn't going to be hurled from the moving car, she decided.

'So Jess, what have we here?'

The voice sounded male and somehow familiar.

She couldn't instantly place it, but had a terrible sinking sensation deep inside that it was someone she had been unguarded with. She tried to remember all the men she had met since arriving in the Lake District, then realised it came from the last person she wanted it to.

This wasn't good.

Not at all.

Margot couldn't stop thinking about Jess. She wasn't sure why, but she just knew deep in her bones that Jess was in grave danger.

'I can't sit here doing nothing,' she said.

'What do you think you should do?' said Tom.

'I don't know,' said Margot. 'Her sidekick at the station sounded worried though, and that makes me *really* concerned.'

'Ah.'

Tony Peters told Bill Harper to find out both who Linno was and who was behind the company names on the ancient email to Bill.

Then several things happened in a short space of time.

Working alongside the forensic accountancy DC from Carlisle, now they had a timeline, albeit one outside their original hypothesis, Bill Harper was able to trace a definite link between Bob Newman and a company named MRNu Holdings. From there they found links to a company called Linnot Ltd. When the council minutes were examined, payments to MRNu Holdings coincided with a raft of planning applications and cash deposits into Newman's accounts that looked very much like backhanders.

'So Councillor Newman appears to have set up MRNu Holdings as a shell company with the sole purpose of laundering money, receiving backhanders in exchange for helping to secure planning permission on various projects?'

The DC added that there looked to be suggestions that someone had attempted very diligently to hide connections to the other shell company, Linnot, which in turn suggested there were not one but two participants in the scam with each potentially comprising many individuals or just one. Either way, both MRNu Holdings and Linnot were offshore, and not paying UK tax, and the name Mike Bowers came up more than once.

Bill Harper went to update Tony Peters, but the DS was looking intently at a phone video of the vigil that had arrived. The man in dark clothing was in frame at a distance for a second, and there was a glint of light at his feet.

'You think that's a reflective strip? said Bill.

'Could be. Or maybe not,' answered Tony. 'I'm going to get it cleaned up and enhanced. I have the authority now to get it fasttracked. Shame there's no view of his face.'

'You should know we've turned up a shady-looking firm called Linnot that seems connected in a peripheral way to Bob Newman. "Linnot" could sound like "Linno". There could be links to another shell company, MRNu Holdings, which Newman definitely seems to have used to receive cash bungs. Mike Bowers seems connected, but in what capacity isn't clear. I can't say it's not all above board and innocent, but neither does it feel kosher.'

'Does it move us on? Is James Garfield named?' asked Tony Peters.

'Yes, and no. It looks like it'll take weeks of work to unravel fully. I've not found Garfield. But it feels like something, don't you think?'

*

'So, Ms Chambers, are you going to make like a good girl, and keep quiet? Or are you going to kick off like an idiot? I'd advise the silent option as being in your best interests, to be honest.'

Jess didn't say anything.

As punishment for her silence even though she had effectively just been told to keep quiet, she was marked on the jaw towards her ear with a quick flick of a Stanley knife. It was a superficial wound but it stung, jolting Jess once more into the panic she had been able to keep under control for more than a few minutes now. And then, as her assailant climbed into the back of the SUV and sat on the seat with his knees not far above her head, Jess saw the grey toecap of a walking boot from the corner of an eye. She knew without a doubt as she stared at the reflective strips at the edge of the toecap, the grey and khaki clothes above and the large hands dangling between the knees cradling the Stanley knife that this was the person who had lurked on Scafell Pike, waiting to ambush James Garfield and tip him over the lip of Piers Gill.

She glanced up and saw the disturbed glint in the eyes fixed upon hers.

'It might help you to know that there's only me and you here. Nobody else around. Nobody here to help you, Jess. Nobody, you hear.'

Jess didn't doubt for a second that this was the truth and her death was imminent, or that however hard she tried to reason or cajole, her words would fall on deaf ears. This wasn't a person open to persuasion.

'Going to be sensible?'

She nodded.

The Stanley knife was held up close to an eyeball, its meaning clear.

'And quiet as a corpse?'

Her nod this time was as fast as she could make it. She needed to buy as much time as possible.

Although her hands remained tied together behind her, the cable tie securing them to the driver's seat was cut. Her kidnapper then kneeled on her uppermost hip and with more than a bit of trouble released her feet from the front passenger seat, again leaving them bound together.

Quick as a flash Jess took the opportunity of her captor's attention being focused on her feet. She reached up behind her and grabbed the nylon strap of her lanyard, leaving her police pass pushed under the seat, and balled the nylon into the palm of one hand. Then she felt the weight lift from her hip, and was roughly hauled from the footwell with several firm tugs on the neck of Margot's coat. Unable to use her feet or hands, Jess tumbled from the SUV down on to the stony ground, taking her full weight on her knees. It was excruciatingly painful, and she retched with the pain.

'Ugh.' Her captor sounded disgusted. There was a snap of plastic as her ankles were released from their cable tie. The blade of the Stanley knife was clearly new and razor sharp, and sliced through the thick plastic of the tie at her ankles as if it were as soft as butter.

'You try to run, Jess, and I swear to God I'll cut the tendons in both your legs, right here, right to the bone.' A finger pressed the Archilles tendon above her left ankle. 'And then you'll be fucked. Really fucked.'

'Okay, Simon, I hear you,' Jess said quickly. 'I'll do what you want.'

He made a wolfish face at her, and she realised he was smirking. For a moment she wanted to vomit. How had she ever found him attractive?

It was a while later that Margot went out on to Scafell Pike.

She couldn't rationalise it; she simply knew Jess was in trouble and Margot had to be there, heading up towards the peak from the Wasdale/Piers Gill route. Tom was heading up to the summit from the other side, the way the majority of walkers and fell runners went up. He'd wanted to stay with Margot, but she had persuaded him to go up the other way.

'We'll cover more ground that way, and I'll be fine on my own.'

'But I might not be.'

'Give over, Tom. Next time you want to go up there, I'll guide you and give you the full works – all my little snippets of info. You won't even have to tip me. But for goodness' sake just do it my way today.'

Tom gave a pained sigh but Margot knew he would do her bidding.

They hadn't been on the mountain for too long before Simon Lindsay realised that because of the smooth and slippery soles of Jess's brogues and her badly bruised knees, if he didn't release her hands from their cable tie, they were never going to get to the top of Scafell Pike. Cutting her hands free would also avoid suspicion if they met anyone else. He wasn't sure *why* he needed

Jess to reach the peak, only knew it was important that they were up there together.

If they couldn't make it all the way up then Plan B was to chuck her into Piers Gill, Simon told her, but that didn't make for such a good story. If he was going to go down for this, he wanted it to be as spectacular as possible, and you couldn't get any better than the top of England's highest peak, could you?

'Simon, you—' started Jess.

'Quiet.' He waved the Stanley knife in front of her face before giving her a kiss on the lips.

Jess found the kiss infinitely more scary than the knife. She realised Simon was totally unhinged. Unfortunately, being unhinged didn't make him stupid. In fact he seemed all too on top of the situation. And Jess could see that he was faster and stronger and fitter than she was and had on the right sort of footwear. Realistically, her only option was to get someone else's attention, but would that help? She might just put someone else's life in danger from this lunatic and his knife.

He seemed to read her mind. 'Jess, if you let out so much as a squeak to anyone else, I'm going to cut their throat then rip out their intestines and wrap them around your neck and strangle you with them. Don't test me on this – you know I've killed twice, and I've no problem about doing it again. Actually, with you watching on, that would feel pretty damn good.'

Jess couldn't prevent a whimper. This was a nightmare to end all nightmares, one in which just as you thought it was as bad as it could get, it got worse, and then even worse.

He told her to speed up and prodded her with the Stanley knife. She felt the point penetrate the padded section where her bra hooked together and nick her skin. Ludicrously, given her plight, what bothered her most at that moment was that Margot's precious coat, the one that had been lent to her so generously, had been damaged.

Jess put her head down and concentrated on staying on her feet, walking as quickly as she could, but it was difficult, her shoes were a real problem, and she simply couldn't go any faster, no matter how much effort she put in.

Margot glanced up at the gathering dark clouds and then scanned around and above her with her father's powerful binoculars. She didn't really expect to see anything significant – she wasn't used to the binoculars and found them hard to focus properly – and was just about to put them back in her rucksack when she caught a glimpse of something.

She fiddled with the focus and then tried to re-find what she had noticed.

After an agonising age she located it once more. She peered, concentrating.

Yes! That's my coat.

Margot couldn't be absolutely certain that Jess was inside, but the hair of the person wearing it was the same colour as the detective's. And there was a larger figure dressed in muted tones beside this person, Margot was certain, although they blended in well with the damp colours of the mountain.

She checked her phone signal. Not one bar. Her back started

to twinge, but still Margot upped her pace, keeping the phone in her hand and checking repeatedly for an improvement.

This turned out to be a forlorn hope.

For a long while Jess kept quiet, stumbling along with her head down. But after at least two hours of hard physical exertion, she looked up at Simon, who suddenly seemed to have reverted to the man with whom she'd had a drink the night before. He was looking at her and grinning his dazzling smile.

He had a shape-shifting quality, his swings in attitude and mood changing his physical presence. She was oddly fascinated but in the way a child reacts to creepy-crawlies when a large flat stone is lifted.

'It's such a shame, Jess –' he broke the silence '– as I think you and I might have been good for one another.'

Knowing what she did now, Jess severely doubted that.

He held out his hand to haul her up a tricky bit, and then after she had taken it and let him help her, and they were back on slightly less steep ground, he linked his arm through hers as rain started to fall.

'But you're too clever by half, and the reality is that you've set off a chain of consequences by not believing James fell into Piers Gill and his death was an accident, which is what almost everyone else would have done. And so you have to pay. Obviously. I'm sorry, but there it is.' Jess thought he actually did sound a little bit sorry, which was bizarre. But then he added, 'This is a place for records, as James was always so desperate to point out, and I'll be achieving a record people will remember for much longer than anything he did. Killing a police officer on the summit. Once I've done it, I'll wait at the top until they come, and then I'll cut my throat before they can get to me, ideally my blood cascading down onto your body as I stand over you. Or I might come down, if I decide I stand a chance of getting away with it.'

As she tried to expel that bloody image from her mind's eye, Jess said, 'They'll shoot you down before you can do any of that stuff standing over me. Nice concept and all that, but I don't think it has a snowflake's chance in hell of coming off.'

'Still a win-win,' Simon told her as if he had indeed won something, and he was so matter-of-fact in the way he said it that Jess couldn't help letting out a hysterical hoot of laughter.

'But why James Garfield, and why Kate Summers? Their deaths seem so unnecessary,' she said.

'That fucker Garfield was going to expose me and his uncle – we'd been raking it in for years. And then a charity Bob Newman had hooked up with got shirty when he suggested a backhander – this was ages ago – and James was involved with the charity too, and he did some digging. And to keep him quiet over this – it's years back, mind – Bob told James about his payola sideline. But when this didn't work, to keep the peace Bob told James he'd stop. But he didn't and neither ultimately did James, and you can see how that turned out for him. He threatened to speak to the charity again and thus turned out to have more of a moral compass than anyone believed.'

Jess thought James's moral compass might have been more about protecting his own business interests – he needed to be squeaky clean – than altruism, but Bob Newman wouldn't care about either of these. He'd assume he'd come up with a fool-proof scheme and that James was daft not to be involved.

The weather was turning truly nasty now, and Simon's body language shifted again, this time to morose. He gave Jess a shove that brought her onto her knees again. She yelped from the pain, but then climbed back to her feet, resolving to conserve her energy and just climb, but her legs and body were soon crying out for a rest, her thighs burning, and she was slipping all over the place on her brogues. But Simon wouldn't let her rest or stop, and although their progress towards the peak was at best steady, it was relentless, and after what felt an age Jess realised the summit wasn't far away.

Margot had managed to alert Tony Peters at last to what seemed to be happening, and although she couldn't one-hundred-per-cent confirm it was Jess she had seen, Tony knew that Jess had been wearing Margot's distinctive coat when she arrived at work, and so after he instructed Margot to stay back and not approach the couple, he said he'd try to raise a helicopter and an armed response unit.

'Armed response unit?' said Margot weakly.

'Jess Chambers is a capable woman, and if she's being forced up a mountain, then whoever's making her is not using sweet talk to do it,' said Tony. 'This says weapons to me, and is why you have to stay back, Ms Voyce. It could get dangerous.'

Margot said nothing as she tried to absorb what she was hearing.

Tony Peters now sounded exasperated: 'Do you understand

what I'm saying, Ms Voyce? You need to turn round and go home. This is a dangerous situation, and for you to go on is not helping anyone. Are you listen—'

Her phone cut out with Margot feeling cross she hadn't asked if the police had any inkling of who the person with Jess might be. In any case, Margot knew she had no intention of going home. And at the very least she needed to warn Tom that there was probably an armed man near the top of Scafell Pike. And she was determined to help Jess if that was possible.

As it turned out, the police had a very good idea now who Jess was with.

Tony Peters had had Bob Newman brought into the station. He'd blustered under questioning at first, but when Tony said, 'Tell me about Linnot,' Bob crumpled and against the advice of his solicitor confessed, although he made it sound like Simon Lindsay over at the CPS had been the mastermind and Bob the underling, and that now his nephew had died in such an awful way, Bob had realised the error of his ways, was truly penitent and wanted to come clean.

At this point Tony paused the interview and left the room. He found Bill and the Carlisle DC and put them on to finding out all they could about Simon Lindsay. It wasn't long before they discovered a trail linking Lindsay to Linnot and connections between Bob Newman's umbrella company MRNu Holdings and Linnot. Back in the interview room and armed with evidence of both a financial and a paper trail, Tony pressed Bob, who stayed true to his promise to sing like a canary.

Simon Lindsay – or Linno as Bob liked to call him – had

developed a lucrative personal sideline to his work at the Crown Prosecution Service. For a fee, Simon could ensure certain criminal cases never came to court, by sometimes tipping off witnesses or losing paperwork. Somewhere along the way Simon had come across Bob Newman's small-time planning-application softeners, and he had suggested a partnership, with Bob asking for bigger softeners and picking up gossip when out and about in order to help Simon work out better targets for his activities.

Bob hadn't needed asking twice about such a mutually beneficial arrangement. Simon had access to tremendous amounts of information about the lives of all sorts of people – potential plaintiffs, their victims and all manner of witnesses – and was ideally placed to spot opportunities that in turn Bob could exploit for his own ends.

'It worked well for a long while,' Bob Newman admitted. 'Essentially I did the non-criminal stuff, and Linno the criminal. But he was sectioned a while back, and he's never been the same since. His behaviour always was erratic, but it's become more so lately.

'And for a long while we were careful to choose our targets carefully, and we were never greedy. But the charity was a mistake, and then once James got on to me, he found out about Linno. And from there, it was only a matter of time till the house of cards came crashing down. But I never thought Simon would kill James. Or that woman from the vigil, come to that. I want to make it clear that I am not involved in either of these deaths.'

'The CPS and a jury might think differently,' said Tony Peters.

Bob lost all the colour from his normally ruddy cheeks but

then pasted an open expression on his face, and said ingratiatingly, 'What else do you need to know? A man in my position is always keen to help the police.'

Tony Peters was sorry Jess wasn't beside him in the interview room. He knew that she would have appreciated the councillor's gall and self-preservation skills. But there was a helicopter to catch, and he left Bill Harper to take Bob to a holding cell so that he could be questioned further later.

Reaching the top of Scafell Pike at last, Jess and Simon slumped down side by side on some large rocks, almost as if they were companions.

Adrenaline was keeping Jess alert despite the climb and whatever he had used on her, but she could see that the climb had taken it out of Simon, his eyelids looking heavy. She wondered if he had taken some drugs, possibly prescription but more likely illegal. If he had, would that help or hinder her? Drugs might make him unpredictable, and she couldn't tell if he was acting or really exhausted.

He rambled for a while about himself and Bob Newman, and how James had been on them over the past few weeks like a dog with a bone. His speech was increasingly disjointed though, and Jess had to concentrate hard to make sense of what he was telling her. She looked about her. The beauty of the scenery seemed a cruel joke.

'I just wanted James to shut the fuck up,' said Simon, 'but he wouldn't. He was laughing on the other side of his face when I pushed him into Piers Gill though – that was a good moment.' Simon then told Jess about working for the CPS.

'So when we met in the Carlisle café, that wasn't an accident?' she said.

'Nope,' Simon replied. 'I knew who you were when you arrived in the office, so I kept out of the way and then followed you, and you chose the cafe where I have lunch! Actually, I've been keeping tabs on you since Bob began taking you about.'

Jess sighed. She'd told Mike Bowers at the time it had felt too good to be true meeting Simon, and her instincts had been right all along. And, fuck it, she really should have checked out his occupation. She blamed Mike Bowers for telling her not to be so suspicious about everything.

'Your mate in the outdoor wear shop told me you were a civil servant, and I suppose you are. I thought he meant you were a pen-pusher in something like DEFRA or something similar,' Jess admitted.

'The good old Department for Environment, Food and Rural Affairs – don't you wish I was?' Simon said, and he took her hand in his free hand. The other was wrapped around the Stanley knife, his huge fingers hiding the knife from the sight of the few walkers remaining on the summit now the weather had really set in.

Suddenly he looked her in the eye calmly but so intensely that even in her precarious position, Jess still felt a sexual tingle.

'So why Kate Summers?' she said, disconcerted.

'I'd been watching you at the vigil, but when she made her speech I couldn't tell what she knew, and the minute she mentioned a television documentary I knew she had to go. I needed to stop *that* in its tracks, as God knows what would have been included. I'm sure it would have been very superficial, but I couldn't take the risk of journalists sniffing around. It was easy. I came up behind her, put my lights on full beam, and she did the rest. I hadn't expected it to be quite so successful – I thought she would hit a wall and then I'd bash her head in. But she managed her own death remarkably well. I stopped in time to get out and see her come to a stop at the bottom. And then I went to the pub, before I returned to watch – I thought you lot would never get there. And that creep who takes the drone footage was there, and Mike Bowers, although God knows why. Then when you and I went out last night, I could tell you were clever, and clever means dangerous. And that to you these were definitely two murders. And your goon Mike was in the pub, which tightened the noose. So here we are.'

'Yes, there is that,' agreed Jess. That confirmed Mike was indeed not squeaky clean.

She looked around. There were patches of mist, but the spectacular views peeked through here and there. In that direction were her and Mike's houses, several miles away, while over there was the police station. She couldn't see any of the buildings, but knowing they were there, solid and stone-built, gave Jess a sense of belonging. If these were her last minutes, there were many worse things to look at, and somehow Jess felt heartened by this thought and that perhaps Cumbria had been able to give her a sense of home that up until then had always eluded her.

'You know this is all your fault, Jess?'

Jess felt nothing could be further from the truth, but she nodded, saying, 'I do, Simon.' She made sure to speak very quietly so that he had to put his head close to hers and concentrate on what she was saying, for behind him, with a rush of something approaching happiness, she could see Margot inching forward, although Jess took immense care to ensure that not a muscle in her face moved.

'Do you want to kiss me again, Simon?' Jess whispered, her mouth almost touching his ear. She absolutely didn't want them to kiss, but she needed to distract him, and it was the best she could think of in the moment.

Simon held Jess's two hands behind her back with one hand, while with the other he pressed the Stanley knife to her neck. As his lips brushed Jess's, Margot clobbered him as hard as she could on the top of his head with a large rock, causing Simon and Jess's teeth to bang together.

It had precisely the opposite effect than what Margot had hoped – he must have a skull like steel, she thought. For Simon let out a roar of fury, dropped the Stanley knife and sprang to his feet. The knife bounced a little way away down the stony slope, and he and Jess lunged for it. Jess was quicker. Snatching it up, she brought the knife up in front of her with the blade towards him as Margot flung herself on Simon's back and tried to ram her fingers into his eyes.

Simon grabbed Jess's feet and upended her, then hurled her downslope. Jess landed on her face and careered down the incline, a metallic, earthy smell in her nostrils as she slid to a halt. But she had kept hold of the knife. Getting to her feet, she scrambled back up the slope to be greeted by the horrifying sight of Margot flat on her back with Simon on top of her, his hands on her shoulders as he raised her torso and repeatedly crashed it to the ground as he tried to fracture her skull.

Jess slashed at his back, but his jacket and hood seemed made of Kevlar, and the Stanley knife wouldn't go through. Groggy again from whatever he had drugged her with, Jess put everything into her final move. Yanking the nylon lanyard strap from her pocket, she threw it round Simon's throat and pulled for all she was worth.

As she was on the verge of passing out with the effort, a couple of walkers dithered over wondering what was happening and who to help, but the furious noises Simon was making kept them at their distance. Jess saw another walker filming from some way away. She couldn't blame any of them for keeping well clear.

Exhausted, battered and bruised, Jess and Margot were saved by the beating sound of the helicopter blades.

'The cavalry, I suppose,' wheezed Simon somehow through the chokehold that Jess was maintaining with her lanyard. Margot had wriggled from beneath him and had pinioned his arms with the straps of her rucksack.

Jess relaxed her grip slightly on the lanyard, and Simon sat back on his heels, taking big gasps of air as the first person jumped down from the helicopter and ran towards them.

Margot let go of her rucksack. Simon shrugged off the straps but remained kneeling and raised his hands high in the air in surrender, looking for all the world as if he and the two women had merely been involved in a mild scuffle.

As Simon was handcuffed and manhandled into the helicopter, Tony Peters and Bill Harper came over to check on the women just in time to hear Margot say to Jess as she stared at her feet, 'Are you ever going to go out on this fell wearing the right footwear?'

'Probably not,' said Jess.

And the two women began to laugh.

Margot looked to Jess like someone who had been in a dust-up but who it wouldn't take too much to clean up. Margot didn't think the same about Jess. When they stopped laughing, she looked her up and down and said softly, 'Oh my God,' and Jess realised she probably didn't look too good.

And once she'd thought this, suddenly Jess really didn't feel very well at all.

'We need to get you to hospital pronto, boss,' said Tony Peters.

Jess put a hand to her face, which was badly grazed, with numerous cuts full of grit, the broken skin bleeding profusely. It hadn't hurt while she'd been struggling with Simon, but it sure as hell did now.

'Fuck,' she said quietly.

Suddenly Jess was hurting all over. She staggered as if drunk, before dramatically crashing to the ground in a dead faint.

'Hell indeed' were the last words Jess heard. They were spoken by Tom Drake, who had finally made it to the summit the other way.

'Perfect example of man-timing,' said Margot soon after-wards as she pushed Tom into the helicopter, having made it very clear she'd walk down Scafell Pike with him if he wasn't allowed in. Tony had insisted she be checked out at hospital immediately. He had seen Simon Lindsay repeatedly smash Margot to the ground and remembered her previously broken back.

'Man-timing?' said Tom once they were airborne.

'Arriving once all the hard work is done,' Margot said.

Tom nodded gravely. 'Years of practice.'

Margot was too tired even to smile; she leaned her head on his shoulder and fell instantly deeply asleep.

It was close to midnight. In her hospital room the small pool of light around Jess's head looked almost like a halo. Her wounds had been dressed, and she had been pumped full of various drugs.

Mike Bowers had been in to see Jess, leaving when he saw Margot arrive. Jess had felt awkward having him there, hoping that he'd take her reticence for the effects of the painkillers. She knew he had been involved somehow with Bob Newman, but was unclear as to how much. She knew she'd have to look into it once she was back at work. Jess had flicked Margot a significant glance when she saw Mike Bowers, although she said hello very nicely to him as he squeezed past her in the doorway.

'Hi, Margot,' said Jess. It was the first time she had used Margot's first name to her.

'How are you feeling?' asked Margot, who had just been X-rayed and told she was fine to go home as long as she took it easy for a few days. She hadn't wanted to leave until she'd checked on Jess.

'Been better.' Her speech was slow and slurred. 'I'm numb all over. They couldn't tell what . . . I needed because of not knowing what Simon . . . gave me. But whatever they did it's working.'

'Good,' said Margot. 'It's not every day you pretty much single-handedly catch a double murderer.'

'Well . . . it's not every day I go on a date with . . . someone who wants to kill me the next morning.'

Margot laughed. 'Really? You went out with him? A date!'

'Just the once. My taste in men . . . Tony Peters told me how amazing you were today. He said . . . you were worried when you couldn't talk to me. What was that about?'

'Tom and I had a spat. He went to the pub and heard some gossip at the bar about somebody on the take who sounded very similar to our friend at the top of Scafell Pike, and in the next breath somebody else mentioned Bob Newman. It all seemed like coincidence and conjecture, but he wondered if it might be helpful,' said Margot.

'If you'd got me thirty minutes earlier, than Simon did, we'd have missed out on a lot of hoo-ha,' said Jess.

'What, not have all that fun?'

'I'm sorry about your coat. They had to cut it off as I'd got a dislocated shoulder and a broken clavicle on the same side.'

'Don't be. It belongs in the past. I'm going to let a lot of that stuff go.'

'Good . . . plan.'

Jess sounded very tired and Margot turned to go.

'Next time . . .' Jess managed, as if talking to herself.

Margot looked back, but Jess was asleep, her meaning unclear.

Standing in the doorway, Margot gazed at Jess and then realised she felt done in too. It was time to find where Tom had got to; he'd gone off to sort a taxi.

What had happened that afternoon had been too close for comfort, and Margot realised that for the first time she was looking forward to being a walking guide. In comparison to today, it should be safe, easy and undemanding. Not far away the majestic peaks rose into the sky and the mysterious lakes at their feet clung to their secrets. Margot shivered with the sensation of somebody walking over her grave, but then the sight of Tom and his shabby coat and untamed hair made her feel warm and happy. He turned to smile at her and she grinned back.

Lying on the thin, plastic-covered mattress in his police cell, Simon leered into the darkness. Those two really are going to pay, he promised himself. He didn't how he would do it, but he would find a way, even from prison. Nobody was going to get one over on him, least of all Jess Chambers and Margot Voyce. Simon's leer turned into a smirk, and the smirk grew into a belly laugh.